GRAY WOLF ISLAND

GRAY WOLF ISLAND

TRACEY NEITHERCOTT

ALFRED A. KNOPF
NEW YORK

Visit us on the Web! randomhouseteens.com

Educators and librarians, for a variety of teaching tools,
visit us at RHTeachersLibrarians.com

Library of Congress Cataloging-in-Publication Data is available upon request.

ISBN 978-1-5247-1530-4 (trade) — ISBN 978-1-5247-1531-1 (lib. bdg.) —
ISBN 978-1-5247-1532-8 (ebook)

Printed in the United States of America
October 2017
10 9 8 7 6 5 4 3 2 1

First Edition

For Matt and Jill,
who have always believed

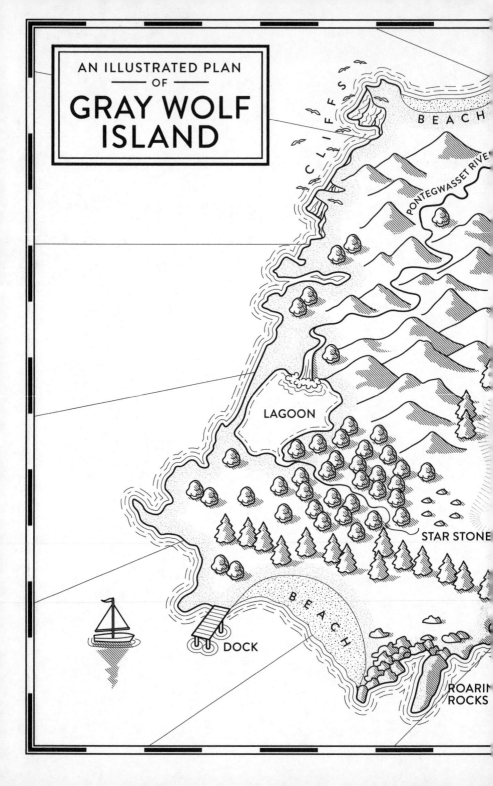

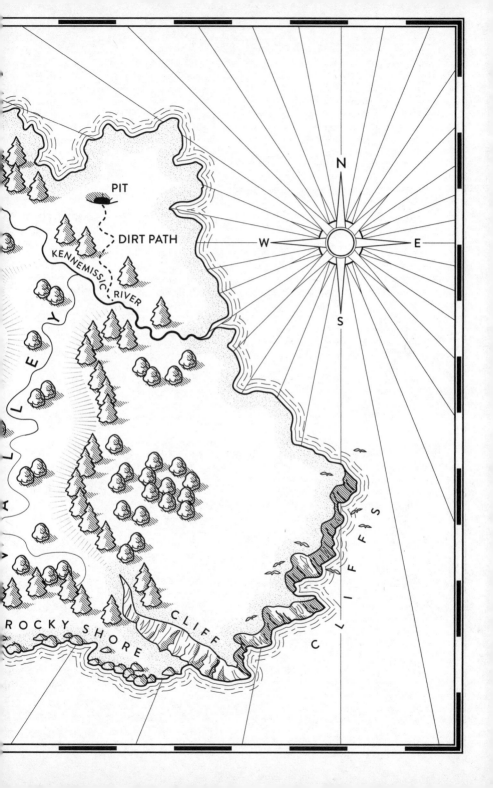

PROLOGUE

RUBY

IT'S NO SECRET THAT SOMEBODY ELSE HAS TO DIE.

In Wildewell, where there's little to do but stare at the sea and think deep thoughts about a deep hole, there's no such thing as a secret. The curse of Gray Wolf Island doesn't even play at privacy. If you know about the eight days of rain each summer that make flowers grow on the ancient tree in the center of town, you know about Gray Wolf Island and the pit in the earth that demands three lives before it gives us anything in return.

My sister finds this endlessly fascinating in the way she's found most things having to do with death fascinating since her diagnosis. She licks her cracked lips, and when she speaks, her voice is scratchy from sleep and sickness. "Murder."

I open the curtains so early-morning sun can warm her

face. A cool breeze sneaks through the open window and ruffles what's left of Sadie's auburn hair. I push the strands behind her ear. "You're truly a creep," I say.

She turns on her side, tugging my arm across her stomach. Her skin looks pale against the jewel-toned pillows, against my tan arm. "I can feel it, Ruby. Like it's calling to me."

It's what people said when they came to Wildewell in its heyday, back when nobody owned Gray Wolf Island and anybody with an ounce of curiosity could hire a boat and try their luck at the infinitely deep pit that legend says promises treasure. But the decades passed and the centuries turned and nobody found the bottom of that hole. Now the corporation that owns the island has long since given up on gold, and only true believers like my sister think anyone will ever solve the mystery.

I think death's calling to Sadie, but the island is easier to accept. "Well, tell it to call back later. You need another nap."

Her lungs rattle when she heaves an exasperated sigh. With a shuddering breath, she lowers her lashes. Beyond her window, the grass gives way to sand and surf. I watch the horizon until my eyes burn, then lower my head to the pillow. Sadie's skeletal body shivers, and I scoot closer to lend her my warmth.

My mother says we left the womb like this, my long body coiled around my tinier twin like if I held on tight enough, she'd never leave my side. Not much has changed in the past sixteen years. There's Sadie, and then there's me, stuck to her like gum to the bottom of a shoe. It doesn't matter that we're twins or that I'm a whole head taller. She's always been my big sister. I'll always look up to her.

Until I can't.

Sadie presses a finger to the window screen, right where sea meets sky. "Murder," she whispers. "That's all that's left."

She's talking about the curse of Gray Wolf Island again. My sister's lifelong infatuation with the treasure transformed into an obsession about the time the doctors gave up on a cure. Now, the worse she feels, the harder she searches, like maybe her body will stick around for the treasure if she wants it badly enough. I use a blanket to wipe sweat from her cold forehead. "There have probably been a hundred murders there. People are generally willing to kill for buried treasure."

Sadie hits me with a look I haven't seen in a while because condescension is tiring for her to maintain. "The suicide and the accident," she says, her voice hoarse. I lift a cup to her lips. "Two deaths. If we'd had the third, if someone had been murdered there, we'd have a treasure."

Maybe there's been a murder there. Maybe not. It wouldn't matter because the legend isn't true. But I smile and nod because Sadie needs it to be true, needs to believe she has a chance to solve the mystery before she goes. "Okay, I'll look out for a murder."

"And if you get lost, just ask Mom, 'kay?"

"Whatever you say."

Sadie doesn't speak for a long while. She's doing that thing she always does, which is stare at me without blinking. Like she can see into my head or something. I'm not sure what she finds, but her attention flips to the window, where the cloudless sky is baby-boy blue. "This is the year you finally live, Rubes."

"Shut up, Sadie. Just shut up." Sadie is convinced her death will be great for my social life. But my life is her life. She dies, I die.

"Promise me something," she says, ignoring my irritation like she always does.

I'm afraid of what she'll ask me to do, and I'm afraid I won't say no. But this is my twin, so I say, "I'll promise you anything."

"If you make a promise, you have to mean it. This is my *deathbed*," she says with the kind of dramatic emphasis she's been using since she was old enough to speak in syllables.

I don't need to know what she wants. Tomorrow I might not have a sister, so today I'll do whatever she asks.

"Find the treasure."

I sigh. "Sadie."

"Ruby." Her hand wraps around mine. "You can have this great adventure for us both. I want you to do that for me. I want you to have the adventure I can't."

I get the sense I'm being manipulated, but I don't care. "Okay."

"Promise it, Ruby."

"I promise," I say. "I'll find your treasure."

This is the first lie I tell my dying sister, but it won't be the last.

Later that morning, while the good people of Wildewell, including my parents, are at church, Sadie asks me to do it. We're curled up on her bed, three blankets covering her thin frame, and I'm fussing with her hair like I used to before it started falling out.

My fingers brush her cheek—too pale, too clammy, all wrong.

A tear leaks from my squeezed-shut eye, and I bat it away. The motion rouses my sister, who snuggles closer. For the past two months, she's been cold when the world is hot, icy fingers crawling up my warm skin and begging me to stay a little longer, stay the night.

"Play me something, Ruby."

It's impossible to play the harmonica without breath, and looking at her steals just about all of mine. "Go back to bed," I say.

Sadie's fingers dance across my temple. "Why are you crying?"

I look at my sister, with her sunken cheeks and stringy hair and defiant eyes that promise to keep fighting, and I tell another lie. "I was dreaming about the day the butterfly was killed."

"Why'd it have to die?" Sadie wheezes as she sucks down a deep breath. The air's a mix of salty sea and the tuberose lotion I rubbed onto her dry hands. She doesn't smell this, of course. She stopped smelling a week ago.

"It was beautiful," I say, and I'm back on that day four years ago. In my mind, the butterfly is a swirl of yellows and oranges. My memory may be more imagination, but when I think of it, when I tell the story, the butterfly is marigold and rust with shots of white and black. In my mind, its wings are torn and its body squished, but maybe I made that up, too.

I remember the next part, though: dark hair hanging over green eyes, rough boy fingers plucking the butterfly from my palm. The rock, the smash. "It was hurt," I tell Sadie even though she's heard this story before. "It was mercy."

Sadie starts to speak, but a cough tears through her. Her body shakes from the force of it, a floppy sort of movement that makes her neck weaken and head roll. I wrap my arms around her, tug her back to my front, and hold tight. I feel the echo of her tremors in my bones.

I rest my cheek on the crown of her head and shut my eyes. I wish I could shut my ears to the sound of my sister fighting with her lungs. My arms are damp with her tears.

When the coughing stops and her breathing steadies, Sadie slumps in my arms. I lower her to the bed, so focused on keeping her steady that I almost miss the red. It takes a curved course over my forearm and onto the blankets. "Oh God, Sadie."

"I'm sorry," she says. "I'm so sorry."

I can't stop gaping at the blood. She's coughed some up before, but never this much. It looks like a crime scene. Like someone slashed my skin to ribbons. *Murder,* my mind says in Sadie's wispy voice. "Stop being sorry. You're going to be okay. This is all—" I scrub the blood from my arms, toss crimson tissues to the floor. "This is all going to be okay."

"Rubes," she says. "I need help." I tell her I'll do anything for her, but she does the thing where she tries to transmit thoughts into my head and, finally, it works. I look at her, knitted brows and face pinched in pain, and I know what she wants.

It's not the first time she's asked. Not even close. Each time she begs, the idea burrows into my brain a bit more. I shake my head—really fast so the idea won't stick around any longer than it already has. "Anything but that."

Sadie doesn't speak at first, just nuzzles her head into the

6

crook of my shoulder. Her cold nose soothes my sunburned skin. Finally, she says, "You know it's coming."

"It'll come when it's damn well ready to come!" I push away from the bed, away from her searching eyes and trembling body and sickening request.

"It hurts."

Murder, my mind says in Sadie's voice, but it sounds a lot like *mercy.*

I look down at my twin, my best friend, the only person in the entire universe who understands me. I've known all along, I realize. It was always going to end this way.

She must see it in my eyes, this horrible decision I've made, because she whispers, "Thank you."

I say, "I love you."

I squeeze her nostrils.

"Don't let go," she says.

A sob escapes me.

My hand clamps over my sister's chapped lips, and I tell my third lie. "This won't hurt," I say, and her eyes are so bright, so full of love and gratitude and relief.

When she starts to struggle, I do what she said. I hold on.

And on.

When the church bells sound in the distance, Sadie's eyes close, and I tell the biggest lie of them all. *Everything is going to be okay.*

ONE

RUBY

One Year Later

EVERYBODY HAS A THEORY ABOUT GRAY WOLF ISLAND. DORIS Lansing has five.

"Pirates' gold." She touches one finger to another. "King John's missing crown jewels. The Holy Grail. The Ark of the Covenant. Or the Fountain of Youth."

We're sucking down milk shakes beneath the lone oak tree outside the Oceanview Nursing Center, her in a wheelchair and me on a stone bench that cools the backs of my thighs. I tie my hair into a high ponytail so the meager breeze can dry the sweat on my neck.

Across the lawn, the bluff drops to a pebbled beach, then miles and miles of ocean. Somewhere too far to see from here but close enough to call our own are Gray Wolf Island and a deep, deep, deep hole.

"Sheriff March thinks it holds the key to all knowledge," I say.

"Ha! That's a myth if I've ever heard one."

They are all myths. It's the lie I tell myself daily because that's what I do now. I lie.

I tell myself there is no such thing as buried treasure. That the source of Wildewell's endless frustration is one very famous sinkhole. That I haven't screwed up my sister's dying wish by being too weak with grief to chase a legend.

Doris's fingers tighten around my wrist. "Are you seeing this, Ruby?"

I lift my sunglasses and blink back the bright. The ocean is almost silver in the summer light, as if the sun has leached color from the sea. A bony finger pushes my cheek, and my head jerks to the left.

"What a babe." Her eyes follow Gabriel Nash in all his crisp-polo glory as he pushes the giant Oceanview lawn mower with an almost innocent unawareness that other people might struggle with the same task only to come away sweaty, wrinkled, and covered in grass clippings. "I always trust a man in a pair of pressed slacks." She slurps her milk shake, then shoots me a serious look. "I bet he's a very tidy kisser."

"Doris!" I should mention that Doris Lansing is one hundred and four years old, and she's only that young because she started counting backward once she hit a hundred and six.

"Not for me." She shakes her head. "Nope, not for *me*."

It's been this way with her since I first started volunteering at the nursing home, one month after Sadie died. I push the wheelchair around the grounds, she scouts for potential relationships. Once, in a fit of exasperation after I told her I didn't want a boyfriend, she told me I could have a quick fling so long as I kept my pants on.

"Which of those boys is he?" She doesn't say it the way most adults do when talking about Gabriel Nash, Elliot Thorne, and Charles Kim, like they're talking about wild boars or ferocious wolves. She says it the way most girls my age do when talking about the trio, like the boys have been dipped in chocolate and sprinkled with gold.

"His mother's the Virgin Mary." It isn't her real name, of course. That's Cecile Nash—three syllables too ordinary for the virgin who gave birth.

My grandpa Sal used to say that simply being near Gabe invited evil into your life. There are stories—this is Wildewell, after all. Some say Gabe brushed against them in a crowded store and, out of their fear of the damned, their shoulders dislocated. Others say Gabe shook their hands and, after they'd come into contact with such evil, burns sprang to life on their palms. And if it wasn't exactly true before, it was once they spoke the words.

But there are also those people who believe Gabe is holy. An angel maybe, because who else but God could make a virgin pregnant? Constance Loyal, whose knees have cracked with arthritis for longer than Gabe has been alive, said she found relief after Gabe shook her hand at church. She was seated at the time, so Mr. Garza, who had burns on his palm from where Gabe had shaken *his* hand at church just last week, cried foul. But Mrs. Loyal just stood without a creak and danced a small jig.

Across the lawn, Gabe whips off his polo and tucks it into his back pocket. Doris sucks in a breath. "I hope the sprinklers come on."

"Doris!"

She shoots me a look that says she's lovingly infuriated with me. "It's okay to joke now and then."

"Fine. Yes, Gabe Nash is an exquisite lawn ornament." But I'm not looking at Gabe. I'm staring at the silver sea. And like I do every time I see the ocean, I think of Gray Wolf Island and buried treasure and a promise I can't keep.

❖

I park Doris's wheelchair at the far end of the library, where a wall of windows overlooks the garden. It's overrun by butterfly bushes, azaleas, hyssop, monkshood, and dogwood trees that spill petals across the lawn. A layer of dirt left over from this week's landscaping coats the outer glass, so the light streaming into the room has a hazy, lazy quality.

Unlike Doris.

"I can't just fall asleep, Ruby. It doesn't work like that," she says, rolling her eyes. I want to tell her that that is exactly how it works, but we've been over this before. And besides, she thinks I only fall asleep so easily because I'm depressed, which I'm not. Not really. Mostly I can't think of anything else to do with my time. And in sleep I can forget what I did.

I don't tell Doris that, though. I don't tell anyone.

"Read me something good." A mischievous smile and a wink tell me exactly what kind of book she has in mind, but narrating sex scenes to an old woman is about as enjoyable as cleaning bedpans. Unfortunately, I have firsthand knowledge of both.

"I'll read you something academic. That ought to put you right to sleep."

"You know what you need, Ruby?"

"A paying job?"

"An adventure." Doris squints at me so hard I'm afraid she's stuck that way.

Then I remember the way she looked at Gabe Nash earlier, like she might gift-wrap him and give him to me with a bow. "I'm not really the adventuring type."

"Oh, fine." She shakes her head. I get the feeling I've disappointed her, but I'm used to it. I disappoint myself on a daily basis. "At least pick one about indigenous peoples. Ours is a history you kids ought to learn."

There is no shortage of historical texts on these shelves. In its past life, this building dealt in the rare and exceptional, and the research within these walls was the first step to discovery. Its former owner, renowned American antiquities dealer Bishop Rollins, was a true believer, and the town's most prominent one at that. Like so many before him, he was drawn to quiet Wildewell by the tempting tale of Gray Wolf Island. He wasn't the first to commission a dig, but he was the only one who stuck around after the money ran out and the treasure, if there is a treasure at all, stayed buried.

My fingers trace worn spines as I walk the perimeter of the room. Paperback romance novels and used sudoku books, which the library has collected in the five years since Rollins's death, squeeze beside books older than my grandparents, giving the wall the appearance of a grin with too many teeth.

In the far corner of the library, towering mahogany shelves hold dense reads with thick spines. I suck in a deep breath, savoring the musty, dusty scent that seems to float like motes in the air. "Smells like knowledge," Sadie used to say when she brought worn books home from the library in her never-ending quest to discover the secrets of Gray Wolf Island. I hated the smell until she was gone. Now I love it.

I walk with my head tipped sideways until my gaze falls on a shelf labeled NATIVE STUDIES. It's packed with cracked spines, monstrous things that promise dry sentences and tedious facts and a nap for a very old woman. I tug *Twelve Thousand Years: Native Americans in Maine* from its tight slot between two equally formidable books, both of which crash to the floor as *Twelve Thousand Years* thuds into my chest. I fumble for the fallen books, but before I slide them onto the shelf, I notice a thin paperback hidden at the back.

Treasure Island.

As I look at the flapping flag on the book's cover—black as sin and adorned with a skull and crossbones—I know with an odd certainty that it was left for me: a gaping grin of bones meant to mock the standstill I've been in since the day Sadie died.

But no, it's more than that. It's adrenaline in my veins. Anticipation in my chest. It's the sense of something more that makes my skin buzz and my arm hairs stand.

I snatch the book from the shelf and walk away.

Doris is asleep by the time I return, white hair fluttering in the breeze from the air conditioner. I tug her blanket to her neck, fingers brushing papery skin, then settle onto a couch so stiff it has to be expensive.

The slim book sits on my lap like an anchor. Holding me here, to this spot in Bishop Rollins's house, to this moment that feels like more than it is.

I fan the pages, skimming the chapter titles and not thinking about the story or even the treasure. My mind is on Sadie and the day she stole lip gloss from the pharmacy. The way she flipped the pages of her book—fast, fast, faster—until she couldn't keep the secret any longer.

My mind is on Sadie's red fingernails the day the butterfly died. The way she let the polish smear against a stark white page because she'd been inexplicably bitten by the poetry bug.

My mind is on Sadie when I discover the treasure map.

The first clue is inked in the empty space after the book's final words—a square with a slash through its center. Slanted writing begins after the symbol and runs onto the next page. I read and reread and reread, not quite believing that the scribbled poem is a map to the treasure. Sadie's treasure. I close my eyes. Take a deep breath. Then I read it again.

Many will try,
will seek, will fail
to discover a treasure
and pull back the veil.

To throw out the false
and welcome the true,
Only one will triumph.
And that could be you.

Your adventure begins
with stars trapped in a sign.
Navigate with them and
our paths will align.

Discover the spot where
morning sun scorches sand
and the ocean beats its anger
into the land.

Head west, dear friend,
if you want to have fun.
Too far to the south,
and your quest is done.

Go down to go up,
pay no heed to the dead.
If you're on the right track,
you'll see gray wolves ahead.

Find heaven on earth—
a sign you will see.
Then let go the lie
and set the truth free.

Into the depths
is your eventual demise.
Part the water instead
for the ultimate prize.

Night descends quickly and
dark is made near.
It cloaks you in shadows,
but strangle your fear.

And in the black
you'll find the star
to guide your way,
to take you far.

Take caution, dear friend.
Do not be misled.
If trickle turns torrent,
you'll soon end up dead.

When narrow opens
up to wide,
take a deep breath
and step inside.

Look for the place
where stone stabs at sky
and the earth sings a mourning song
for your echo to reply.

Search for the six,
sturdy, solid, and true.
For centuries they've been waiting,
waiting for you.

Hidden stays hidden
until the ray
that guides your gaze
does a secret betray.

Only the worthy
can see the clue
to the greater treasure:
to know what is true.

I leave you now
With an immense quest.
Your strength, your intellect,
your honor it will test.

But if you are brave
and if you are wise,
if you're determined,
you—only you—will find my prize.

My body vibrates, each part of me moving at a different frequency so the whole feels disjointed and dizzy. How is it that Bishop Rollins never found this? A treasure map. In *Treasure Island*. A heavy laugh escapes my lips, and I clap a hand over my mouth so I don't wake Doris.

It has never been my adventure, this Gray Wolf Island business. That was all Sadie, and I was just along for the ride. When she died, it never felt right, me continuing on without her. But now I feel a wave of pure want for an adventure.

So I steal the book.

TWO

RUBY

Poppy March looks like she's seen a ghost. Blond hair swishes in the wind, but when I step onto the sidewalk, the strands sort of freeze in midair. All of Poppy freezes, really, except for her thin lips, which puff out a breath too soft to hear. Doesn't matter. I can see what she says as if she shouted it. *Sadie?*

"I'm sorry, no."

She blinks once. Twice. She shakes her head and slaps on a smile. "Oh . . ."

"Ruby."

"Right, Ruby. I'm sorry—" She waves her hand around, like she's trying to erase the past minute. "I forgot."

People have a tendency to do that, forget me. Ronnie Lansing, the degenerate Sadie dated for half of freshman year, went a good two months before realizing I wasn't just Sadie's ghost going about like death never happened. It's understandable, really. Without Sadie, there's not much of me to remember.

Besides, this is Sadie's turf. She spent countless hours locked in the back room of the Wildewell Historical Society and Museum, trying to piece together the mystery of Gray Wolf Island. *I'd* assume I was her if I hadn't—

I'd assume I was her if she hadn't died.

"She asked you to find the treasure," Poppy says. At my shocked expression, a bittersweet smile crosses her face. "About a month before she died, she told me you'd be coming here for information about the treasure and that I should help you. When you didn't show up, I figured she never . . . well, that she never got the chance to ask."

I stare at the sidewalk. A crack splits the concrete, and in that space a yellow dandelion pokes through the earth. I used to think that kind of thing was beautiful, but really it's just a weed. "I should have come sooner," I say.

Poppy's face softens. "Don't be so hard on yourself—you'd just lost your sister."

For one sinful moment I drink up her sympathy, but then I remember. I didn't lose anything. I *took* something.

"I have to run an errand, but my nephew's inside. He can show you around the treasure room." She shoots me a sad smile before scurrying toward town. "And, Ruby? It doesn't matter how long it took you. She knew you'd get here."

I only nod. I think what Sadie knew was that I couldn't say no to her.

I thunder up the museum's wooden steps. Back when

boatmen got fat making regular trips to Gray Wolf Island, this was someone's home. The museum retains the original architecture—something my Realtor mom likes to point out each time we pass—with grand gables, a rounded tower covered in gray shingles, and a porch that hugs the whole house. I yank open the door and step from muggy afternoon into air-conditioning.

A lonely chair sits behind the information desk, and I release a sigh of relief. This task feels too personal—too tied up in my life with Sadie—to include a museum worker. I climb to the second floor, past empty exhibit rooms with pieces of historical Wildewell. It's the stuff of endless field trips: a warped mirror that shows inverted images, an iron lantern that only burns during daylight, a giant clock with two faces that tells time forward and backward.

But nobody visits the Wildewell Historical Society and Museum for that. They come for the room at the end of the hall. Today, sunlight is streaming through windows set high in its rounded walls, highlighting motes that seem suspended in air, like the room's holding its breath until tourists take over. My footsteps break the quiet, a steady *thud, thud, thud* until I'm inches from Gray Wolf Island. The mural is longer than I am tall, swirls of brown and green alone in a sea of blue brushstrokes.

I'm not sure how long I stand there before metal clinking against metal pulls me from my thoughts. I whip around to find Elliot Thorne squatting in front of a display case. He's curved over a small lock attached to the glass.

"It's your fault for leaving me without keys," Elliot says

without looking away from the lock. His words jumble around the paper clip between his teeth. Long fingers jiggle two other paper clips in the lock. "Besides, I don't work for you."

"Well, if you did, you'd be fired," I mumble.

Elliot's head jerks up. Dark hair flops into his eye, and he bats it away. "I thought you were my aunt."

"Your aunt thought I was my dead sister, so this is an improvement." I turn back to the mural, studying the way the eastern cliffs drop into the sea, the jagged line of the mountains that peak in the northwest, not far from an almost insignificant dark spot. It's strange to see the island's greatest mystery—and its greatest lure—reduced to a fist-sized splotch of brown.

"Hey, give me a hand."

I'd like to ignore Elliot, tug *Treasure Island* from my bag, and match parts of the poem to points on the map, but I figure at some point I'm going to need to see whatever's in that case, so I drop my purse on the floor by the mural and cross the room. "It's your lucky day," I say, squatting beside him. "I have two."

Elliot rolls his eyes. "See that plastic piece at the top? I need you to press it up as I turn the pick and open the door."

I do as he says, and in seconds the glass door slides to the side. "Of course you know how to pick locks."

"Of course," he says, smirking. This is a thing Elliot has been doing for the past two years, ever since he went from class brain to tattooed bad boy. It's annoying, and not just because smirks are always annoying, but because Elliot Thorne is the worst bad boy I have ever met.

I was as fooled as the rest of Wildewell before Sadie pushed me into my one great act of disobedience. She'd spent sophomore year pointing to Elliot's long body in the crush of students, watching intently as he strolled out the front doors and never came back. "You could learn a lot about independence from that guy," she said.

I scowled and hated Elliot a little more. Later that week, on a day that smelled like damp leaves, Sadie and I spied Elliot leaving school before fourth period. "He's all alone," she said. "He's having an adventure."

"I don't want an adventure." That was Sadie's job.

She leaned her head on my shoulder and whispered in a voice almost too faint for me to hear, "Sometimes it's okay for us to be apart."

I shot to my feet. Didn't even look back as I fled from Sadie. And that afternoon, when I should have been in gym, I followed Elliot as he skipped the second half of school. After all Sadie's speculations on Elliot's solo activities, I expected to witness vandalism, a drug deal, or some petty theft. Instead, I ended up on a public bus to the nearby university. I ended up in the back of a lecture hall, falling asleep to a lesson on a subject I forgot on my way home.

Since then, I've had a hard time taking his bad-boy act seriously, and now is one of those times. I leave him in front of the gaping glass case and return to the map. My copy of *Treasure Island* is familiar beneath my fingers, and I flip to the last page on the first try.

"You've heard about the Star Stones, right?" Elliot appears beside me, bringing with him the scent of lavender. I realize his mom probably buys his laundry detergent, but who ever heard of a lavender-scented bad boy?

His fingers trace the mural where six stones nestle among

trees in a valley that dips between mountain and cliff. To help people who can't see the star symbol, the artist painted a light yellow line from one stone to the next.

"I'm not new." Everybody knows about the Star Stones, just as everybody knows about the hole and the Virgin Mary and Sadie's cancer. Everybody knows about everything in Wildewell.

"Doris Lansing says they have nothing to do with the pit," I say.

Elliot scoffs. "You don't erect stones at each point of a star for no reason. Unless you're an asshole."

"Maybe the treasure's buried there."

"The team that found the stones in 1886 thought the symbols covering the northern Star Stone were a map. They did a dig a few years later. There's a cave below—a whole system of limestone caves—but that's it. Decades of searching since, and nothing but empty caves." He traces the shape into the wall, pressing hard enough to turn his fingernail violently white. "They missed something."

In Elliot's mouth, the word *they* is a slur. But he's a Thorne. They've always found the idea of other treasure hunters particularly distasteful.

I leave him there, fingernail scratching at the mural as if the treasure's buried behind it. As if a hole in the wall will sate his curiosity about a hole in the earth.

"Holy shit," Elliot says, and in the silence of the small room, the sound seems to shout. He gapes at me with eyes so wide I can see the whites from across the room. "Ruby," he says.

I'm surprised he knows my name, and not because most people call me Sadie's sister or nothing at all. I'm surprised because Elliot and I have spoken only twice, years ago when he was a different person.

He widens his eyes even more. *"Ruby."*

Even before he redecorated his wardrobe and his body, Elliot had this look about him—a certain slant of the lips and squint of the eyes—that gave the impression he was in on a secret no one else was smart enough to learn. But now he's looking at me with a smile that says we're partners in something, something rare and important.

It's a frightening thought.

I drop my gaze, and that's when I see it. Caught in a death grip.

A black-and-red cover and a bone-white skull.

THREE

RUBY

STEALING BACK MY BOOK IS AN UNBELIEVABLY EASY TASK. Elliot's staring at the map when I cross the room and snatch *Treasure Island* from his fingers.

His eyebrows lower. "I saw the poem. You know what that is, right?"

"Of course I know what that is," I snip. I'm no good at this. I used to deal with Sadie, and Sadie used to deal with everyone else. Now I have words in my head that want to be words on my tongue. Only, my words are rough, not the pretty things Sadie tossed around.

But I don't need to talk about this at all. I need to turn a poem into instructions, and miles of empty darkness into a hiding place for lost treasure.

I wander to the display cases, which house the only objects the stingy pit has coughed up since it was discovered in 1845. My breath fogs the glass as I read about a coin found in 1943. It's not the perfect circle of the chocolate coins in the museum gift shop. It's hardly a circle at all anymore. The right side is straight and thinner than the rest. It's silver—I know this because everybody knows about the coin—but it's a dull gray, not shiny like a dime.

Elliot elbows me aside, sinks to the floor, and sticks a couple of paper clips into the lock. "Do you know who wrote it? Have you decoded it?"

I press the plastic latch. "No."

I hoped he'd take a hint and drop the topic, but feeding Elliot information is a lot like tossing bread at a seagull. One piece is never enough.

Besides, this isn't just any information. Doris says the first word Elliot uttered was *treasure,* just like his father and grandfather and probably every other Thorne before them.

I'm saved from answering by the pop of the lock and the shudder of the glass door on its metal runner. I pluck the coin from its perch, let the heavy metal cool my palm as I examine it. Its face is stamped with a worn-down crest, flanked on the right with a *P* and an *S* and on the left with an 8.

"Piece of eight." Elliot might not be an employee here, but he's been hanging around the museum for so long—since Bishop Rollins died and the prospect of another hunt went with him—that he knows the exhibit like he's being paid to.

"Where are the other seven?"

Elliot sighs, and it sounds like the precursor to something

violent. "It's not part of a gift set. Pieces of eight were Spanish dollars minted around the seventeenth century. They were basically a worldwide currency through the late eighteen hundreds."

"Could this be part of the treasure?" It doesn't look like much, that's for sure.

Elliot shrugs. "Maybe. Or maybe it's from the first treasure hunter."

I flip the coin to find its date: 1677. "Shouldn't we be wearing white gloves or something?"

"I'm a rebel, Ruby."

In my defense, I try very hard not to laugh. He scowls, then snatches the coin from my fist, returning it to its box.

"You want to see something cool?" He leans against the display case, twirling an enormous knife.

I shrug.

Elliot crowds beside me, shoves the knife handle at me. His finger rubs at a curlicue carved into the handle. "See those words? They're Dutch. You know what that means?"

"A Dutch guy lost a knife on Gray Wolf Island?"

His gaze flits to mine before returning to the intricate design. "It means this knife could have belonged to Michiel Andrieszoon, a Dutch buccaneer who visited New England in the late sixteen hundreds."

"So it could be his treasure," I say.

"Maybe." Elliot spins the knife in his hand with the ease of someone who is used to handling sharp objects. If I'd never followed him to the lecture that day last year, I might imagine him twirling the dagger before pressing the sharp metal against someone's throat. Instead, I picture him practicing with plastic knives in front of his bedroom mirror. "I used to think the Knights Templar buried the Ark of the Covenant there. It seemed like the coolest idea."

"Cooler than endless knowledge?"

Elliot smirks again. "Seeing as I already have endless knowledge . . ." I roll my eyes, and he laughs. "Okay, yes, that'd be cool. But the Ark of the Covenant is at least within the realm of possibility. And even that seems farfetched."

I sigh. I can't help it. "*All* of it seems farfetched."

He searches my face. "You're hunting a treasure you don't believe in?"

"Yes." I think of the book in my hands and the eighteen stanzas weighing me down. "No. I don't know anymore."

"It's real." His words sound like both an invitation and a threat.

I push away from the case of ancient finds, away from Elliot and the interest written all over his face. I poke at a miniature model of Gray Wolf Island that stands on a pedestal in the center of the circular room. Stick my pinky finger down the pit.

He bites his lip, right where a silver hoop sinks into soft flesh. "Let me see the map."

It feels wrong to share. Right now, this search is between me and Sadie, held together with a fragile string that bridges life and death. If I open the book, if I let Elliot look, his knowing will make him a part of it.

Still, I find myself approaching the display case. I think about Sadie on the warm summer day when the air smelled like tuberose and sea salt and how it was just her and me and a promise. Then I think about discussing the treasure, which wasn't as terrible as I'd imagined.

It's strange how someone can so hate loneliness and cling to it all the same.

My fingers shake as I find the poem, as I slide the book across the glass case. Elliot's eyes devour the words. When he's done, he looks at me. Looks through me, mind on an island or down a deep ditch.

"We're going to find the treasure." His mouth kicks up into a genuine grin, but I don't join in.

"No. No, no, no. There's no *we*, Elliot Thorne. There's me, the girl who's going to find the treasure for her sister. And there's you, the Wildewell Historical Society and Museum volunteer, who's going to tell me everything he knows about Gray Wolf Island."

"I don't volunteer here." The poem must have scrambled Elliot's brain because he has this dazed look on his face, like maybe he climbed through a portal and found everyone speaking another language or walking on the ceiling.

"So you know nothing about the island?" This, I know, is false. There are people who know a little about a lot of things. Elliot knows a lot about a lot.

Elliot launches himself onto the display case. His boots bang out a violent beat against the wood. "You can't just use me for my brain."

I want to tell him that people use people all the time and that being used for your mind is infinitely better than being used for something else, but I just raise an eyebrow and wait.

"I have needs, Ruby."

"You can't just use me for my body."

Elliot's jaw unclenches, and though he still looks stern, I

can tell he's fighting a smile. "Forget your body. I want in on the hunt."

"No, this is something I have to do alone. I'll share the treasure with you, though." This is incredibly generous of me, especially since I'll be doing the hard part in traipsing across the island. But Sadie never said I had to keep the treasure, just that I had to find it.

Elliot tugs at his hair. "What the hell's the point of a treasure you don't have to search for?"

I slap *Treasure Island* shut, return it to my bag. "I'll see you around, Elliot."

I turn for the door, but he yanks me back. Elliot's face is stone, but his Adam's apple gives away his nervousness. It bobs and bobs in his throat before he speaks. "The poem—you'll need my help to decode it," he says, but he means so much more.

Elliot is brilliant with words. Piercings, tattoos, and a new wardrobe can't change that. Mrs. Thorne is a linguist. I'm not entirely sure what that means, but I do know that Bishop Rollins hired her to translate the strange symbols covering the northern Star Stone.

More than that, I remember how Elliot used to be: a know-it-all who'd go to war over incorrect word usage or blabber on about the etymology of a term you really didn't care about. So if anyone could decipher the map in the poem, it'd be the boy who wields knowledge like a battle-ax.

But he's a Thorne. "You'd want to do things your way and do them yourself, and a few days later this would be your expedition, not mine."

"Please," he says, and his voice is hoarse with desire. I know the feeling, have since I found the book yesterday. Sometimes I think I can feel the cool waters that pool fifty feet down the hole, the cruel slap of the wild wind that attacks Gray Wolf Island but leaves Wildewell alone.

So I say the only thing I can say. I say yes.

FOUR

THE BOY

It's dark when I wake. The smell of dirt assaults me.

It may be daybreak. Maybe nightfall.

My mouth tastes like dirt.

Where am I?

Who am I?

That last one sends a shock through my system. I jump to my feet. The world goes topsy-turvy, and I stumble forward a few steps before it rights itself.

Up. Down. Those I know.

I scan my body. Injury-free and covered in a layer of dirt. There's a lot of that around here—packed dirt, upturned dirt. Beyond that, a small shack, some shovels sticking out of the earth. To my right, there's a white cross. Straight ahead's a cluster of construction equipment. And behind me is the most massive hole I've ever seen.

Or maybe not. I wouldn't remember.

I peer down the hole. A bunch of black and no help at all. I chuck a rock down there and wait for the *crack* against stone or *plop* into water, but nothing.

I try the shack. Empty and locked. I don't have keys, so it must not be mine.

Who the hell am I?

The question's even more annoying than the more pressing "Where the hell am I?"

I decide to focus on that even though the only way I'll find out is by walking. Luckily, I'm wearing sneakers. I pick a direction by shutting my eyes, spinning in a tight circle, then walking in the direction I'm facing when my eyes open.

So I've learned one new thing about myself: I'm a complete idiot.

It's green. Up, down, wherever I look there's green, green, and more green.

Green grass. Green trees. Green moss.

It's boring, but more than that, it's not helpful. I need street signs.

Unless the green is the clue. Could I be in Ireland? That sounds green.

Maybe I'm Irish. "Maybe I'm Irish," I repeat, out loud this time so I can hear my accent. American.

Useless information. So what if I'm American? I could be

an American lost in China for all this godforsaken wilderness is telling me.

More trees, a river. Grass, flowers, blah, blah, blah. I'm not really stopping to smell the roses here. I'm looking for two things and two things only: signs and people. It's probably an idiot move, but I already established I was an idiot back at that hole.

Hours pass. I estimate it's about eight in the morning.

I can remember how to tell time from the position of the sun, but I can't remember anything about my life. It's really an unfair trade-off.

Giant flies bite my legs. I squash one on my shorts.

The land pitches downward, and my thighs ache with keeping me upright. Halfway between standing and rolling down the steep hill, I smell it. Briny, fishy, salty air.

When the trees clear, I stand on an overhang and view the beach below.

"I live on the beach," I say, testing. It doesn't feel true and it doesn't feel false.

I scan the shore. Jagged rocks. Yellow sand. Deep blue sea.

There's a dock. And bobbing by its side is a boat.

It's spring going on summer. That's another fact I've picked up sometime between waking up beside that hole and reaching the beach. It was warm before sunrise, and now it's sweltering.

I wipe my sweaty brow with the back of my hand. Almost there.

The boat practically glows in the sun. I have no idea if it's nice or anything, but it looks nice. Real shiny.

"Hello?" Water crashing into the shore shushes my shout. "Anyone there?"

The dock creaks underfoot. It's rickety, maybe dangerously so. I study the water lapping its legs.

Can I swim?

I'd like to think that if I couldn't swim, some kind of innate fear would wash over me. My brain's way of saying, "Get off the dock before you drown."

Then again, my brain hasn't been so good to me today.

I listen to the *whap, whap, whap* of wind around sailcloth. Kick the side of the boat with the tip of my shoe and ask, "Are you mine?"

"Son, if the *Gold Bug* were yours, she'd kick you right back for that."

There's a man behind me. He's older than me, but by how much I don't know. I haven't exactly seen myself. At any rate, I feel a lot younger than he looks.

I wait for a reaction. Relieved hug. Questioning look.

His weather-beaten face gives away nothing.

The man tosses a bag onto the boat. Runs a finger along the hull, right where I kicked it. I think it's to make me feel bad. Honestly, though, I can't feel much worse than I did waking up without a past and trekking across this stupid green land.

The man looks over his shoulder at me. "You stealing my boat, boy?"

Boy. So I must be pretty young. If the ocean weren't so active here, I'd peek over the edge of this dock for a glimpse of my face. "Do you know me?"

"You come with the Belfast crew to help at the dig?"

"We're in Ireland?" This is doubly surprising, because the old man has an American accent, too.

His features screw up in a way that makes him look both refined and mocking. "Not my new assistant, that's for sure." He laughs. "Ireland."

"It *is* green."

"Course it's green. It's spring."

My head starts pounding, probably from too little memory. "Look, I don't know anything about anything except pointless things like the sun, so could you just tell me where we are?"

"Gray Wolf Island," he says.

"Okay, but *where* is Gray Wolf Island?"

"Off the coast of Maine." The man squints at me. "What's the matter with you?"

I flop onto the dock, not even caring that I might fall into the water and maybe drown. "I woke up next to this massive hole, and I have nothing in my head. Not a fucking thing."

"Don't curse," says the man.

"I'm sorry."

He shakes his head. "You look young, but . . . You have an ID on you?"

It didn't even occur to me to check for a license—more proof I was either born stupid or had it knocked into my head when my memory was knocked out.

I fumble through my pockets. All empty.

My shoulders droop.

"C'mon," the man says, hopping aboard the boat like he's a kid or something. Nimble and quick. I follow him. Not much else I can do. "We'll take you around town, see if any of the tourists might have lost you."

37

I close my eyes as he works the boat. The insides of my eyelids go red in the sun.

Who am I?

Who am I?

Who am I?

"Nameless Boy," he calls. I open my eyes to a salty sea breeze. Water splashes my cheeks as the boat speeds along. "Never did introduce myself. I'm Mr. Rollins at the dig site, but you can call me Bishop."

FIVE

RUBY

THORNE MANOR SITS GRANDLY ON A STRETCH OF GREEN SET apart from the larger, more modern homes on the street. Weathered stone gives the home an unrefined look, but the widow's walk atop the roof elevates its status, as if the Thornes need another way to stand above us all.

The imperious attitude of past Thornes had less to do with intellectual aptitude, as it does with Elliot, and more to do with a very old shoe. Harry Thorne, who heard the island's call all the way from California, spent five long years digging in that pit before its walls coughed up a worn leather shoe. That was 1876, and though no Thorne has unearthed an artifact since, they like to think they could.

I follow a walkway as it curves around the side of the house. With a connecting stone wall crumbling down a rocky crag and into the shore, Thorne Manor appears fused with the beach, as if the house itself is trying to sneak closer to the island.

Elliot answers the door less than a minute after I ring the bell. His dark hair is in disarray, the longer top section nearly standing on end. He runs a hand through it. "I was worried you weren't going to come."

"I'm here," I say, but I almost wasn't. I had second thoughts about our partnership a dozen times last night, my mind flipping back and forth like a girl plucking petals from a flower. *He can help me. He can help me not. He can help me . . .* And that's what I decided. As much as I want this experience to be about me and Sadie, about me finally atoning for what I did, I need help.

"Elliot, who was— Oh, hello." Mrs. Thorne is a giant of a woman, nearly a head above my five-foot-eight frame. Her smile is warm and weepy, the same smile she's worn every day since Elliot's dad took that gun to his face. She reaches a skeletal hand toward him, but he shoots her a glare and she snaps it back.

Elliot shoulders past his mother. "C'mon, Ruby. We have a lot to do."

I glance between mother and son. The tension in the foyer is as heavy as a grown man. "Nice to meet you," I tell Mrs. Thorne with a smile.

She nods, scurries away.

Elliot is all stiff shoulders and silence as we walk upstairs and to his room. Heavy boot meets blond wood, and his door flies open. It clatters against the wall and shakes his shelves.

I notice Charlie first, almost too late. My shoe nearly crunches his fingers into the floor, where his lanky body is contorted like the chalk outline of a dead boy. It's as angelic as Charles Kim has ever appeared.

Elliot kicks his side. "Quit playing dead," he says. "It's disturbing."

The spell is broken when Charlie's eyes shoot open and his face takes on a familiar impish appearance. In a swift motion, he jumps up—he's always jumping: over things, onto things, off things—only to flop back down on a beanbag chair, where he sits like a crumpled piece of paper.

Elliot takes the only available chair, which he collapses into with a thud before thunking his feet on his desk. I resign myself to the bed, across which Gabe Nash has draped himself like a muse waiting to be sketched. I perch at the edge of the mattress, worrying at the hem of my jean shorts as I wait for Elliot to kick the boys out so we can get down to business.

"So, did you bring it?" Elliot asks.

My jaw clenches. I have a feeling our treasure-hunting team of two has doubled. "I thought we were going to talk about . . ." I widen my eyes. "You know."

"The treasure? We are. They're part of the team."

"The team, Elliot?" I take a deep breath. "You have commandeered my mission."

"No, I invited friends."

It's times like these when I wish Sadie were here to save me.

My fingernails bite my palms. My voice is as calm as the sea before a storm, but inside I'm the wind that riles the water and lets grown men drown. "By inviting *your* friends, you have stolen the leadership of this mission. You are a leadership stealer."

"Right." He turns to the boys. "Ruby's in charge."

"Cool," says Charlie.

"Cool," says Gabe.

I release a low groan. This is everything I don't want. Sadie never specified that I have to do this alone, but I don't think she'd support the idea of these boys finding her treasure.

That's another lie.

"Fine," I say, because I knew my twin better than I know myself, and Sadie would never turn down a trip with three cute boys. Their eyes are glued to my fingers as I unzip my bag and remove the book. The mattress bounces as Gabe scoots closer, peering over my shoulder at the worn novel. I flip to the final page. Skim my fingers over the simple words that will lead me to the treasure.

Gabe's chin presses into my shoulder, and warmth tickles my ear as he lets out a breath. "No way."

"Um, yes," I say, politely inching away. "Yes way."

His body sways into me. Palm to forehead, I push him out of my personal space. I stand, pressing my back against the wall.

Guilt flashes across Gabe's face, but only for an instant. He laughs and retreats to the other side of the bed, reclining in a position that would give Doris another heart attack. "I thought *you* were supposed to find the map," he says to Elliot. "What kind of Thorne are you?"

Elliot flinches at that, and I get the sense that he's the kind of Thorne who'll spend his life trying to live up to the expectations of six little letters. "Does it matter? We have the map, and we're going to have the treasure, too."

Elliot leans forward as if there's a string between his chest and the book, and by opening the cover, I've given a not-so-gentle tug. I read the poem aloud, barely looking at the words on the page. I've studied them so often they've burrowed into the folds of my brain.

When I'm done, Charlie tilts his head back and releases the loudest laugh I've ever heard. "Dude," he says, glancing at Elliot with watery eyes. "You look like you're going to tackle her."

Elliot sinks back into his chair. He chucks a balled-up sock at Charlie. "Ruby's protective of her book. But," he says, focusing on me, "I can decode the poem if you'd let me have a look."

I hug the book to my chest. "So you can solve it on your own?"

He stares at me—eyes narrowed, tongue tangling with the hoop at the edge of his lower lip—but that's about as far as Elliot's intimidation goes. "I wouldn't do that."

"Uh, yes you would." Gabe plucks the book from my fingers.

"Shut up, Gabriella," Elliot says.

Gabe's fingers tighten on the pages, but his face reveals no tension. "Dick."

"Least he has one," Charlie contributes to this pointless conversation.

Elliot ends up with the book anyway, because he snatches it from the bed as Gabe leaps at Charlie. They roll around on the floor like a couple of feral animals, nearly knocking Elliot's dresser over in the process. Elliot, for his part, grins as he reads the book, as if the fight was his plan all along.

"Take it back or I'll shave your eyebrows," Gabe says, his muscular frame pinning Charlie to the floor.

"It's like I'm being mauled by a gorilla. Not that I've ever been mauled by a gorilla. Or been mauled. Or seen a gorilla." Charlie tries to kick the back of Gabe's head, but mostly he just flails like a toppled giraffe. "Fine, I take it back."

Gabe eases off Charlie, swipes at his ruffled brown hair, and collapses back on the bed with a satisfied sigh, as if Charlie's proclamation of his masculinity is the only reason it's real.

"You find the treasure yet?" Charlie asks Elliot from a splayed-out spot on the floor. Sweat sticks his hair to his skin, and he wipes it away with the back of his hand.

Sadie always said Charlie was about as exciting as Wildewell got. He does the things no one else is brave enough or stupid enough to do, and he does them with an air of fearless nonchalance that makes him appear larger than Wildewell will ever be. When he went cliff diving during a thunderstorm, Sadie decided he'd be her one true love.

This had more to do with the fact that she was dying and everyone knows Charlie is going to go someday soon. It might have been romantic if she hadn't gotten worse before Charlie figured out his end of the whole thing.

Elliot runs his fingers over the slashed square at the top of the page. "You ever see this symbol before?"

Only every time I close my eyes. "No. Could it be one of those old letters, like from Viking times?"

"Runes? Unlikely. I'm pretty familiar with the runic alphabet."

And Sadie thought *this* boy could teach me about adventure?

"My mom taught it to me when she was trying to translate the Star Stone markings, which turned out not to be runes." His mouth tightens, and for a minute it's just Elliot and his thoughts. Then he flicks the page. "Anyway, this symbol isn't part of the alphabet."

"It could correspond with the third stanza." I gaze at the ceiling and pull the poem from my memory. " 'Your adventure begins with stars trapped in a sign. Navigate with them and our paths will align.' Maybe we find the symbol in the night sky and it'll point to the treasure."

Elliot's "No" bites off the end of my sentence. "It's too easy to connect the stars into this shape. We could make dozens of squares with lines down the middle."

"It's a constellation that corresponds with the signs of the zodiac," Gabe says. "We find the right one, we use that to navigate."

"Celestial navigation doesn't work that way. The stars can tell you where you are or which direction you're headed, but they can't give turn-by-turn directions for a location even we don't know. And," Elliot says, swiveling to Gabe, "how the hell do you know about zodiac constellations?"

"What? Kiera James likes to do my horoscope. And I like to do—"

"The next stanza," I say before the room fills up with any more testosterone. "We should talk about that."

Elliot unrolls a map of Gray Wolf Island. It's from the museum gift shop, so there's a crispness to the otherwise antique-looking paper. " 'Discover the spot where morning sun scorches sand and the ocean beats its anger into the land.' That's talking about a beach."

"Where's the water roughest?" I ask.

"Two places," Elliot says. "Before Rollins Corp. bought the island, a kid died while swimming by the cliffs in the southeast.

A wave crashed him against the rocks. But in the northwest there's a small beach and another set of cliffs with violent waves."

"One of those is where the ocean beats its anger into the land."

Elliot appraises me with something like admiration. "Exactly. The only dock on the island is in the south, so we'll start with those cliffs. If that doesn't lead to the treasure, we'll start over and follow the map from the northwestern cliffs."

Charlie unearths a tennis ball from beneath Elliot's bed, chucks it against the door. "You realize Rollins Corp. still owns the island, so you'll be trespassing."

"And you care?" Gabe asks with a laugh. He and Elliot share a look that says Charlie is out of his mind. I think it's a valid question.

Charlie rolls his eyes. "Obviously, no. But *I'm* not going."

This sends Gabe and Elliot into a minute-long discussion spoken solely in eye movements. It feels sort of intimate, and I press my back against the wall until I feel myself go a little invisible.

The tennis ball clatters against the door again. "I can hear you," Charlie says.

"We're not talking." Gabe grins, but Charlie is too busy chucking the tennis ball against the door to notice.

"Whatever. Not even a killer cliff dive could lure me to that deathtrap."

My eyebrows jump to my hairline. Charlie Kim isn't afraid of anything.

Everyone remembers the scared Korean kid who never removed his bike helmet, not even indoors. Wade Kim. It's the name Charlie used to go by, back when he was a scared slip of a thing. The summer he got cool enough for boys to call him by his last name, he went around answering to Kim. That confused all the old people in town, who knew one or two other Kims, all of whom were women. When his father died that fall, Wade stole his name, and he's been Charlie ever since.

Connecting Wade with Charlie is almost impossible. This boy has free-climbed Wildewell's highest cliffs. He's gone skydiving and white-water rafting and heli-skiing. He shouldn't be afraid of Gray Wolf Island. Of all of us, he shouldn't be afraid.

I glance between Elliot and Gabe, then finally look at Charlie, who leans on his elbows, feet still splayed to the sides. He sighs. "It's the legend."

He's talking about the three deaths the pit needs before it gives up the treasure: an accident, a suicide, and a murder.

"The pit's a greedy bastard," Sadie used to say. "It got its accident. It got its suicide. And it's still demanding murder."

Charlie hurls the tennis ball across the room, hard enough to smack Elliot's door shut. "I'm not going to be the pit's murder. I could *die*."

"I'm not talking about your fucking death again," Elliot snarls before he storms out of the room.

Charlie's gaze locks with mine, and for the first time in a very long time his eyes are haunted. "That's the thing, Ruby. I'm going to die on Gray Wolf Island."

SIX

RUBY

The Boy Who Is Going to Die. That's what they call Charles Kim. Not the Boy With the Virgin Mother, like Gabe, or the One Whose Dad Blew His Face Off, like Elliot. Ever since he had his first vision at age six, Charlie has been the boy who would die.

It's absurd, really, that title. We're all going to die. The only difference is that Charlie's time is coming soon.

This knowledge is as much a part of me as the fact that Wildewell daffodils stay shut until a band of yellow-rumped warblers sings the buds into bloom. I don't remember a time when Charlie wasn't on the cusp of dying.

But I didn't know he'd do it on Gray Wolf Island. Or that he'd do it quite so soon.

Elliot and Gabe knew this already. Their eyes didn't bug

out of their heads and nearly bounce across the room like mine. Still, Charlie's declaration officially ended our meeting, and I've been avoiding the boys ever since.

Now, two days later, I've decided to go alone. It's not just about Charlie. It's that any of them could die, and it'd be my fault for finding the map. I've done enough murdering, thank you very much.

But then the doorbell rings and they lure me right back in.

"We need a boat, Ruby." Elliot pushes his way through my door with such authority I feel as if I'm the guest. I should have known he wouldn't give up.

Charlie pauses for less than a second before disappearing through the wide French doors to my left. He shouts something about food that gets muffled as he moves farther into the house. If I hadn't spent the past forty-eight hours contemplating his imminent death, I'd tell him how much my mother hates when anyone wears shoes in the house. But I feel bad about him dying sometime soon, so I stay silent.

He wanders back into the foyer, granola bar between his teeth and crumbs dusting his T-shirt.

"Can't bring him anywhere." Gabe's breath is warm on my ear. "Me, though? You can take me *anywhere*."

"You have a problem with personal space," I say, then turn to Elliot. He's in full thug mode today, muscle tee baring his inked-up arms, shorts hanging loose and low. "Also, I don't have a boat."

"I know," Elliot says without glancing up from the book he's pulled from thin air. He's standing in front of a window that gives his hair a halo of light, as if the sun itself has anointed him the leader. "I arranged an appointment with someone who does."

"How anyone believes you're anything but a control freak with initiative, I have no idea," I say, forgetting for a moment that when I speak without thinking I almost always say things that are rude. Sadie would be rolling her eyes at me right about now.

I dare a glance at Elliot. He seems surprised for some reason. Maybe he believes he's a better bad boy than he actually is.

"Don't you have a boat?" I ask Charlie, whose stepdad is rich enough to own a fleet.

Charlie mumbles something, spitting a few pieces of granola in the process. Gabe translates. "Charlie broke the last boat when he tried to see if a case of soda stuffed with firecrackers would blow up."

"It was an experiment," Charlie says. "Like, with science and fun."

I'm supposed to carry out a serious treasure hunt with these people? "This is going to take longer than a day. I doubt our parents will let us spend a week on Gray Wolf Island."

Elliot shrugs. "I wasn't planning on telling my mom."

"We'll say we're visiting colleges," Gabe says.

I sigh. "Who are we bribing?"

"No one," Elliot says. "Gabe mentioned you visit Mrs. Lansing all the time. She'll let you borrow her boat."

A laugh bursts from my chest, bounces around the foyer. "I'm not the one who should be asking her," I say with a pointed look at Gabe.

"Me? I've met her, like, twice."

"Well, she knows you." I really do try to contain the giggles that spill from my lips. "You in those sensible khakis and starched shirt. You without a shirt, covered in sweat and glistening . . ."

Charlie drops to the floor with laughter, and Gabe lunges for him. Charlie dodges, then flees out the front door.

"She thinks you'd be a very tidy kisser."

Gabe follows Charlie's howling outside. Elliot looks up from his book, glances around the room, and shrugs. "Let's go."

And then he's gone, too, and I'm left with a choice.

So I walk out the door.

"If I'd known *you* were coming, I'd have worn my fancy sweater." Doris fluffs her hair and gazes at Gabe over her shoulder as we spill out of the Oceanview Nursing Center.

I walk beside her wheelchair, carrying a bundle of sweetgrass. When she was younger—and younger for Doris means forty, even though that's not young at all—she and other Native American women founded a basket-weaving band. Together they'd canoe out to Arrow Isle and gather heaps of sweetgrass from the marsh, then sleep under the stars.

She can't make the trip herself anymore, so sometimes I get up early and hitch a ride to the island on a lobster boat. It's how I spent yesterday, so she'd have the sweetgrass for the apprentice she's teaching in a couple weeks. But instead of being grateful, she won't let me push her wheelchair because Gabe is here and have I seen his muscles?

"You have just lovely features. Like a young Cary Grant." Doris has been in love with Cary Grant since before color TV.

Gabe winks at me. "Not nearly as lovely as yours, Mrs. Lansing."

I roll my eyes. Doris laughs. "So polite. What'd I tell you, Ruby? This is the kind of boy you want to marry." Gabe's face pales. Either he's grossed out by the idea of marrying me or he's grossed out by marriage in general. Probably both.

Elliot's shoulders tighten. He can't help that people see *his* lovely features and imagine the man who bit the barrel of a gun. And Charlie? Well, no one considers Charlie for the long run.

Elliot sits at the base of a wide tree, crosses his ankles, and opens his book. Charlie disappears into the foliage. I get the sense that dealing with these boys is going to be more difficult than finding buried treasure.

"Excuse me, Mrs. Lansing?" Gabe with manners is actually kind of cute. I bite back a smile and focus on Doris, who's straightening the pile of sweetgrass I dropped on the ground.

"Call me Doris, dear. I'm not that old." The tree guffaws. Doris glares at the branch above our heads. "Keep laughing, Charles Kim, and your time will come sooner than you've seen."

Leaves rustle overhead. Then a body soars toward the wall that forms a barrier between the nursing home's land and the ocean beyond. Charlie teeters at the top of the wall, arms pinwheeling as his body tilts toward the sea below. But he rights himself, brushes his shaggy hair from his eyes, and winks. "Don't worry, Mrs. Lansing. I can't die until it's my time to die."

Doris shakes her head. "It's not a question of when that boy's going to die. It's a matter of who's going to kill him first."

Charlie cracks up at this.

"Today it's going to be me." Elliot glares at Charlie. "We're off topic."

I should care that we haven't secured a boat yet, but mostly I'm enjoying being in on the jokes, even if all I've done so far is sit and watch without a word.

Gabe smiles at Doris. "We're going to discover the Gray Wolf Island treasure."

"Of course you are. You have this one leading you," Doris says with a head tip to Elliot. As if simply being a Thorne makes him more capable of finding the treasure. I behead a purple clover.

"Well, uh, we need a boat," Gabe says. "To get there."

"I see." She meets my gaze with a single raised eyebrow. "And you thought I'd be more inclined to loan it to you if Gabriel here asked?"

"Yes?" I squint at her through the sunlight. "Is it going to work?"

Doris sighs. "Of course it's going to work."

Elliot's head jerks up, revealing wide eyes and an open mouth. Gabe huffs. "You always underestimate my charm."

Doris pats his head. "So which of you boys knows how to sail a boat?"

"I do," Charlie says.

Doris's thin lips are a slash of coral against her tan skin. "Try again."

I shake my head. Sadie was afraid of the open ocean, so we never learned to sail. Gabe looks the part, but he informs Doris that he wouldn't know a boat's left from its right. This seems to dampen her opinion of him, because she spends a full two minutes explaining that boats have port and starboard sides, but not lefts and rights.

"I know how to drive a speedboat," Elliot says. "And I'm a fast learner."

"Oh no." Doris shakes her head, then rolls her eyes for extra effect. "Bishop would have a fit just thinking about you taking the *Gold Bug* to that cursed island without a bit of sailing know-how."

With a flick of his finger, Elliot's Wayfarers slide from his head to the bridge of his nose.

"What you need," Doris says, "is someone like my great-granddaughter."

I'm sure Doris would volunteer herself if she actually knew how to sail, but she inherited the *Gold Bug* long after old age made her landlocked. So while Bishop Rollins left the sailboat to Doris when he died, he really left it to Anne Lansing. Unlike Doris's daughter and granddaughter, Anne had both the time and patience to learn.

A dark eyebrow rises above cherry-red shades. "You trust her more than me and Charlie?"

"Guess we know how I'm dying," Charlie says.

Doris shrugs. She and about everybody else in Wildewell stopped guessing how Charlie will go a long time ago. "I suppose you could just give up."

I groan. At this rate, the entire town may as well migrate to Gray Wolf Island for the hunt.

"Thanks anyway, Doris. But I think we'll forget about the treasure." Elliot peers at me over the top of his sunglasses. "Our leader is a bit antisocial."

I shouldn't care that he's right. I shouldn't want to be like these boys, who cease to exist without each other. It's a dangerous thing, flinging open your chest and begging another person to burrow inside without breaking anything.

After Sadie, I should want to be alone. But that's the thing: In a flash, alone becomes lonely. Maybe I've been waiting for someone to push me. That's what these boys are doing, I think. They're forcing their way under my skin.

I drop my gaze to the ground. "No," I say. "We're going."

SEVEN

THE BOY

I LEARN LITTLE THINGS ABOUT MYSELF BETWEEN THE MOMENT I board Bishop's boat and the moment I know I belong to no one.

It starts with the waves. Rolling, playfully nudging the boat. We rock, tilt, dip, and rise.

I don't get seasick.

Of all the pointless things I know about my unknown self, this one finally works in my favor.

I ask Bishop about me as we sail to his home. Try to soak up as many details as possible. Hoping something will tug at my memory.

"And this," I say, yanking at a chunk of hair. "What's this look like?"

Bishop's doing all this stuff with the boat, so he barely gives me a look. "Brown."

"There are a million shades of brown," I say.

"Thought you didn't know anything."

"I don't know anything about myself. I know plenty about other things. Besides, even if my brain was totally blank, I'd know brown isn't brown isn't brown. Your face is brown, but it's darker than the dirt on that damn island."

"Don't curse," he says. "And, fine. Your hair's the color of Indian laurel."

"That a flower?" I tug my hair forward, but I can't make out the ends that brush my eyebrows. "Am I the kind of guy who dyes his hair the color of a flower?"

"It's a type of hardwood. I have a desk made from it— a nice, rich brown."

I open my eyes really wide. "What about my eyes?"

"Ah, you've got Gray Wolf Island eyes."

I blink against the drying wind. "I don't know what that means."

"Green as the grass in the valley."

"Humph," I say, still sore at all the green for its uselessness.

Land rises in the distance, a smattering of houses and hilltops. As we near, I make out a small marina, a cluster of buildings painted a dozen different colors, a tall cliff, and a giant house perched at its edge.

"Who lives there?"

Bishop glances at the estate. "An old man on an even older quest."

There's a bed-and-breakfast in the center of Wildewell that looks like a frosted gingerbread house. It's dark brown, maybe Indian laurel brown. The trim's turquoise. Some kind of white wood made to resemble lace dangles from the roof.

Inside, it looks like a candy store exploded. The furniture's a rainbow of gumdrop colors. The wood stairs are bubblegum pink. The painting behind the reception desk is a lollipop swirl. I eye the jar of jelly beans on the counter.

"Go ahead, have some." The receptionist is younger than Bishop but old enough to have some gray hair. She has kind eyes. Makes me think I had some kindness in my past if I can recognize the kindness in her.

I shove a handful in my mouth.

"Maybe you're part animal," Bishop says, popping jelly beans in his mouth one by one. "You eat like one."

"I can't remember the last time I ate," I say around a mouthful of candy.

"You can't remember anything."

"Not a thing?" Bed-and-Breakfast Lady asks.

I shake my head. "Do you know me?"

I've spent the past hour asking that question. Bishop looks less hopeful than he did when we first set foot on land. Looks about as hopeful as I feel.

"Wouldn't know," she says, pointing to her eyes. The pupils have gone hazy gray. "The morning fog got caught in my eyes, and I can't seem to blink it out."

"But you might know me."

"Maybe." She shakes her head. "But right now you're as big a mystery as that island."

❖

The porch is empty, aside from a kid wearing a helmet who's staring into space. "Weird," I mumble.

Bishop slaps me upside the head. "C'mon, Nameless Boy. Time to go to the police."

I stop him in front of a blue cottage with a billion buoys hung from its side. It's been hours since I woke up beside that pit. Hours to wonder who I am. How I got there. Why I'm as dumb as the day I was born.

I'm sick of being an unknown. "I don't want to be Nameless Boy."

"How about Bart? It fits you."

"I look like a Bart?" I blow out a low breath. I'd forgotten about finding a mirror while we searched for someone who knew me. I'm tempted to find my reflection in a car window, but this day keeps getting worse and worse, which means I'll probably find out I do look like a Bart.

Bishop rolls his eyes, which is strange for a guy so old. "The way you act. You have a Bart-ness to you."

"What the hell's that even mean?"

"Don't curse," he says. "And it means that I had a really nice dog named Bart and you remind me of him."

"I'd really rather not be named after a dog."

"He was a good dog."

"How'd you like it if I called you Rover instead of Bishop?"

"You have a dog named Rover?"

I slump against the store window. A flyer for the one hundred and fifty-eighth annual Festival of Souls scratches at my neck. "Obviously I don't know that. I don't know anything. But I could."

"Oh, do whatever you want. It's your fake name."

I roll my head. COOPER COUNTRY STORE screams in yellow.

"Cooper," I tell Bishop. "My name's Cooper."

EIGHT

RUBY

THERE'S A BATTLE GOING ON, AND I'M NOT THE ONLY ONE
watching. I stand in the lone shadow amid the swirling lights
of the merry-go-round, letting my body fade until I'm as vis-
ible as the wind. Across the dirt path, Elliot, Charlie, and Gabe
grab their guns. A bell dings, and the boys shoot, streaming
water at moving clamshells with bull's-eyes on their backs.

Elliot grins at Gabe. It's the kind of smile I imagine the
devil might have before he swindles you out of a soul. Water
arcs over the clams, over the counter, over Charlie. Lines of
wet crisscross Gabe's chest. Elliot laughs, and it's loud and
deep and magnetic. It's a sound I swear I've never heard before.

My mouth smiles without my permission. I'm high on
their energy, their excitement, their hope. Sadie would tell me

61

to barge in on their fun and make some for myself. But I can catch the buzz just fine like this.

A group of Sadie's friends approaches, and I'm glad I didn't bridge the gap between me and the boys. With me, the effervescent mood would flatten. It always does. I don't even blame them—I'd have a hard time talking to someone who looked just like Sadie, too.

Elliot cranes his neck and scans the crowd. I feel it the moment he senses me, a warming of my skin that makes my body reappear.

"Ruby!"

I give a single wave, then shove my hand in my hair. "I think I need a funnel cake."

"Wait!" He jogs across the dirt path, kicking up pebbles as he goes. "You disappeared there for a bit."

I shrug, embarrassed. "Nice game."

"If you haven't noticed, I'm kind of a badass these days."

I'm pretty sure badasses don't go around telling everyone they're badass. I do my best to hold back a smile. "I do not think that word means what you think it means."

"Inconceivable. I'm a linguistic prodigy, you know."

"That I believe."

He laughs, then it's back to business. "C'mon, let's round up the guys. Anne's meeting us at the Ferris wheel at eight-thirty."

While Elliot wrangles Charlie away from the pirates' ship, I head for Gabe, who's on the verge of disappearing for an entirely different reason.

He's sandwiched between two girls on a picnic table, beneath a sign that shouts, 165TH ANNUAL FESTIVAL OF SOULS

CARNIVAL! His shirt hangs from his hands, swaying in the slight breeze. I'd like to pretend I don't notice his muscles, but it's hard not to with the sunset giving Gabe's skin an unnatural glow.

"Your shirt's dry," Elliot says as he approaches the table.

"Looks like the fun police have officially ended this party," Gabe says with a pout, though he almost looks relieved. He trades phone numbers with the girls as Elliot reads a book and Charlie unwraps a lollipop the size of his head.

"Want a lick?" Charlie leans his shoulder against mine, sticks his rainbow pop in my face. I shake my head. He touches the sticky candy to my lips. "It's okay. I don't care about your germs."

I lick the top because it makes Charlie smile. He's going to die soon, so the least I can do is eat some of his candy.

"Finally," Elliot says when Gabe saunters over. "Let's go find Anne."

As we wander the carnival, the purple-streaked sky darkens to deep cerulean. Fairy lights flicker on, illuminating trees on the outskirts of the grounds. Chinese lanterns strung overhead light the walkways with brilliant color.

My neighbor Alfie Barker sidles up to Gabe. "Got a job interview tomorrow. If I don't get it, I'll be bent-backed by sixty for all the clam digging I'll be doing. Could really use some divine intervention, if you don't mind."

He won't say no. Hasn't since he was ten and ran from a lobsterman looking for a bit of luck. When the season was bad, half of Wildewell was sure Gabe cursed us all. I've always felt a little awful for him, all those people thinking they can treat him like a charm. It makes me glad I'm so unremarkable.

Gabe sighs, opens his arms. The older man engulfs Gabe in a hug.

I wait beneath a fat tree. Miniature wolves spot its branches, foam-and-fur creations with clay fangs. The Junior League makes them each year, a nod to the famous island that we pin to the old tree with our greatest desires.

"I'm going to wish your lips here," Gabe tells me, tapping his neck with a wolf's Styrofoam snout. He attaches his wolf to a low branch, then stands in front of me, waiting. A shadow passes over his face, and I look up to find a tall Native American boy with spiked hair blotting out the lamplight.

"Hey, Gabriella." Ronnie Lansing smiles like he knows a joke and Gabe's the punch line. "Things so desperate you have to beg a ghost to get with you?"

"Last night it was your girlfriend doing the begging."

"You don't talk about my—"

Elliot's fist shoves the rest of Ronnie's words back into his mouth. "The next one's on Gabe."

"Unhinged." Ronnie spits blood on Elliot's shoe. "Just like your dad."

Elliot lunges for Ronnie, but Charlie holds him back.

"Move," Ronnie says. "Unless you want me to be the one who kills you."

"You could," Charlie says. "But I can't promise I'll stay dead. Not to say you'd be an inefficient murderer or anything. It's just that I'm planning to die somewhere else."

"You have fun with that." Ronnie turns to Gabe with teeth

made of razor blades and tongue spitting blood. "Let me know if you find that Y chromosome."

And then he's gone.

Elliot jerks out of Charlie's grasp. "I was handling it."

Gabe wraps an arm around my shoulder, tucks me into his side. "Ronnie's totally jealous of my good looks and raw masculinity, isn't he?"

It's a dark sort of magic that can turn a person's anger into something potent enough to poison lives. I'm just thankful Ronnie's picking on someone who has enough ego not to feel its effects.

"So jealous," I say as I approach the wishing tree. Two dollars gets me my own wolf. I pick a higher branch, one not already covered in artificial wolves. I close my eyes, real tight. *I wish Sadie were alive.*

The boys find me like that, too afraid to learn my silly wish didn't come true.

"So, what was your wish?" Elliot says when we've left the tree and our hopes behind. "To find the treasure?"

I don't say anything at first, then I whisper, "I wished my sister back."

He nods. "I waste all my wishes trying to bring back my brother." He's talking about Toby, who was so taken with the idea of a treasure that at age ten he attempted to walk straight through the ocean to Gray Wolf Island. "Think one day it'll work?"

"I think if grief and hope could bring people back from the dead, Sadie would be leading this treasure hunt."

The boys are quiet for once, letting the carnival swallow us whole. The Tilt-A-Whirl plays an upbeat song and the air is a mix of spun sugar and salt. If it weren't for the person missing from my side, this moment would be perfect.

I'm a liar, so I tell myself it's perfect anyway.

❖

We find Anne by the Ferris wheel, its blinking lights turning her shirt green then blue then purple and back again. She's the exact opposite of Ronnie—all soft edges, wide eyes, and a dreamy smile—yet she's unmistakably his sister.

Anne cranes her neck to look at Charlie. Her crown of flowers slips to the side. "I was just thinking of candy."

She plucks the lollipop from Charlie's fingers and takes a cracking bite. A soft breeze sticks her chin-length hair to the rainbow surface. "Don't worry," she says, returning the lollipop to Charlie, "hair's clean."

Charlie shrugs and licks away. "They need your help, Anne."

She tilts her head to the side. "I'm cheapest in the summer, but I still charge based on interest. I may have more hours in the day than the rest of you, but I don't like to spend them bored."

Gabe turns to Elliot. "What's she talking about?"

Anne's small nose scrunches. "Buying hours."

Everyone knows that Anne Lansing doesn't sleep. She hasn't needed to since her parents took off that hot summer night. Since her aunt and uncle, both important people with too little time, prayed for more hours in Anne's day.

But the ever-churning Wildewell gossip mill has never whispered about an hour-buying business.

"My spare time," she says, head tilted back to watch the Ferris wheel make its slow circle. "Buy hours, and I'll spend them doing whatever you need to get done."

"Yeah, we're not buying your time."

"What Elliot means," Gabe says with the kind of smile that should come with a license, "is that we're inviting you on a trip."

"As friends?" Anne's big eyes widen. She looks so small beside the towering ride, next to these towering boys and me, the tower of a girl.

"Well, as our sailboat captain." Elliot grunts as Gabe's elbow meets his stomach. "But also as friends."

If possible, her eyes get even bigger. "I don't have any of those."

It's probably true. Sadie thought Anne lived in her own head a little too much. I never said so, but I always liked that about her. I got the sense that if we ever became friends it'd be because she liked me for me, not because my face matched Sadie's.

"We're searching for the Gray Wolf Island treasure," Elliot says. "Your great-grandmother already said she'll cover for you with your aunt and uncle. So you're coming."

"This is so exciting!" Anne shouts, and it'd be ear-piercing loud if it weren't for the carnival music that muffles everything else. She bounces on her heels, jostling her flower crown. "So, when do we go?"

NINE

RUBY

My mother can't contain her excitement. She tucks her bare feet beneath her, bounces on the oversized armchair. Wild auburn hair and a red-lipped smile make her look younger than she is, though there's a chance her skin has been wearing crushed daffodil petals, which she swears can reverse aging. "It was awfully nice of them to invite you."

"I invited them." A ladybug lands on my bare knee. Little legs tickle my skin. When we were kids, Sadie and I made wishes on the insects, rubbing their backs three times for good luck. This summer, the house has been so overrun by ladybugs that my mother has started sucking them from the windows and curtains with a vacuum. With that many around, it seems less like random signs of good luck and more like, well, an infestation of insects.

"In what I may later consider a spell of terrible parenting, I'm going to overlook the whole trespassing thing. But only because Bishop Rollins is dead and nobody polices the island." She's talking about the treasure hunt. I considered lying—I'm a liar, after all—but I knew I wouldn't need to. "I know how much she wanted this for you. *I* want this for you."

I can't look at her with all that love just spilling over, everything I don't deserve puddling in the space between us. Times like this, I wish she'd figure it out—that Sadie's eyes weren't bloodshot from sickness, that I'm filled with a disgusting darkness.

But my parents will never suspect that evil lives in me. And I'm too much of a coward to tell.

My mom leans forward, squeezes my hand. "I would have hated to see you miss out simply because you can't go alone."

"I can go alone," I say.

"No, you can't." I open my mouth, but she cuts me off before I can respond. "That was an order, not a challenge."

My dad appears in the doorway, keys dangling from his fingers. Straight from work at the law firm, he's polish and poise, hair combed to the side, tie tight around his neck, jacket stiff over his sturdy frame. His gaze ping-pongs between me and my mother. "Is this a girl thing?"

My mom waves him into the living room. "A group of kids invited Ruby on a camping trip. Isn't that wonderful?"

"I invited them."

"That's great, sweetie," he says, stealing a bowl of honey-roasted peanuts from the coffee table and tossing them into his mouth one by one. "I'll get the tent from the attic for you."

"We're not camping," I say. "We're going to find the Gray Wolf Island treasure."

I expect him to choke on a peanut in surprise, but he doesn't even lift his eyes from his honey-roasted fingers. "You'll still need a tent for that, right?"

"How about the red one we used a few years ago? That fit you and Sadie comfortably," my mom says. "Unless Anne's sharing a tent with her great-grandmother—then you can use the small blue tent and the boys can use the red if they need one."

"Doris is just lending her boat. She's not coming with us," I say. "I mean, c'mon, Mom, she's like a billion years old."

My mom seems to sink into the chair. "Well."

My dad shakes his head. "You're not attending an unchaperoned camping trip with teenage boys—"

"And Anne," I say.

"Teenage boys and Anne to a potentially dangerous hole in the earth, all of which requires trespassing." He turns to my mother. "This doesn't concern you?"

My gaze jumps from my dad to my mom, who, while not quite bubbling like she has been, gives me a suspiciously sincere smile.

"Of course it concerns me. She's our . . . daughter," she says, and my mind adds *only* in her slight pause. "But I'm just happy she's getting out of the house. Talking to people other than us or Doris. It'll be good for her to act like a kid again."

"But that Wade kid is wild. What if he asks her to jump off a cliff?"

"He isn't even going," I say. "But if he was, why would he ask me to jump off a cliff?"

My dad's too busy being outraged to answer. He moves

70

closer to my mom. "And Elliot Thorne is a hoodlum. Aren't you afraid he's going to coerce her to, I don't know, steal something?"

I flop back into the couch, letting the puffy cushions swallow me whole. "That's the whole point of a treasure hunt, isn't it?"

"I hate when you use logic on me," my dad says over his shoulder. He refocuses on my mom. "This could take a long time. She could get pregnant spending so much time with those boys."

"It doesn't really work that way," my mom says with a laugh. "Besides, we'll give her one week—no more."

Another ladybug lands on me, a fat one that's more rust than red. I scoop it into my palm, let it walk down my forefinger. "She wanted me to go."

My dad looks at me. Really looks at me. "I know," he says. "I know you miss her."

He says it like I'm the only one who notices Sadie's gone. Like he doesn't read poetry in the dark just to feel close to her again. Like my mom doesn't wash her pillowcase in tears. Like the entire town doesn't miss her, even Kit the cat, who came by every Thursday for the milk and tuna Sadie would leave for him on the front porch. One Thursday after she died, I saw the stray moping about like he'd lost *his* twin.

"She made me promise. Please don't make me break it."

"You fight dirty, my child."

My mom glances at my father with thick brows raised high. He nods, as if she's spoken aloud, and I'm reminded of Elliot and Gabe's silent conversation the other day. Of so many conversations with Sadie. It's what happens when two people's lives are linked for so long. Their thinking becomes so familiar they stop needing to speak to say what they mean.

"I trust you," my mom says. "So go. Have fun and make new friends—do things you'd normally do with Sadie, or even things you wouldn't have done if Sadie were here."

"Safe, legal, and moral things," my dad says with a grin that slowly slides down his face. Without it, he looks like something old and worn. "And whatever you do, don't fall down that pit."

TEN

RUBY

A WEEK LATER, MY PARENTS DRIVE ME TO TOWN. WE ROLL down our windows, let the scent of summer swirl through the car—bark mulch, fresh-cut grass, and the lavender that turns the rolling hills purple. My mom cranks the radio, and the Violent Femmes sing about blistering in the sun. Her shoulders shimmy and my dad shakes his head, but the skin by his eyes crinkles.

It's times like these, when everything feels so absurdly perfect, that I miss Sadie most. She'd be smiling right about now, high on the anticipation of an adventure. She'd tilt her head way back, thrust her arm out the window, and open her hand wide to feel the air between her fingers.

It's a shame I'm the sister who got to live.

We crawl in tourist traffic down Main Street, past shops

painted every color of pastel. My dad parks in front of Cooper Country Store, a blue-shingled cottage covered in a rainbow of old buoys. "Don't forget to call home," he says, engulfing me in a hug. "Don't hike at night—it's dangerous. And always use the buddy system, okay?"

"I'll be fine, Dad."

He squeezes me one last time, then lifts my backpack onto my shoulders. He grips the straps and says, "She'd be proud."

I nod, then follow my mom's bouncing ponytail around the side of Cooper's. Gabe's leaning against the building, hands shoved casually into his salmon-colored shorts. He looks like he should be holding the kind of old-fashioned tennis racket nobody uses unless they're wearing Ralph Lauren and appearing in an ad campaign. Elliot stands beside him, looking like the kind of guy who'd beat up a Ralph Lauren model.

My mom waits until we're two feet from the boys before discussing my underwear. "They're lightweight," she says, shoving five more pairs into the mesh pouch on the side of my backpack. It's one of those tall ones people use when traveling around Europe and staying in places that have bedbugs instead of bellhops. Though I filled it to nearly bursting—I'm in charge of toiletries and one of the lightweight backpacking tents Charlie lent us—I'm sure there's a spot inside that could hide my zebra-print panties.

She shoots the boys her mile-wide smile and shakes her head. "Nothing worse than dirty undies."

My face flames. "Oh God."

Gabe drops an arm over my shoulder. "So hot-pink zebras . . ."

"Komodo dragons," Elliot says. At our blank stares, he

rushes on. "Scientists used to think the bacteria in their mouths killed their prey, but really they're venomous. Well, that and they have serrated teeth that'll tear a chunk of your flesh off. But the venom makes you bleed faster. That's a lot worse than dirty underwear."

"Listening to you lecture is worse than dirty underwear." Gabe shoves Elliot toward Cooper's. "I'm going to buy Ruby's love with sugar."

Elliot punches Gabe in the stomach, then waves at my mom.

"I like him," my mom says.

"He has piercings. And tattoos."

She straightens my ponytail. Kisses my forehead. "This will be good for you."

I leave her there, white blouse billowing in the breeze, and follow the seashell-covered path that leads to a private marina. A clutter of bobbing boats with bare masts edges the dock.

Captain Thirwall, an old sea salt with worn-leather skin and hair the gray of the ocean during a storm, sits at the stern of his boat, chewing a pipe he never lights. A blue captain's hat sits atop a cooler on the dock, but he uses a hand to shade his eyes as he watches me approach the *Gold Bug*. It looks like a toy boat come to life: gleaming white bottom, teak deck, and polished oak trim.

"Do something about that Indian girl," the captain grumbles. "Been lying there since noon."

I follow his gaze to the end of the dock, where Anne's lying on her back. She gazes up at me with one eye. "I lost a bet with myself."

"Then I guess you also won," I say.

75

She rolls her head from side to side. "Self-bets don't work that way. See, I was getting the boat ready this morning and I got a feeling like maybe four of us wouldn't be leaving for Gray Wolf Island. I told myself I didn't have to share my jelly beans if that happened."

"And you thought I'd be the one who didn't show up?"

"Of course," Anne says. "But only because you hate adventure. And maybe people."

A laugh bursts from deep in my chest. Her lips tip up into a soft smile.

"Anne Lansing, you sorceress." Gabe taps her foot with his. "What magic made our surly Ruby laugh like that?"

"I'm funny, Gabriel." She rises to her feet, picks up my backpack—which is nearly as tall as she is and probably just as heavy—and heaves it onto the boat. Gabe follows her instructions as she prepares to set off, their bodies wrapping around the mast and each other as they tighten cords and remove the sail cover and make a million small adjustments only a seasoned sailor could keep straight.

I turn at the sound of approaching footsteps and catch Captain Thirwall eyeing Elliot as he strolls down the dock. Elliot fits with the peaceful marina about as well as a nun in a knife fight: black pants, tank top with a grinning skull, and tattoos on display. As he passes the captain, Elliot sneers and extends his middle finger.

He stands beside me at the end of the dock and says, "The sky was red last night."

"Well, it's blue right now."

The sun glints off the silver hoop in Elliot's lip when he smiles. It's a tiny, unsure thing that makes me think it's not so absurd to hope we'll one day be friends. "Yeah." He tilts his head way back. "It's just— Well, it's about how the sun's light is scattered through the dirt in the atmosphere. When it's red at night there's high pressure, so the weather will be good the next day. Today."

He sits on the captain's cooler and spends the next ten minutes asking over and over if I've packed *Treasure Island*. As if I could possibly forget it.

"All aboard!" Anne shouts.

The captain chews the end of his pipe. "You kids have permission to use that boat?"

He says "you kids" but he's looking at Elliot. Anne bounds from the boat. "Don't worry, Captain. My great-grandmother knows we're using it."

"You stay far from that island. Even the ocean around it is cursed. No place for a bunch of kids." He shakes his head, extra slow so we know he finds our adventure especially silly. "No place for a couple of girls, and it sure as hell ain't a place for a boy who might bite the barrel of a gun on a good day."

Elliot shoots to his feet. Stomps down the dock, launches himself into the boat with such force I'm amazed he doesn't fall straight through the bottom. I hop aboard, strap on a life vest, and settle on the empty oak bench at the stern. Anne's small body flits about the compact space as she tests the wind and positions the boat. A clobber of footsteps joins the scraping-metal sound of the sail rising up the mast. Charlie appears at the edge of the dock, backpack slipping down his shoulder.

"Hurry, before my mom finds out I'm gone!" Charlie tosses his bag onto the boat, then leaps into the cockpit, nearly decapitating himself on a long beam that juts from the mast.

"I thought you weren't coming because you're going to die," Elliot says.

"Probably will." Charlie flops down beside him. "But imagine the fun I'll have first."

I tilt my head to the sky and close my eyes, letting the rocking boat lull me into almost-sleep. Serenity stops when a stream of swearwords rumbles from Captain Thirwall's lungs like a fit of coughing. Furry eyebrows meet in the middle of his red face. "Don't think you'll get away with this!" he yells to Elliot, who's grinning beneath the captain's sea-beaten hat.

"Sorry, can't hear you!" Elliot yells. The captain flings a few more curses our way, but Elliot just tips his hat.

"You look ridiculous," Gabe says. And he does, but also kind of nice.

In the honey-hued light of early evening, with my entire life behind us and Gray Wolf Island somewhere ahead, I get the dizzying sensation that everything that comes after this will belong to a new girl.

ELEVEN

COOPER

Two months, and here's what I know: I have dark brown hair. The color of Bishop's desk. I have green eyes. Bright as island grass.

I stood naked in front of the bathroom mirror the night Bishop brought me home and studied myself. Looked for the familiar.

Didn't find it.

All that really matters about me is the hair Bishop called Indian laurel brown and the eyes he said are Gray Wolf Island eyes. It may not be who I was before, but that's who I am now.

I know I can't fish, but Bishop says I'll learn. I can mow the lawn, but Bishop says I do a shoddy job. I know I can read and write, and now that's my job.

Bishop never did hear from that new assistant, so I've slid

into the role like my entire life was waiting for it. Sometimes I wonder if *I'm* the missing assistant. If I went to meet Bishop on Gray Wolf Island, knocked my head on something hard, and landed right where I was supposed to be.

That's not what happened.

The assistant was older, and Bishop estimates I'm between twelve and fifteen. I tried to tell him I'm twenty-one, but he just shoved a cold soda in my hand and took a sip of his Scotch.

Two months, and here's what I know: I haven't been reported missing.

I am no one.

But Bishop's making me into someone.

I'm sitting in Bishop's immense library, sifting through a stack of books, when Bishop walks into the room.

He's not a big man. Barely taller than me. But he's got this presence about him. Bed-and-Breakfast Mary calls it a largeness. Makes him feel about twelve feet tall.

"Listen up, Bart," he says, sitting in the chair next to me. Everyone else in Wildewell knows me as Cooper, but Bishop's convinced I'm Bart. It makes me feel mildly repulsive, but it makes him happy so I go with it. "I'm going to bury a treasure on Gray Wolf Island."

"There's already a treasure on Gray Wolf Island."

Mary calls Bishop a true believer. He came to Wildewell thirty years ago. He'd made a bazillion dollars in the antiquities business, which he still sort of dabbles in. He'd heard about the Gray Wolf Island treasure pit from a lobsterman up north, who said the Ark of the Covenant was buried somewhere down that hole. Bishop knew that was one hundred percent horseshit, but he was drawn to the pit anyway. When Gray Wolf Island calls, he says, it holds you by the balls and doesn't let go.

It's true, too. For years he tried to forget about the island and the hole, but it just kept calling *Bishop, Bishop, Bishop!* until he had to come to Wildewell and he had to buy up Gray Wolf Island and he had to excavate the site in search of treasure.

Even now, over a decade after he shut down the dig, he's still searching on his own. Can't get the island out of his head.

I've spent two months poring over dusty books. Looking for clues. Looking for missed details.

It's the most fun I've ever had. Pretty sure I'd think that even if I could remember myself.

I hold up the book I'm reading, *Norwegian Runes and Runic Inscriptions.* "What do you think all this is for?"

Bishop laughs. "You becoming a believer?"

I roll my eyes, but he knows it's mostly for show. He smiles like I belong to him. Sometimes I wish I did.

"Why are you burying a treasure on Gray Wolf Island?"

He fiddles with this smiling Buddha statue on the side table. "You remember that trip I took last month?"

I nod. He was gone eight days.

Eight days is a very long time.

"It was my last trip to the island, Bart. It's been three decades and I'm an old man. It's time to call it quits."

"You're giving up on the treasure?" I don't know why, but this makes my throat tight.

He ruffles my hair. I'm too old for that, but I let him do it because it makes him happy. "Time to give something back."

"You can give back and keep searching."

"I could," he says. "But I'm tired. I'm not sure anyone will ever find it, and that's . . ."

"That's what?"

I've never felt more like I belonged than right now. With Bishop's tragic eyes.

He doesn't show those to just anyone. Maybe to no one else.

"That's sad, Bart." He stares out the window. The library overlooks a garden and a tidy lawn, then turns rocky. Below the cliff is the deep blue ocean. He's looking there, at the invisible speck on the horizon. At Gray Wolf Island.

"It'll be my legacy," he says after some time.

"Okay."

The old man shakes his head. "You're too young to understand."

"Maybe I'm older than we think."

"Maybe you're younger than we think. You know, your voice cracked the other day."

"I'd just woken up."

"Okay."

"I'm serious."

"I'm serious about this treasure." He turns to me. "You know I never married."

I nod.

"There were women," he says. "There *were* women, Bart."

"I believe you." Bishop is super rich. I bet all the ladies wanted to date him back in the day. Even now, when he's all wrinkled and gray, Doris Lansing—who's even more wrinkled and gray—says he's as handsome as Sidney Poitier. I have no idea who that is.

"But I never married. Never wanted to settle down. Was always looking for the next adventure." He sighs. Deep, trouble-bearing sigh. "I've lived a good life. Been all over the globe. Never had kids, though. They wouldn't have fit into my world."

He calls me a kid, and I fit into his world. I don't say that, though.

"I'm eighty-six years old, Bart. I have all this—" He waves a hand around the library. It's loaded with books and antiques he collected over the years. "And when I go, the memory of me goes, too. No one's telling stories about me around the dinner table. No one's remembering that Christmas I wore a Santa costume."

He stares at the ocean again. "No legacy but a buried treasure."

"I'll help." I open my mouth. Pause. Shut it. Best leave it alone.

"Whatever it is, say it." He's straightforward like that. It's one of my favorite things about him.

"I'll tell stories about you." I look away from him. "I'll remember."

"You can't even remember your own name." His voice is gruff but kind.

"Maybe it's Bart."

TWELVE

RUBY

FORTY-FIVE MINUTES LATER, I'VE HAD ENOUGH OF ADVENTURE. I bolt from the boat, clattering down the dock as fast as I can go with a heavy pack on my back. I zigzag on jelly legs until I'm away from that infernal boat and its diabolical captain.

"That was . . ." Anne searches the clouds for words. "Well, I really like you, Charles Kim, but I won't ever ride a boat steered by you again."

To be fair, Anne wasn't much better. She nearly sideswiped another boat, which is why Charlie took over in the first place. He moved about the boat with a keen understanding, like he grew up with a hard back and sails for skin. But Charlie likes to fly. He caught the wind and let it push the boat to stomach-dropping speeds. He rode with the port side lifted in the air and the starboard kissing the sea.

"Elliot, what's the etymology of *adventure*?" Charlie hikes his backpack higher on his shoulders. The shovel attached to the outside clanks as he races ahead. "Elliot, answer me. What's the origin of *adventure*?"

"In the late fourteenth century it meant 'a perilous undertaking,' which is also the definition of a sailing trip with you."

There is something seriously wrong with these people. I should have hired a real captain to bring me to the island, someone with leathery skin and wrinkles to prove he's been at sea often and still hasn't died. I should have rebelled for once and come here alone. Now I'm stuck on an abandoned island with a group of people who talk nonstop and hardly ever leave me alone.

I scan the desolate beach. A stretch of sand is the toothy smile beneath a thick mustache of pine trees. *Welcome,* the island seems to say with a rustle of branches and the gentle *shh, shh* of waves hitting the beach.

"We can make it before dark."

I follow Elliot's gaze to an outcropping that divides the beach in two. The boys are unreasonably excited to see the Roaring Rocks formation. It doesn't match up with a clue from the poem, but daylight's fading—Gabe worked this morning, so we got a late start—and it's as good a place as any to camp for the night.

We leave footprints in the unspoiled sand as we trek down the beach. How many footprints has the ocean licked away, erasing all signs of discovery and exploration but the stubborn dock? If I crossed the beach and strode into the forest, would I find grass worn to dirt by trucks and excavation equipment, or has the island devoured those, too?

"So, Ruby, with only two tents, you and I might have to share." Gabe appears at my left, having somehow defied the wind that whipped everyone else's hair into tangles during the boat ride here.

"I'm with Anne."

Anne races to my side, sneakers swinging by laces knotted around her backpack strap. Her feet slap shallow water. It's clear blue, not murky like the ocean that hugs the mainland. "I've never been invited to a sleepover before."

"You don't sleep," Gabe says.

"Sleepovers aren't about the sleep, Gabriel. They're about what comes before."

"That," Gabe says, "is exactly why I want to share a tent with Ruby."

I roll my eyes. How Gabe gets so many girls with his over-the-top flirting is a mystery.

We walk in a strange silence full of sound: the whisper of waves, the crunch of sand beneath our feet, the caw of gulls overhead. And when the wind blows a moment later, a whirling, belligerent thing, it seems to suck the sound from everywhere that's not here.

An hour and a half later, we stop on the last stretch of smooth beach before it turns rocky. After setting up the tents, we wander toward the Roaring Rocks—a collection of boulders jutting into the sea. They curve around a narrow inlet and connect with a twelve-foot-high crag on the other side. Beyond that are more beach and a cliff that may or may not be our starting location.

The sun dips its belly into the water, and my shadow steps away from me. I know I should follow Anne and the boys into the ocean, but I just need a moment. A short little second to get past the fact that I'm here with four people and not one of them is my twin.

Elliot squints in my direction, lips slowly tipping into a smile. It's the kind of look that makes me want to be seen. "Get over here, Ruby!" he yells. "You're blurring around the edges."

I wave but stay put. Sadie never understood it, but I'm a perfectly content observer of fun. The boys don't know this.

Elliot shakes his head, mutters something to Gabe. I can already tell it's nothing good because Gabe's face takes on an expression that, I've learned, foreshadows roguish behavior. I'm proven right when he scoops me up from the stone, flings me over his shoulder, and carries me to the rocky inlet where the others have gathered.

Charlie smiles when he sees me. "You can't miss this, Ruby. Well, I guess you could, but then all of us would be laughing and telling stories about the Roaring Rocks and you'd be left out. Then we'd feel bad, and it'd ruin the whole memory."

My cheeks warm with embarrassment, but I'm smiling. There's something about Charlie that feels like magic, like just being near him might bring the dead to life.

I toe the edge of the rock and peer over. The water recedes down a narrow passageway walled in by tall rocks, revealing a small, semi-submerged cave.

"This is the best time to see it," Elliot says. "Before high tide, when the waves are high and fast like this."

I glance at his profile: eyebrows raised, teeth biting his lip ring. He cranes his neck to the ocean. "Are we waiting for something?" I ask.

The look he gives me is an unnerving mix of mischief

and glee. "When waves push down this channel with enough power, air gets trapped in that cave. It's supposed to make this rumbling sound before the water escapes. It's why they call this place the Roaring Rocks."

"That's not even the fun part," Charlie says. He says something else, but his words are lost in the ferocious water that rockets down the passageway and into the cave. White surf hits the back of the cave with a thunderous reverberation. Water in the channel is frothy white and rising, and when it leaves the small cave it shoots skyward, drenching us from head to toe.

I push salty strands of hair from my eyes and watch the water recede before it spits a shorter blast of ocean at us. Elliot is whooping. Anne and Gabe are giggling. I'm smiling in a way I haven't for a very long time. And Charlie, well, he looks like he's soaking up all the life he can before he goes.

The sun drips light down the face of the sky, fierce reds and oranges pooling on the surface of the water. For the long moments before the sun dunks beneath the waves, we're kings and queens with skin like fire.

THIRTEEN

RUBY

Your adventure begins
with stars trapped in a sign.
Navigate with them and
our paths will align.

We head back to the beach, solid figures turning to shadow as twilight descends. Anne and I shuck our soaked clothes while the boys collect wood from the edge of the forest, mysteriously unaffected by cool night air against wet cotton. The island doesn't have cell reception, so I use the satellite phone we nabbed from the *Gold Bug* to call my mom, who wants to know if I have a best friend yet and if he's covered in tattoos. It's a short call.

I emerge from our tent to find half the contents of Gabe's

backpack strewn across the sand: a bear-proof canister filled with food, a sealed bag containing collapsible bowls and a handful of sporks, a container of oil, and a titanium pot with a lid that doubles as a pan. He and Elliot are kneeling beside a pile of wood. Elliot flicks a lighter, touches flame to firewood, and waits for the burn.

When the fire's warm and strong, Gabe sticks five foil-wrapped somethings in the pan and holds it over the flame.

Charlie kicks up sand as he approaches. He's shed his shirt, and his skinny chest shines white and bright as the moon. "I want steak."

"We're not carting a cooler around the island," Elliot says. "You want meat, go dive for some fish."

Gabe removes the pan from the fire, then tosses us each a foil packet. My fingertips burn as I unwrap the package, releasing a puff of steam and the scent of banana and peanut butter. My tongue's a riot of sweet-and-salty flavor.

"You know, food is the way to a man's heart," Charlie says around a mouthful of sandwich. "Is that why I'm finding you strangely attractive right now?"

Gabe rolls his eyes.

"I'm serious. It's like eating love."

A nervous look passes over Gabe's face, but it's gone in an instant. He winks at me. "What can I say? I'm good at love. Real good."

"Sex," Anne says. "He's talking about the sex."

I don't dare look at Gabe. I'm thankful for the dusk that masks my blush, thankful for Elliot's obsessive focus on the treasure. "See, Ruby? You can trace a hundred slashed squares in the stars."

I follow his gaze to the pinpricks of light now appearing in the dimming sky. "We kind of already established you're always right."

Elliot traces a square into the sand. He draws a line through the center of the square, starting an inch above the shape and extending an inch below. The side of his hand erases the symbol, and he starts again. "But if it's not related to the poem, then what's the point?"

Nobody knows, so nobody responds. Charlie breaks out the Captain Morgan, which he stole from his older brother's stash because it had a pirate on the front and we're looking for treasure. Anne takes a sip before passing the bottle to Elliot. She turns to Charlie.

"Are you here to disprove destiny?" Her large eyes look watery in the firelight. "Or are you chasing your death?"

Charlie groans. "I'm here because I can either change my fate or I can't."

Elliot lobs a shell at Charlie's face. It bounces off his forehead. "And I'm either going to punch you or I'm not. How is that an answer?"

"Look, if I can change what I saw, then I can stay alive. If I can't, well, then I was always going to end up on the island, wasn't I?" Charlie laughs, and it's like a stone sinking down a bottomless pit. "I just wanted to get it over with."

Anne leaps to her feet. She rounds the fire, sinks to the ground in front of Charlie. "I believe you can question fate. I believe you can use your visions to beat fate." She bites her lip, then unwinds a leather bracelet from her wrist. "Are you wearing this in your vision?"

Charlie shakes his head, and Anne loops the leather around

his arm. She sits back on her feet. "We're going to save your life, Charles Kim. As long as you wear that, your vision is wrong. If that can be wrong . . ."

"So can my death." A flash of a Cheshire cat smile. Charlie raises the rum above his head. "To the treasure! And to staying alive!"

Elliot's shoulder bumps mine. "Play us something." At my blank look, he says, "I heard you play at school one day. You were waiting for your sister. I was on the bench next to you, and—" He sort of stops there. Nothing but a sigh and a quick glance away.

"Keep going," Charlie says. "I don't think she sees you as a full-on stalker, but I'm sure you can change her mind."

"Shut the hell up, Charlie." Elliot looks at me from the corner of his eye. "You brought your harmonica, didn't you?"

"Yes." I bury my head in my hands. "But I can't play in front of people."

Something taps my head, and I look up. My Marine Band diatonic dangles from Anne's fingers. "This is a moment," Anne says. "We need a soundtrack to remember it by."

I run my fingers over the cover plate. Sadie had it engraved with my initials for our twelfth birthday. My blood stirs at its touch, notes itching to slide out.

I wrap my hands around the instrument and press it to my lips. A single note, that's all they're getting. At least it is until I taste the music in my mouth. Then I'm closing my eyes and shaping the sound into something bluesy. I try to hold tight to the music, keeping it slow and low, but it rips right from me.

I let go. I'm breathing impossibly fast, kicking up the beat, bending notes and pulsing sound with a flutter of my hands. I blow the final note and with it escapes the scent of tuberose, as if my music has drawn a little bit of Sadie from my mind.

❖

When the sky is black and the fire's a struggling thing, Elliot draws another slashed square in the sand, then promptly curses its existence. He doesn't use expletives this time, but even *God* is a blasphemy when the word's sliding off Elliot's tongue.

He kicks the symbol away. "I have met my nemesis."

"I thought your family had a direct line to the island itself." I edge my fingers closer to the fire, letting the meager flames chase away the night's chill. Smoke dances from the fire and burns my eyes. There's a filmy otherness to the beach, everything light and smudged. A few feet from me, Gabe helps Anne bury a sleeping Charlie in the sand, and he looks practically angelic. But then I blink the world into crisp and clear.

Elliot lets loose a string of swearwords, and I turn to find him tangled in Gabe's backpack and splayed out in the sand.

"Are you, like— Is this you drunk or something?"

"Am I slurring my speech?" He rolls his head in my direction. "I could be having an ischemic stroke."

Well, that answers that.

"You're fine," I say. "I thought maybe you'd poured your clumsiness from a bottle."

"Because tough guys like me always get drunk?"

It's too dark to tell if he's joking. I sincerely hope he is. "Because guys pretending to be tough generally get drunk."

"Except here's the thing," he says, shifting closer. He smells like salty sea and smoking wood. "Actually, no, I'm not going to tell you."

I look out to the ocean, a writhing black mass. In the dark, we're even farther from Wildewell than we were in the light. "That sort of teasing is against the laws of the universe."

Elliot's smile cuts through the night. "So arrest me. It'll up my street cred."

I groan. "Now you're just being ridiculous."

"Okay, fine. Here it is: I don't really like the taste of alcohol."

"Scandal."

He shrugs. "It's not very good."

Elliot has a menacing look about him in the daylight, but at night he's the sort of boy who inspires mothers to buy their daughters Mace. So when he's like this, all boyish grins and startling charm, it's a lot like sticking your hand in a fire and getting frostbite.

I smile at Elliot, but he's not looking my way. His gaze is fixed on the sand.

"Holiest of all shit. I figured it out."

We move closer to the firelight. Elliot draws six dots in the sand. "Four corners of the square and the top and bottom of the line, right?" He connects the dots to form the slashed square.

With a grin, he clears the sand and draws the six dots again. "Or the six points of a hexagram."

"Is there a purpose to this geometry lesson?"

"The purpose," Elliot says, connecting the lines into a six-pointed star, "is that this is our star trapped in a sign."

FOURTEEN

RUBY

Discover the spot where
morning sun scorches sand
and the ocean beats its anger
into the land.

It comes to me as the sun is poking its nose over the earth. "It's sunrise!"

Gabe grins around his toothbrush. The air's soaked with the scent of mint and brine. "I'm honored to be here for your first time."

I'm too excited to roll my eyes. But really. "No, I figured out the next clue."

He stares at the pink sky and says, "Nice day to discover a treasure."

The mere mention of the treasure draws Elliot from the boys' tent. He stumbles onto the beach without a shirt, tattoos on full display: designs on each arm, a colorful circle over his heart, and a wolf spanning the length of his right side. In this moment, Elliot Thorne looks every bit the rebel he professes to be.

But then he opens his mouth.

"The average teen needs nine and a quarter hours of sleep each night for optimal functioning." He staggers to the ocean, bends low over the shallows, and sticks his head under the water. "Four hours! You gave us four hours!"

Anne shrugs. "People sleep for a long time, and it feels longer when you don't sleep."

Elliot collapses onto the ground. His hard gaze finds Anne. "Look, you can borrow a book, but—"

"Your backpack was for maps, flashlights, and our tent." Gabe spits toothpaste into the sea. "If you could fit books, you could've fit the extra cooking supplies you made me leave behind."

"What the hell are we going to do with a Dutch oven, Gabe?" Elliot glares at Anne. "You can borrow a book, but I need to sleep at least three hours past sunrise."

I raise my hand. "I'd also like that deal. Also, I'd like to not wake up to your face six inches away."

"I wasn't that close all night," she says. "It's just that sometime after dawn, I started thinking you'd been asleep for an awfully long time and maybe you'd died. And then I started worrying I was sitting in a hot tent with a dead body, so I had to check."

Instead of answering, I take a giant bite of my Pop-Tart.

The ocean air has turned it soggy, but it's still cherry-sweet and a good distraction. When I'm done, I kneel in the sand and draw the slashed square. And I explain our latest discovery.

"So," Elliot says, "the map tells us to navigate with the stars trapped in a sign. I bet we have to look for the slashed square along the way."

Charlie groans. "This is literally going to take forever."

"Is it, Charlie? Is it *literally* going to take forever?" Elliot rolls his eyes. "Look, all we have to do is search for this symbol in the place where 'the ocean beats its anger into the land.' Either the northwestern or southeastern cliffs."

"Southeastern," I say. "I figured it out this morning."

Elliot tugs at his hair. Uses both hands, too, in case I thought he was only mildly irritated. "And you let me discuss Dutch ovens—"

"I could have made vegetarian chili," Gabe grumbles.

"Dutch ovens," Elliot says. "Instead of your breakthrough."

"I was luxuriating in the knowledge that I solved something a Thorne couldn't."

"Well," he says, "if you're done savoring your own brilliance, care to fill the rest of us in?"

"Don't mind him." Charlie waves a lazy hand in Elliot's direction. "He's a viper before noon. After that, he's . . . a slightly less venomous snake."

Gabe nods. "So, Ruby, tell us about the sunrise. Feel free to mention the way it accentuated my eyes when you tell the story."

Waves roar at the shoreline. The wind batters our tents. I raise my voice and say, "I was staring at the sunrise, which accentuated the flecks of yellow in Gabe's eyes, making them look jaundiced—"

"More like golden."

"All of a sudden the poem clicked. 'Discover the spot where morning sun scorches sand' is talking about sunrise." I pause for emphasis, the way Anne does when she tells a story. "The sun rises in the east. The poem's talking about this beach."

"I think Ruby's more of a Thorne than you are," Gabe says. I wait for Elliot to snip at him, but he smiles instead. And then he breaks out the big laugh. The rest of us join in, and the morning crankiness dissipates like predawn fog. By the time we've reached the southeast end of the beach, we're practically glowing.

It's low tide, so the rounded rocks that lead to the cliffs are slippery but not submerged. The cliff seems to grow as we near it, stacked rock soaring so high I have to crane my neck to see the top. With the full force of the early-morning sun, the tan stones are lit like pirates' gold.

We're almost positive this is the spot mentioned by the map, but to be sure, we fan out and search for the symbol. The sun bakes the back of my neck as I scour the base of the cliff. Charlie finds it fifteen minutes later, a palm-sized sign carved into the stone.

Anne runs a fingernail through the groove. "I can't fly."

"What's she talking about?" Gabe asks Elliot.

Anne flings a piece of seaweed at him. "Flying, Gabriel. I can't do it, and neither can any of you." She points to the highest bluff, which has a flat top bare of trees. "So how do you suggest we get from here to there?"

I bite back a grin. I know Sadie said Anne was odd, but it's a good kind of odd.

Charlie backtracks to where she stands. "Do you trust me, Anna Banana?"

She tilts her head, stares at the sky from the corner of her eyes. "I don't think so."

"Yeah, that's probably a good idea," he says. "But you kind of have no other choice."

At my and Anne's skeptical gazes, Charlie agrees to take everyone's backpacks up first. Gabe grumbles about being manly enough to climb with his own pack, but even he relents in the face of Charlie's obvious glee. He's all smiles as he jumps onto a boulder. The way his body moves, smooth and precise, leaves me with no doubt this will be an easy climb for him.

Charlie is covered in sweat but only mildly exhausted when he returns to the beach for the final time. Anne follows his path up the rock, slow but surprisingly skilled.

I'm not convinced I can do it without serious bodily injury.

"It's really not that hard, Ruby. Those smaller rocks are like stairs." Elliot falls into step beside me. He's wearing a pair of translucent orange sunglasses with dark brown lenses. They match the orange shorts slung low on his hips and the orange lettering on his white tank top.

"Are you . . . color-coordinated?"

Elliot follows Gabe onto a jagged boulder. His back muscles bulge as he moves from this outcropping to its taller neighbor. When he's standing steady, he peers down at me. "Can't I be smart and fashionable?"

I laugh, but it sounds more like a grunt because I'm

somewhere between up and down. "You can be anything you want. Except a badass."

A gap between the crag I hold tight and the one Elliot stands on yawns at me, sharp rocks at its base ready to bite me if I fall. Elliot points to a jag along the rock face. "Put your left foot there."

I do as he says. Left foot, left hand. I'm nearly there, spanning the rift like an X that marks the spot. I'm nearly there, reaching my right hand for a knob of stone.

I'm nearly there when I slip.

My feet scrabble against stone.

One hand holds fast to a protrusion. The rest of me dangles twenty feet over razor-edged rocks.

A scream rips from my throat. My fingers are slipping. Quickly? Slowly? I can't tell through the terror.

Elliot's hand shoots out. Clenches around my wrist.

For a moment, we're frozen. Time stops and it's just me and Elliot and a whole lot of relief. "I have you," he says. "It's okay to let go."

People always do this in the movies, give up a tight hold for a strong hand, but I can't imagine it's a safe idea in real life. "I have a vision of us both falling to our deaths."

"I *have you*, Ruby," Elliot says before he tugs my arm off the rock and up, up, up. Nothing but me and Elliot's hand and too much empty air. My stomach swallows my throat. I land on my knees, which burn against the hot rock.

Elliot presses two fists to his forehead. "Holy shit. I thought for sure I was going to drop you."

"Not the kind of thing a girl likes to hear after dangling

twenty feet off the ground." I'd like to sock him in the gut for that one. I form a fist but change my mind. My finger presses the underside of his forearm, where a compass tattoo puts me at due north. "Thanks for hanging on."

Elliot has a look about him, like he has a mouthful of letters and is deciding which to swallow. I take strange satisfaction in the fact that of all the words Elliot knows, he chooses my name.

And then he's shouldering his pack and hiking across the flat outcrop. From here, the path to the top is clearer: a rugged climb along a narrow stretch of rock that's covered in dirt and spindly pine trees. We reach the others, then walk single file along the coast as the cliff climbs higher and higher and the trees thin. At the top it's nothing but tan rock, long grass, and salty sea air.

Charlie wraps Anne in a bear hug, lifts her off her feet, and twirls her around. His shovel clunks against his pack as he spins. "How about now, Anna Banana? Now do you trust me?"

She gives him a soft smile. "Anywhere but on a boat, dear Charlie."

Elliot turns to the forest behind us. "It's out there," he says in a voice so soft and deep it sounds almost reverent. "I can feel it."

I can't feel the treasure, but I can feel the weight of this moment. It's heavy like salty water in your stomach and lungs. But it's light, too. Buoyant as a body floating on its back.

"It's like nothing exists anymore," Anne says. She's right: There's an infinity of blue on one side and an infinity of green on the other. And somewhere buried in that abounding nature is my treasure.

"Read from the book, Ruby," Elliot says.

But I can't. I can't open the cover and flip to the back. I can't run my finger along the lines of poem or trace the slashed square. Can't do anything with the book when it has completely disappeared.

FIFTEEN

COOPER

Laura gives me a discount. Says I remind her of her son.

"Maybe I *am* your son." Wouldn't be a bad thing. "You lose one a few months back?"

She rolls my poster board, snaps on two rubber bands. Later today, I'll start a map of Gray Wolf Island so Bishop and I can plan where to bury his treasure.

Laura hands me the bundle. "Now that you mention it, I did. Pretty thing, but wouldn't remember his name unless it was tattooed to his palm."

"Isn't it rude to make amnesia jokes around an amnesiac?"

She waves me off. "You're not offended."

I'm never offended, even by those people in Wildewell who think a boy with no past is bad luck. Sometimes I catch a whisper not meant for me.

"Bet they grew him that way," Captain Thirwall said one day last week. I was standing in line at the market, waiting for the day's catch. Bishop was teaching me how to cook lobster. "Doesn't need to know he's Jason Bourne to butcher us all. Best to get him out of town now."

I told Bishop about it. "Is my name Jason Bourne?"

He laughed. We watched a spy movie that afternoon, and then I understood.

"No," I tell Laura now. "I'm not offended."

I tuck my poster board under my arm. Grab my bag from the counter.

Outside, the breeze off the ocean ruffles my Indian laurel hair. Car windows flash the sun.

Tourists clog the sidewalks. I don't consider myself one of them. I may not be from Wildewell, but I'm a Wildewell boy now.

The main road ends in a rotary. The arm to the northwest will take me up the steep hill to Bishop's house on the cliff. I stop before the turn.

Across the street, Captain Thirwall sits on a shaded bench in front of the grocer's. He's not actually the captain of anything, aside from his own boat, but he likes people to pretend he is.

Today he's wearing a white tank top, showing off faded tattoos and sagging skin. It's my least-favorite thing I've seen since I woke up on the island.

I put on a pair of sunglasses Bishop lent me the other day. They're from the fifties and make me look like an old-time spy. The poster board under my arm kind of ruins the effect, but whatever.

I cross the street. Pick up my pace. Jason Bourne always moves fast because someone's always on his tail.

The captain peeks at me over his newspaper.

My mouth's a tight line, like I'm concentrating really hard on being a sniper or learning my spy past or generally being dangerous.

When I'm a few feet past the captain, I glance back. He's watching me with narrowed eyes. "You're nobody, boy."

My stare is long enough to be unsettling. Then I raise a finger.

Here's something I just learned about myself: Sometimes I *do* take offense.

I take a shortcut through the park.

Dozens of kids race around a grassy field ringed by trees. The air's full of their shouts.

I sit on a bench in the shade. Try to imagine myself with a bunch of friends.

"Push down," says a soft voice. It belongs to the skinny kid I saw at the bed-and-breakfast when I first came to Wildewell. He's still wearing a bike helmet.

I slide over.

He sits next to me. Back straight. Eyes zipping up, down, all over the place.

"You all right?"

He bounces his feet against the ground. "So far."

"What's with the helmet?" There's no bike in the park. "You have epilepsy?"

"That's not how I die." His hands clench on his lap.

"A little early to be thinking about death."

He puffs out his chest. "I'm twelve."

He looks a lot younger. Especially with that helmet.

He wiggles a finger between his head and helmet. Scratches. "I should have picked a helmet with more ventilation."

"If you're so hot, why not just take it off?" I kick the ground. "Worried about falling a foot onto the padded grass?"

"I'm not worried about falling." He heaves an exasperated sigh. Makes me think he's told this story a few dozen times before. "I'm worried about something cutting my skull open."

"That's pretty morbid."

"It's going to happen. When my hand's larger than this"— he wiggles his fingers—"but before it gets wrinkly."

"Uh, okay."

"It's true. When I was little I used to see my hair, and there was blood on it. I wasn't even asleep. Now I see my hair with the blood, a dirty hand a little bigger than mine, and the back of my head. Only there's a big chunk missing. It's really gruesome."

"So your mom makes you wear a helmet all the time?"

"No." A truck backfires, and the boy jumps off the bench. Kids screeching. An airplane overhead. Tweeting birds. When that's all we hear, the boy sits back on the bench.

"My older brother said I look slow in it." He tilts his head. Squints at me. "He wasn't talking about how fast I run, you know."

"I know."

"Yeah, well, it's a really mean thing to say when you mean someone looks like a freak. My brother got grounded for it.

106

But then my mom felt bad for me, so she said I didn't have to wear it if I felt like a freak."

"And yet you're wearing it."

He scratches beneath his helmet again. "I just don't want to die is all."

I take a long look around the park. Everything here's alive. Thick grass. Sturdy trees.

Kids running circles. Parents fanning themselves in the heat.

Bees. Birds. That dog with the golden fur.

He's the only thing not living in this park.

"What's your name?" I ask the boy.

"Wade Kim."

What kind of parents give their kid a verb for a name?

"Well, Wade," I say. "You ever think you spend so much time not dying you don't really live?"

"Aren't they the same?"

"No," I say, thinking of the map I'll be drawing later and the lobster I cooked the other night. "No, living and not dying aren't the same thing."

I woke beside a giant hole, and I didn't die.

I crossed a wooded island, and I didn't die.

I climbed down steep hills, and I didn't die.

I met Bishop and earned a job, and I'm finally, finally alive.

Wade purses his lips. "You mean how I'm over here and not with friends?"

"Exactly," I say. "You've got a lot of living to do before you die."

He gives me a smile like Bishop's grinning Buddha. "My head's hot."

"Give it some air."

SIXTEEN

RUBY

HEAD WEST, DEAR FRIEND,
if you want to have fun.
Too far to the south,
and your quest is done.

The book is well and truly gone.

We empty our backpacks. Shake out our sleeping bags. Send Charlie back to the beach, but he finds only sand.

Every bit of excitement has been sucked out of me. I collapse to the ground, not even caring when Elliot warns of snakes. I dig my fingers through the rough grass and yank.

"Well, that was exciting," Charlie says from his splayed-out position on the ground. "Can we go find this treasure now?"

Elliot groans, but the roaring wind steals most of the

sound. "By following directions on a map we no longer have? No, Charlie, we can't do that."

"I memorized the poem. That's not what worries me." I watch our boat bob beside the dock below. The sea's a desperate gray with the threat of a storm. I'd like to shine a spotlight on it, see if there's a soggy *Treasure Island* somewhere at the bottom. But the ocean would tell me what I already suspect.

There's nothing down there for me.

"You're sure you packed it?" Elliot asks for the eleven-billionth time.

"Positive." The recollection is twisted around a memory of Sadie, and those remain the clearest of all. I remember opening my desk. Top drawer on the left. Out came the bookmark, the metal one. The one with the glassed-in vintage map at the top. *So you can find your place when I'm not there.*

I remember sliding it between the pages of *Treasure Island.* Zipping the book into the side pouch of my bag.

I remember smiling. Crying. Knowing there was a piece of Sadie coming with me.

"Could it be—" Anne shakes her head, starts again. "Maybe the island disappeared it."

I stare at the only boat beside the only dock on Gray Wolf Island. What started as a hunch has sunk its claws so deep into my skin it's become a fact. I say, "Someone stole it."

"No, you forgot to pack it," Elliot says like *that* is a fact.

I scrabble for my belongings, which are strewn throughout the itchy grass. "Were you there? No, Elliot Thorne, you most definitely were not."

"Who cares?" Charlie jumps to his feet. He's constantly moving like his bones have been replaced by springs, but boredom makes him extra bouncy. "Ruby knows the poem. Let's get the treasure already."

"Then we go west." Elliot leads us across the windy cliff toward the thick woods that cover the eastern half of the island. Chipmunks and squirrels scurry across branches. A lonely hare bolts at the sight of us.

We follow Elliot's compass west for two hours, crunching over sticks and leaves and pinecones. Here the world's the kind of green that belongs in tales of fairies and gnomes who hide beneath ferns or on the heads of flowers. Green grass, green leaves, green moss climbing the trees. If the air had color, it'd be smoky jade.

"How far west is too west?" Charlie asks after another half hour.

I recite the instructions from memory. " 'Head west, dear friend, if you want to have fun. Too far to the south, and your quest is done.' "

"Thanks, Robert Frost, but that doesn't actually answer the question." Elliot drops his pack to the forest floor. He digs around, pulls out a rolled map. A dirty finger lands on the cliffs. "We started here. Where 'the ocean beats its anger into the land.' We hiked west, which should bring us to about here."

His finger taps a forested area close to the middle of the island. "What comes next?"

" 'Go down to go up, pay no heed to the dead,' " I say.

"Right. That's the pit and the grave." Elliot's finger traces from the forest to the pit. "We'll have to travel north. Once we hit the Kennemissic River, we can follow it up to the hole."

"Except the poem doesn't tell us to go north," I say.

Charlie's smile is an impish thing. "But it doesn't tell us not to go north."

"All I'm saying is that maybe we should keep going west toward the Star Stones. They could be the 'six, sturdy, solid, and true' from the end of the poem."

Elliot studies the map. "Yeah, but the stanza that sent us west says, 'Too far to the south, and your quest is done.' The Star Stones are in the south."

Four sets of eyes turn to me. Pink creeps up my neck and over my cheeks. Sadie would have taken me aside, hands on my shoulders, and said, "How much does this matter, Rubes?"

I'd say what I always said, which was "Not much at all."

And it doesn't—we're closer to the pit than the stones. I clear my throat. "I guess it couldn't hurt to look for the symbol there."

Charlie grins. "So you're saying we can still go to the hole? Because I really want to go to the hole."

"We go to the hole."

SEVENTEEN

RUBY

I'M THINKING OF A GIRL WITH MY FACE AND LONG AUBURN hair, bare feet on bark as she scales a twisty tree. I'm thinking of her hands on coarse rope, legs pinwheeling in open air. A drop, a splash. I'm thinking of her smile and the scent of sap and the crinkle of leaves when Elliot says, "Murder."

A branch thwacks me in the face. Ten feet ahead, Charlie jumps onto a fallen log. "I bet I'm the murder," he says, slitting his eyes. "And one of you kills me."

"You're disturbed," Elliot says, pushing him off the log.

"Ruby found the map in Bishop Rollins's copy of *Treasure Island*. You don't think he went through all those books before? The guy was the biggest believer Wildewell has ever seen." Gabe hikes his backpack higher on his shoulders. "No, Ruby found the book with the poem because sometime after Bishop Rollins died, the hole had its third death."

"That's not how the legend goes," Anne says. "It's three deaths for the treasure, not the map. We could still be waiting on the murder."

"No," Elliot says. "I can feel it. The treasure's waiting for us."

"Yeah, waiting for one of us to be murdered." Charlie swats away a massive blackfly. "I'm talking about me, by the way."

"The pit has probably seen dozens of murders over the centuries," I say. "Besides, if it happened recently, someone would have reported a missing person. That sort of news doesn't sneak around Wildewell."

It'd be the talk of town. People don't go missing from Wildewell. They hardly leave at all. Doris says the air on the outskirts is thicker than the rest, so when you try to get by, you're reminded you don't really want to leave.

It happened once, though. But nobody talks about Elliot's little brother, who disappeared on a foggy morning when I was twelve years old. Later that same day, his dad blew his brains all over the beach.

"Maybe it was a tourist," Gabe says. "Someone nobody knew."

"Hmmm," Anne says with a tilt of her head. "First, lunch. Then I'll tell you something you don't know."

Fifteen minutes later, we're shedding our socks and shoes beside the river that will lead us to the pit. It's hemmed in by moss-covered rocks. A flat one holds an otter, who's tossing a stone between his paws, oblivious to our arrival. Another otter waits in the river below, lolling on his back in a spot of sun.

It's the single most adorable thing I've seen in my entire life.

"I don't think I've ever seen you smile so hard," Elliot says from beside me. "I'm a little worried, to be honest."

"You don't understand, Elliot. They're *otters*." I place a palm to each cheek, feel the heat rising from all the excitement. "Did you know they sometimes hold hands while they float?"

"I did."

"If they start doing that, I won't make it to the treasure because I'll be here. Dead."

"This . . ." He chokes back a laugh. "This is not how I imagined you at all."

I take a deep breath. The air has that sunny scent you can only catch on very hot days. "I know. It's a weakness I hide well."

Elliot nods. "At least it's not cats."

"Cats are the worst," I say. It's the one fact Sadie and I ever debated.

"They really are. They're like the scheming overlords of the animal kingdom."

I give him the kind of smile only shared between two people who desperately hate something and thoroughly enjoy hating it together.

"When I'm rich from the treasure, I'm buying a house with a river and a whole romp of otters—that's my favorite word for a group of them—and I'll wear T-shirts with floating otters instead of cat faces."

He bumps my shoulder. "I'll buy you an otter shirt when we get home. And I won't even make fun of you for wearing it."

And that's the moment I start to not hate Elliot Thorne.

❖

Anne removes her shirt as she walks to the river, revealing a lime-green sports bra. Gabe stays silent but trips on a tree root as he rushes for the muddy shore. His cheeks go rosy, and his ears aren't far behind. Anne fixes him with a stern look. "Be a gentleman, Gabriel."

"Whatever," he says, voice tight with something like shame.

I dip my water bottle into the river and add a filtration tablet. A deep drink, then I'm sinking my feet into the clear water, letting it chill me from toe to head. I shiver despite the sticky sweat that covers my skin.

"The Kennemissic River." Anne floats on her back, dark hair fanning around her. "There's a Wildewell legend about it, you know. An island surrounded by salty sea with only a trickle of water to drink from. Two pirate ships crashed into Gray Wolf Island, sometime after dehydration drove my ancestors to the mainland and before the island called them back. The crew that made it to the small spring first was a cruel and greedy lot, threatening a sword through the stomach for anyone who tried to steal a sip. Crazed with dehydration, a trio of pirates bartered the cook's daughter—a Jamaican girl who'd stowed away when the ship left port—for a few drops to drink.

"The girl knew her fate. Not in a Charles Kim way, but in the way all girls know their fate when faced with dirty smiles and eager hands. And as the merciless pirate captain's fetid breath smacked against her cheek, she discovered water."

"She used a desalination process to turn salt water into drinkable water?"

"Elliot, please," Anne says. "This is a *legend,* not a science lesson. So, no, she didn't do that. She let out a cry so deep and powerful it quaked the island and broke the earth. Water filled the fissures, creating the Pontegwasset River in the west and the Kennemissic River here in the east."

"I wish there'd been a sword fight," Charlie says.

I don't. I like that one girl's voice could rattle the world.

"Let's eat," Anne says, emerging from the river like a drowned nymph. She pushes wet hair from her eyes and teeters as her bare feet navigate the rocky bank. "Then I'll tell you where you went wrong."

This sounds both promising and ominous, but none of us question her. Elliot follows me to a fat log that spans the width of the river. Part of me wants to turn back, head south to the Star Stones. But even I can't deny that "go down to go up" sounds a lot like instructions for the pit. I hang my feet over the side of the log and watch as Charlie pulls himself to a rocky ledge ten feet over the river. He releases a roar that could shake the leaves.

"Calm the hell down, Charlie," Elliot says. "What's wrong with you? You said you're going to die here."

"But," Charlie says, toeing the edge of the rock, "I'm not going to drown." And then he's plunging into the water feet-first, a straight line of skinny boy. I have a fleeting thought that maybe he's wrong, that maybe this is how Charlie dies, but he kicks to the surface and hoots again. He smacks Elliot off the log before splashing out of the water and onto the grass.

Gabe rifles through his bag, all shirtless and glistening. He looks like the sort of thing you might collect and polish every so often just to make sure it doesn't get scuffed. Elliot lounges beside him, bare-chested and graffitied up. Skin full of stories—that's what Sadie would say. I'm feeling particularly literary at the moment, so I quickly look away.

Gabe hands us each a protein bar and some beef jerky, crackers, and dried fruit, and I've never wanted ice cream more in my life.

"The problem with your murder," Anne says, twisting her head to tear at her jerky, "is it doesn't account for love."

Gabe turns to Elliot. "What's she talking about?"

"Love, Gabriel. I'm talking about love." She closes her eyes and rubs her head with a sigh. It's something my dad does when he's exasperated, but it looks odd coming from this delicate girl. "There's more to the legend about these deaths."

"We know," Elliot says. "Accident. Suicide. Murder. Three deaths before the pit reveals the treasure."

"The island, not the pit. And that's only part. Bishop Rollins told my great-grandmother the truth." She frowns at Elliot. "How is it you don't know this?"

He huffs. "I'm a Thorne, not omniscient."

"But Bishop—"

"Knew the truth. Which is?"

She holds Elliot's gaze before continuing. "First, a ruse that results in an accident."

"Nineteen twelve," he says. "An excavation team thought

they'd hit the bottom of the pit at a hundred and twenty feet, but the thing was booby-trapped and the floor dropped. The pit flooded and a worker, Clarence Goldhammer, drowned."

Anne nods. "The second: suicide from despair."

"Nineteen seventy-four. Michael Harwell sank close to a million dollars into excavating the site, but after ten years they'd found nothing and Harwell went bankrupt. He spent a final night on the island, where he chased a bottle of pills with a bottle of vodka."

"But that's not the real story." Anne lies back on the grassy riverbank. "Michael Harwell left the island that night, checked into the Wildewell Inn, and overdosed there. So you see, the deaths are tied to the island, but they don't necessarily happen at the hole."

"What about your dad?" Charlie says. Elliot's head jerks up, and a hard look settles over his face. I had the same thought, only I wasn't brave enough to ask. It seems, though, that Patrick Thorne's particular bloodline might have given him the unquenchable thirst for Gray Wolf Island treasure that Thornes are known for and that maybe he felt so hopeless about his search that he decided to swallow a bullet.

Elliot's voice is cold enough to ice the river. "No. It wasn't my father."

"Elliot's right," Gabe says to Charlie with a long look that says a whole lot more. "Mr. Thorne gave up on the treasure a long time before he died. Harwell is our suicide."

Charlie nods. Elliot attempts to soften his glare.

Anne's hands flutter at her hair. "Right, so we have a suicide. Perhaps I should go on?"

"The murder," I say.

This seems to snap Elliot out of his angry trance. "Ruby and Gabe have a point. Even if the murder happened off the island, it had to have been a tourist or someone from long ago whose death went unrecorded."

"But you see, just like the others, there's more to the legend," Anne says. "Love. The last death is a murder out of love."

I'm frozen. I expect my heart to race, but it's covered in ice crystals and barely beating. I've stopped breathing, but if I did exhale, I'd leave smoky puffs of cold in the air. It's one thing to wonder at the truth. It's another thing entirely to know.

But I always knew, didn't I? I knew the island needed three deaths. I knew it'd had its murder. I'm not like the boys or Anne. I wouldn't have come to Gray Wolf Island if I didn't know there'd be a treasure.

"Maybe it was a stalker," Charlie says. "Like, I love you so much I'm going to go completely psycho on you and kill you so no one else can have you."

And I'm a liar, so I say, "I think I read something like that. In the newspaper."

I lie because I have to. Because I can't tell them. I can't tell anyone.

EIGHTEEN

RUBY

Go down to go up,
pay no heed to the dead.
If you're on the right track,
You'll see gray wolves ahead.

When it's over, when I'm on the mainland with a few thousand gold coins, maybe I'll remember the hike. But right now there's only this: dark hair weighed down with water, childlike hands flittering in the air, and lips that form the words *murder* and *love*.

In death, Sadie unlocked the door to a mystery she'd spent years trying to solve, and yet here I am, shuffling over fallen leaves and crooked tree roots while she's lying under a weeping willow and six feet of dirt. The reality of that is about the only thing left in my head.

Guilt whispers in the wind that shakes the trees. Its harsh voice pushes me farther into the forest. Farther, farther, until the whisper turns to warbling.

> *Ruby Caine with the sin-blacked soul*
> *had a sister, but let her go.*
> *Gripped in her hand a sharp sharp knife*
> *and Ruby Caine took her sister's life.*

"That's not what happened," I say, though I'm not sure the difference really matters.

"I'm a little strange," Anne says, startling me out of my thoughts. "You might have noticed. But I'm a talented listener. If you want to talk about it—the thing making you wander off on your own."

I blink away gritty dirt. It's just me and Anne and swaying pines. I twirl in a circle. "I don't know how I got here."

"Your problem isn't that you don't know how you got where you are. It's that you don't know how to get where you need to be going." Times like these, I get the sense she's ageless—or every age all at once. "Fortunately for you, I never get lost. Now talk."

Her stride is short, but she's fast, and I hurry to catch up. Now that she's not staring at me, it's easier to say what's on my mind. "Can people who do bad things ever redeem themselves?"

"Do you mean one person who does multiple bad things or multiple people who each do one bad thing?"

"A single person who does one bad thing."

Anne stops short. I nearly topple her, but steady myself

before we both go down in a tumble of backpacks and limbs. "You can redeem yourself."

"I didn't mean—"

She cuts me off with a shake of her head. "I don't know what you did, Ruby, but I don't believe you're a lost cause."

I nod. Bat away a stray tear. Without another word, she scrambles over a log and pushes between two tight trees to reveal three boys making war with acorns. For the first time in a year, I understand why Sadie wanted more for me. Maybe she was right all along.

My skin's slicked with sweat when the path appears. It's rutted and dusty, much of it covered in tall grass and weeds that itch my ankles. Blackflies nearly the size of bees bite my bare skin.

But after snaking alongside the river for hours, I think the path is downright beautiful.

We're betting the trail was worn by centuries of treasure hunters traveling between the pit and the river for a quick plunge into cool water. "This is it," Elliot says. "I can feel it."

Ten minutes later, we break through the forest. A dilapidated wooden shack welcomes us to a land of dirt, dry stone, and abandoned metal, its door waving on its hinges. We pass an empty dumpster with rust climbing its sides, some chicken wire rolling against the ground, and a hammer with a split handle. Lording over the lifeless spot of land is a white cross going brown.

Elliot grins at me. "Say it, Ruby."

It's the grin that has me shouting it loud. " 'Pay no heed to the dead'!"

Charlie responds with this adorably awkward victory dance that breaks what heart's left in me because it's one more thing about him I'm going to miss when he's gone.

We continue on the path, faster now. A mound of dirt blocks our view, but only for an instant, and then we're there, toeing the soil that surrounds a gaping hole in the earth.

"I thought it'd be bigger," Gabe says.

Elliot rolls his eyes. "When have you ever seen such a fucking huge hole in the ground?"

"This could legitimately lead to hell," Charlie says, peering over the edge. Rusted steel hugs the walls, and a thin ladder bolted to the shaft descends into the depths of the pit.

"The first platform was there," Elliot says, pointing to a spot about fifteen feet down the hole. He's told us this story before: how fat logs spanned the one-hundred-and-fifty-foot-wide hole, how excavators knocked them down only to find another platform at the thirty-foot mark, then another at sixty feet, and again at one hundred and twenty.

"What's the point?" Gabe asks. "Are they a trick?"

"Some people think they're false bottoms—make treasure hunters think they're close to gold when really there's just more cold dirt below." Elliot's voice is faraway, as if it's coming from wherever his mind has wandered. "Or maybe whoever buried the treasure needed the platforms to climb out of the hole."

Elliot digs through his pack, flicks on his flashlight. We gather around to watch the dark swallow the light. I kick dirt down the shaft. "Maybe there's nothing below and the pit's a giant ruse."

"Maybe," he says. The word's as flimsy as tissue paper. I can see hope in his face, the way his eyes glitter in the warm evening sunlight, how hungry he is for the truth of Gray Wolf Island. But more than anything, Elliot believes. He might even believe enough for both of us.

"This was exciting for about ten seconds. Now it's boring," Charlie says. "Are we going down the hole or what?"

"We're going down the hole." Elliot holds up a hand to pause Charlie's body, which is already two feet closer to the ladder. "But we're going tomorrow. We'll need as much daylight as possible."

"Oh, good," Anne says, dropping her pack on a mound of dirt. "I could use a brief repose."

"Is she serious?" Gabe turns to Elliot, eyebrow raised. "A *repose?*"

"A state of relaxation," Elliot says.

"I know what a repose is. I studied for the same SATs as you." Gabe turns to me. "If you don't feel like lying in the dirt, we could find another way to relax."

I release a groan. "Do these lines fall out of your mouth when you open it or is there some brainpower involved?"

"I'm hurt that you think they're lines. I thought we had a deep and meaningful connection." He grins, then busies himself with dinner prep. I help Elliot and Charlie set up camp in the shack, a reminder of Gray Wolf Island's heyday that has me imagining a dig site crowded with workmen in overalls, machines meant to dig through dirt, and pumps intent on siphoning water. The small space is large enough for five sleeping bags, but it's a tight fit.

I leave the boys as they begin searching the dig site for the slashed square. There's a small island of thirsty grass in this sea of dirt, and I settle onto it to call home.

"How's the hole?" my mom says when she's done making sure I haven't lost an appendage or anything.

"Deep." I trace a design into the dirt. It looks like a maze. "Hey, what'd Sadie mean all those times she told me that if I got really lost, I should ask you?"

I don't tell her I'm feeling pretty lost right now.

"She knew you wouldn't need to ask. The day her tests came back—" My mom clears her throat. "That day, she told me about the book she'd found in Bishop Rollins's library. She said, 'Ma, it's a *hunt*. She has to discover it herself. I'm telling you just in case.'"

"What book?" I whisper.

"*Treasure Island*. The one with the poem in it. Your sister was convinced it was the map. You know how she got about the treasure." She laughs. "Our true believer."

"Sadie found the map? But . . ."

And the words won't come, stuck in a sticky pit of why why *why*. Why didn't she set off to search for it before she got too sick? Why didn't she tell me?

"But she lived for the treasure."

And I truly believe that. That treasure gave her purpose, and that purpose gave her months of life no one thought she'd have.

"She lived for you." My mom sighs. "Oh, sweetie. Your

sister wanted you to have a life when she was gone, a full life. Even fuller than the one you had when she was alive, always stuck to her like a shadow. She may have been mooning over that treasure, but in those daydreams she saw you there."

We hang up after that, after both of our throats are too clogged with sadness to speak. I clutch the phone to my chest, thinking about Sadie's secret. An adventure for her non-adventurous sister. It's the best and worst gift anyone has ever given me.

❖

Elliot's about ready to breathe fire.

We're sitting on a group of stones set in a circle—another holdover from island excavations—while Gabe cooks up personal-sized pepperoni pizzas using pancake mix, a can of crushed tomatoes, and freeze-dried cheese.

"It says to navigate with the stars trapped in a sign—the slashed square," Elliot says, taking a violent bite of pizza. "Well, where the hell's the symbol?"

"Maybe it's down the hole," Charlie says. "We should still go down the hole."

Elliot considers. "Excavators added the metal walls down to the twenty-foot mark sometime in the eighties. If the map was created after that, there could be a slashed square etched into the metal."

"I'll check!"

"Tomorrow," I say before Charlie can hurl himself down the bottomless pit.

Gabe hands us each a golden cookie. "Brown-butter oatmeal cookies filled with peanut butter and caramel." He takes a giant bite. "Got the recipe off this lady's blog."

Charlie catches a string of caramel with his tongue. "It's like you took everything good in life and baked it into a cookie," he says. The compliment so invigorates Gabe he nearly floats. He's like a balloon in that, always needing someone else to fill him up so he doesn't deflate.

I use an extra bottle of water to wipe down the dishes and pan while Gabe stashes the bear-proof food canister a hundred feet from where we'll spend the night. Elliot disappears into the shack, but the rest of us goof off until the moon knocks the sun from the sky. I play a boy band song on the harmonica, and Anne sings along in a voice that's like a shot of summer to the veins. Charlie and Gabe are cracking up, and the whole world feels impossibly bright.

Until Elliot returns.

He drops to the ground beside the fire. It casts him in shadow, a black slash with stooped shoulders. He doesn't say a thing. Just sucks up all our joy like an emotional black hole.

"Hey, Elliot," I say. "Mind toning down the excitement? Some of us are trying to have a miserable time here."

He meets my gaze. Opens his mouth like he's ready to share. Like he hasn't kept us in suspense for an entire eternity.

But he says silent.

"He gets like this." Charlie glances from me to Anne. "Don't worry—he's mostly harmless. Unless you're allergic to brooding looks or clenched jaws."

"You really never know," Anne says.

"Well, *I* know, and I'm deathly allergic," Charlie says. "Get me out of here, Anna Banana, before I go into anaphylactic shock."

They zoom toward the shack, Gabe tripping after them. Charlie's laughter catches on the night breeze, and I know I'll never forget the sound, not even after he's gone.

I peek across the fire at the Elliot-shaped shade. "Are you just going to sit there?"

"No. I was going to come over." And he does. "I was always going to come over. Sometimes it takes my body a long time to catch up to my brain."

He tosses a handful of pine needles into the fire. The air smells sweet like Christmas. "Tell me something I don't know."

"Oh God, Elliot. Is there even such a thing?"

He rolls his eyes. Nudges my foot with his. "Tell me a story about you and Sadie."

He might as well ask for my entire heart. "When I was fourteen," I say, "I snuck down to the beach in the middle of the night to see the sky."

"To see the Perseid meteor shower." He delivers a hesitant smile. "I heard Sadie telling someone about it that Monday. It's just . . . I was out there, too."

"See? There's not a single thing you don't know."

"I don't know *your* version."

"I guarantee it's not nearly as exciting as Sadie's," I say. "I walked a ways down the beach, and when it was time to come home, I was lost. I didn't know what to do, so I walked toward a light."

I toss handfuls and handfuls of needles into the fire. Take a deep breath of pine-scented night. "Sadie had woken up and seen my empty bed. And she flicked our bedroom light on and off to help me find my way home."

"She was your North Star," Elliot says.

"No, not even. She was like the entire night sky, everything from stardust to galaxies." I turn to find him already looking at me. "Imagine the universe winking out in a day."

He hands me a fistful of pine needles. I toss them into the fire.

For a while we don't talk, and then I say, "I discovered a really great word one day when Sadie was sick: *Ya'aburnee*. In Arabic, it's hoping you die before someone you love because you can't bear to live without them. There's no English word for it."

Elliot watches the fire like it might escape and set the whole world to flames. He's still staring at it when his hand lands on mine. It's soft and sticky with sap. A firm squeeze, and then it's gone.

If Sadie were here, she could translate that touch. But she's not, so I stare straight ahead and say, "Go on. I know you're dying to give me a vocab lesson, too."

He watches me, doesn't even blink. I'm trapped somewhere between *Talk to me* and *Let's never say a thing*.

"Fuck," he says.

A whole language full of words, and that's the one he chooses.

He runs both hands through his hair. "The way I treated you today . . . I feel like such a tool."

"You *are* a tool, Elliot." I mean it, but I also don't. "You're one of those big ones that are like a cross between a shovel and a rake."

"A hoe?"

I grin. "That's the one."

"If I were Gabe, I'd use this as an opportunity for some serious innuendo."

"Let's be thankful you're Elliot."

"Here's the thing," he says, eyes so wide I can see the fire dancing in his pupils. He tosses me Sadie's bookmark, the bookmark that should be inside *Treasure Island,* and says, "We're not alone."

NINETEEN

RUBY

"Who did you tell?"

We're sardine-squeezed into the shack, lit by the light of the almost-full moon and swallows of dark rum. Thick air curls the ends of my hair and slicks my skin. I'm sitting on my sleeping bag, back against the wood wall. Gabe's sprawled out to my right, eyes raking over Anne's bare legs.

"The map." Elliot chucks a tennis ball at Gabe's head. "Who did you tell?"

Gabe rubs his forehead. "Why do you automatically assume it was me?"

Elliot releases a long, deep breath. If anyone could give life to a sigh, it'd be Elliot. His are constantly crossing their arms and rolling their eyes and raising disapproving eyebrows. "You have the most friends. And you're always trying to impress them."

Gabe scowls. "I don't need to lure girls to me with a treasure map, Elliot. Unlike you."

Charlie grins, and his teeth make a blinding smile in the near-dark. "You think Elliot would tell girls and risk someone else discovering the treasure?"

The boys are having a glaring contest, and I get the sense this fight could go on indefinitely. I flick my flashlight in each of their faces to break the spell. "That's not even the biggest mystery."

"It's the how," Elliot says. Deep lines crease his forehead when he looks at me. His teeth worry at his lip ring. "Gray Wolf Island is all rocks on the west coast. There's a small beach in the northwest, but it's hemmed in by rocks, and the water's too rough to bring a boat to shore. The southern beach is the only place to dock. And ours was the only boat there the night the book—with that bookmark—was stolen."

Charlie unearths the tennis ball from beside Gabe's sleeping bag. He pitches it at the ceiling. "I bet it's not someone from Wildewell. Bet the thief's been living alone on this island since Rollins Corp. left a decade ago. Like, he has no way back so he has to kill animals with spears he whittled himself."

But that's not the suspicion gnawing at my brain. "It's not someone trying to survive on Gray Wolf Island. It's a treasure hunter."

Elliot bangs his head against the wall. The longer hair on the top of his head flops over his eyes. "Ruby's right," he says. "An island hermit living off the land would steal food, water, or clothing, not a book. We have to assume the thief is looking for the treasure—and now has the map."

"We should put Anne on guard duty overnight." Charlie's

body is a skinny slash of pale in dark shorts as he dives for the ball. A *whump, whump, whump,* and then he says, "If only she had a sword. Why don't we ever have swords when we need them?"

"There's not a single time in my life I've needed a sword," Elliot says.

"Well, that's because you have no imagination."

Charlie tosses the ball at Anne's feet, and her head jerks up. For a moment she looks as lost as I felt today in the woods, face blanched in the moonlight. She blinks once, twice. "Oh. Right." She thuds her heels against the cabin wall, walks her feet up the wood as far as they'll go. Her toe taps the solitary window. "That's why you asked me here, isn't it?"

"No," Elliot says, skipping the part where our real motivation was just as self-serving. "But it'd be nice if the person who doesn't sleep made sure wild animals didn't try to eat us or treasure hunters didn't steal our map."

"This is my fault." Her voice is two sizes too small. "I didn't mean—"

"Don't listen to Elliot," Gabe says with a soft smile. He squeezes her hand. "You didn't do anything wrong."

She nods and says, "So what now?"

"Now we look for the wolves," I say, but my words taste all wrong. Sour like mistakes. My mind plays the poem again and again, and it finally clicks: I realize what's been bothering me about the pit. I cast an apologetic look at Charlie and say, "I don't think we're supposed to go down the hole."

Elliot groans. The silver light sculpts his bare chest into granite, makes his skin look paler and his tattoos even darker. My eyes trace the lines of the intricate wolf on his right side. "It says, 'Go down to go up, pay no heed to the dead.' That's the hole and the grave marker out there," he says, pointing in the direction of the once-white cross.

"The poem also says, 'Into the depths is your eventual demise.' What if *that* is the hole?" I thunk my head against the wall of the shack.

Elliot pinches the bridge of his nose. "Then we missed whatever it was we were supposed to go down."

"There is a bottomless pit thirty feet from here," Charlie says. "I'm going down it."

"It's like you're trying to die," Elliot says.

"I'm *trying* to live." Charlie takes a swig of rum. "And I'm going down that hole."

Gabe and Elliot have a wordless conversation. A couple of hard stares, a raised eyebrow, a shake of the head. Not for the first time, the boys leave Charlie to be Charlie.

"It seems to me," Anne says, laying a hand on Charlie's forearm, "that the best way to live is to not die."

"Living and not dying aren't the same thing." Charlie wipes his forehead, fist around the neck of the bottle. Rum sloshes against its sides. "I used to not die all the time."

It's difficult to remember the weird boy who wore his fear like body armor. As still as he sat, always on the sidelines, he was constantly in motion: deep brown eyes scanning the room for sharp objects, structural problems, the random light fixture that might fall during third-grade reading lessons.

"Someone once told me I had a lot of living to do before I died." Charlie watches Elliot with raised eyebrows.

Elliot scowls. "Not by climbing down a pit that might still be hungry for another death, I'm sure."

"But—"

"But it's easier to chase death than let it chase you. Yes, we understand," Anne says with a stern expression. "But I'd still like a little more time with you before you drop yourself down an endless hole."

Charlie is made of fire and fun, but not much fight, so he drops his shoulders and nods. "Sure thing, Anna Banana."

Gabe swallows a gulp of rum. Shakes his head. "Of course he gives in to *you*."

"Because I'm nice."

Elliot sends her a teasing smile. "*Nice*. First used in the late thirteenth to fourteenth centuries. From Old French: foolish, stupid. From Latin, *nescius:* ignorant."

"You're studying words with your mom again?"

Gabe's remark seems to beat every bit of happy from Elliot's body. He stares at Gabe for a minute, twisting the hoop in his lip. "I'm done with that," Elliot says, but it sounds a lot like "I'm done with her."

If the air itself weren't sweating in this heat, I'd burrow in my sleeping bag to avoid this conversation. It feels wrong to sit in this small shack as Gabe and Elliot talk around a secret meant for friends.

Gabe leans forward, shoulders rounded. He's the distorted-mirror image of Elliot, all soft edges against Elliot's sharp points. "Good God, Elliot. It's been two years. So she bad-mouthed your dad. You can't ignore her forever."

"That's exactly what I'm going to do," Elliot says. "I didn't tell you the whole story. My dad's dead and she—"

"You're taking the easy way out, and you know it." Gabe shakes his head. "Stop holding a grudge and be a man."

"How could you possibly understand?"

Gabe's muscles tense. "You saying I'm not a man because I don't have a dad?"

"I'm saying you have no idea what it's like to lose a dad the way I did, so you can't call it the easy way out."

"No," Gabe says. His eyes are wild, almost glowing in the moonlight. "No, you meant that I'm not a man because my mom's a virgin. That nothing male made me, so how can I be? You meant it like all those other people mean it when they say I'm unnatural."

"You know I don't think that," Elliot says.

Something in Gabe's eyes tells me he's past the point of understanding. That the rum in his blood has him voicing a conversation he has with himself all too often.

"Of course we know you're a man. You've been with girls, Gabriel. They talk," Anne says. "Though I suppose that's your intention."

"You think I put them up to it? That they're all lying?" Gabe's face is red now, so red I worry he'll start sweating blood.

"That's not what I meant."

"Whatever, Anne." Gabe turns to me, and I push my back into the wall. If I sit really still, can I bleed through the wood and into the night air?

Of course not.

Gabe's gaze locks on mine for only a moment. I see pulled-together brows and flared nostrils and angry eyes and lowering lashes, then nothing because Gabe's lips crush to mine. The kiss is hard, demanding. Rough fingers hold my head still, digging into my scalp. I push at Gabe's shoulders, but he doesn't budge. His mind's on his tongue slipping into my mouth.

"Stop," I say before his lips can be back on mine. I feel his pain and confusion, and there's nothing romantic about it. I push against him again, harder. "Gabe, stop."

He moves fast, so fast. I blink and he's across the room, sinking into the corner like a skittish animal. Anne reaches for him, but he shoots to his feet.

"It's okay," I say, rubbing my swollen lips.

"No. It's really not. You said stop." Gabe rubs his head with both hands. He stares at Elliot and Charlie. "She said stop."

And then he's gone. The door clacks against the frame, revealing a glimpse of dark earth and a dark sky and a deep, dark hole.

Elliot squats beside me. "You okay?"

"I'm fine."

He stares at the door, and when he speaks again it's with vicious calm. "I'll handle this."

Then he's gone, too.

Without a clock, I can't watch the time tick by, but I know we wait a long time for Elliot to return. Alone. Anne sets up outside the shack to wait for Gabe, so Elliot, Charlie, and I go to bed.

But I don't sleep. I picture Gabe stumbling over a cloak of guilt and rage and falling down that endless pit. And when I slide from awake to asleep, I picture his bones at the bottom, and a skeletal smile and the tortured eyes he wore after our kiss.

TWENTY

RUBY

GABE'S ALIVE.

No, *alive*'s not the right word for the boy who's standing over the pit with terrifyingly empty eyes. He's here. And he's breathing. That seems about all we can ask for this morning.

Charlie kicks a stone down the hole. "An hour. Only an hour."

He spent all of breakfast trying to convince us that a brief stop down a dark hole is the best way to start the morning. "I get that you have this pathological sense of adventure," I tell him. "But I won't help you die."

"Ruby." He says my name like he's pulling taffy. "Are you not filled with curiosity? Like, an hour's worth of curiosity?"

Right about now, Sadie would look me in the eyes and somehow read my mind. She'd step into the spotlight for me, part sexy, part sweet, and she'd remind Charlie that she was in charge. But it's only me now, and there's nothing sweet or sexy about my response. "Someone's on the island with our map. We've seen no star symbol and no wolves, so we're not wasting time down a hole that may or may not be our eventual demise." I shoulder my pack. "We'll backtrack until we see the clue. And *then* you can attempt to maim yourself."

I head for the woods.

"Well done," Anne says, jogging to match my stride. I slow so we can walk side by side. "A fantastic dismissal. Elliot just about tossed himself down that hole with all the laughing he was doing."

"Sadie was the nice sister," I say.

"Which sister were you?"

"I was the nice sister's sister."

Anne links her arm through mine. "And now?"

"I don't know." I'm less me than I was in Wildewell. It's as if the island has taken the me-ness out of me. Or maybe it's sucked the Sadie out of me, and since all I've ever been is wrapped up in my twin, there's not much of me left.

"Sadie once said she hoped I died first so she could make sure my name got on my gravestone and not 'Sadie Caine's Sister.'"

My words linger there, a line of lyrics to the forest's orchestra. The insects and birds chirrup the kind of song I'd like to play right now, something like breathing my soul into the harmonica and having a song slip out the other side.

I clear my throat. "The next night she left me behind when she went out with friends."

"Yeah, my great-grandmother says when love's involved

someone always gets left behind." Anne swats at the monster blackflies that swarm the forest. "She says my parents loved each other so much that it created the kind of heat everyone could feel. It got too hot for them to live in Wildewell—or anywhere with other people, really—so the summer I turned six, they left me and my brother with our aunt and uncle. I think they're out there somewhere, burning everything up. Or maybe they're in the Arctic."

"You miss them?"

Anne trips over a tree root. Her cheeks are rosy. "We should be searching for wolves." Her eyes dart away from mine. "You don't want to hear any more about me."

The strangest thing of all is that I do. I tug her to a stop. "Do you miss them?"

"It's stupid. I know what Ronnie says about our parents. I should hate them like he does. Maybe I should hate everyone whose parents stuck around. Ronnie does. But I have a lot more hours to think than he does. And I can't seem to think myself into anger." She sighs. "I'm a hopeless optimist."

"Optimistic is good, Anna Banana," Charlie says, approaching from behind. He ruffles her hair. "Now, bossy . . ." He pretends to glare at me, but Charlie's face only holds angry for seconds before it reverts to affable. They chatter as they crunch over the broken limbs of half-felled trees.

Elliot appears on my right. Today he's wearing aviator sunglasses with blue-mirrored lenses and a *Treasure Island* T-shirt.

I tug his sleeve. "Highly appropriate attire."

"Let no one say I'm too tough for good fashion."

"Elliot." I don't even try to hold in my laughter. "That's not a thing anyone would ever say."

He knocks his shoulder into mine and sends me stumbling a few steps. That cracks him up, but only for a minute. He gazes at me from behind those stupid blue lenses, and it's like staring at the sky. "Are you okay?" he whispers. "After last night?"

I nod. "But I should talk to him."

Elliot aims a glare in Gabe's direction, then jogs ahead.

I fall into step beside Gabe, whose stiffening posture is the only sign he sees me. I scan his frame, slumped beneath something heavier than his backpack. He's got a tangle of brown hair and is wearing yesterday's clothes, creased and covered in dirt. "Gabe? It's okay. I'm okay." Seventeen steps and he's still silent. "Can we at least talk about it?"

He looks at me, not in the sultry appraising way he's done in the past but with an achingly honest expression. "Do you think we can ever be better than our worst?"

Anne spouts wisdom like a faucet, but I come up dry. How can I answer a question I've asked myself a million and one times, not once learning the answer? "I don't know," I say. "But if you knew what I've done, you'd understand why I want to believe we can."

He nods. Slows his steps. I may not know what's eating Gabe Nash, but I know he wants to work it out on his own. I leap over a warped tree root. Trample a waving fern. The forest comes alive, composing a song of crinkles and chirps and the ring of wind through the leaves.

Go down to go up. Go down to go up.

It repeats enough in my mind that I stop seeing a bottomless hole. I see the cliffs to the east, the flat plain where I noticed the book was missing. I see the thick forest that leads north to the deep, dark pit. I see the trees that continue west to the valley, to the mountains, to the great, wide ocean. "I see where we went wrong."

"But do you see how to turn the wrong right?" Anne yells from up ahead.

I race to catch up. "I'll need to see the map, but I think I know the way."

Elliot pauses on a sloping rock. His sunglasses perch on his head like a crown. Hands on hips, shoulders back, chin held high—he looks like the king of something significant. "What's the plan?"

"The poem's deliberately misleading," I say, unrolling the map on top of the rock. I stare at it, running the poem through my head.

Elliot's brow furrows as he catches my gaze. "Tell me you have a brilliant theory for us, Rubes."

At the moment, I have a head full of warm air and a fizzy feeling like champagne bubbling in my chest. How have I lasted so long without hearing my nickname spoken aloud?

It's not just about Sadie or what she used to call me. It's what it means to hear it roll from Elliot's tongue like *a, and,* or *the.* Like a million other words he says every day. Like *friend.*

My cheeks flush, and I duck my head. "Probably not brilliant, but an idea." I take a deep breath, then say, "Once we climbed the cliff, I think we were supposed to go down the hills to go up and out of the valley—which would have put us by the Star Stones."

Elliot leans over the map, hands splayed wide on the rock. I press a finger over a forest on the eastern side of the island. "The poem said, 'Too far to the south, and your quest is done,' so we went north here. But even though the Star Stones are in the south, they might not be *too far* to the south."

"So we need to hike southwest across the valley to get back on track." A small smile inches across his face. "This is it."

A loud squawk cuts through the forest, and I nearly jump a foot. Anne tilts her chin to the sky. "Birds," she says. "We've seen birds and rabbits and squirrels and otters and deer. We heard that owl and those awful screaming fisher cats."

"Okay, Ranger Anne."

"Don't mock me, Charles Kim. I'm simply pointing out all the animals we've seen and heard." She turns to Elliot. "So where are all the wolves?"

TWENTY-ONE

COOPER

Fifteen minutes into our trip around Gray Wolf Island, the boat lurches in the water and I drop the egg.

"Gotta move with the boat," Bishop says, shaking his head.

The deck's a mess of gold shells and yellow yolk. I scoop up whatever I can, toss it overboard. The rest I rinse with bucketfuls of seawater.

"Next year, Bart." He steers the boat around the curve of the island. A cliff of tan stone towers above, its flat top covered in waving grass. "Starting tomorrow, we'll practice until you can hold an egg in that spoon while dancing a jig. The cup will be ours."

He's talking about the golden chalice, a stand-in for whatever treasure's buried in that pit. It's the prize Bishop and I would have won if we'd sailed around Gray Wolf Island faster than anyone else participating in Race 'Round the Island and I hadn't dropped the egg. "Fecking egg."

I'm trying to curse less.

Bishop shakes his head. "How's the map coming?"

We're rounding the west side of the island, the spot I was studying before Bishop's last trip. He returned from it last night, just in time for Wildewell's Festival of Souls.

"I decided something about myself, Bishop."

"That you're scrubbing egg from my boat tomorrow morning?"

"That I'm not an artist." I learned this the day I started drawing the treasure map. Up until last week, I'd resigned myself to creating a really terrible map. "I'm making a word puzzle instead."

Bishop takes a while to respond. He's doing something with the sails and lines—I don't know what. He hasn't taught me to sail yet. "Like a treasure crossword puzzle?"

"Like a poem." I like this idea more than I'm letting on. I'll keep going with the stupid drawing if he's stuck on the idea of an old-time treasure map. I'll even color it with tea and burn the edges like he wanted. It's his treasure, after all.

But I've already started writing the poem. Words are as easy as breathing. Drawing's kind of like drowning.

"Will it rhyme?"

I search his eyes, but the bill of his hat hides them with a shadow. "You want it to rhyme?"

"Of course I want it to rhyme, Bart."

I smile. "It rhymes."

We've rounded the island. If I hadn't dropped the gold-dipped egg, we might still be in the race for the chalice. Since we're not, Bishop sails at a leisurely pace. He leans back, crosses his ankles. "And how far along did you get?"

"To the Star Stones." I think it'll be a good part. There's a lot that rhymes with *star*. I'm trying to work it so I allude to the island's possible pirate past. *Aarrrh.*

I tilt my face into the sea spray. "How'd they get there?"

Six towering stones squat at the base of Gray Wolf Island's tallest mountain. Back in 1886, a treasure hunter named George Aston figured out that when you connect the stones, it makes a six-sided star. If the treasure's not down the pit, then it's below those stones. That's what I thought. That's what Bishop thought. I guess every treasure hunter who's ever struck out at the pit has thought that about the stones.

They dug. Found an empty cave—a whole system of empty caves. No treasure.

"Who put them there? What's their purpose?"

Bishop tips his head back. I do the same.

Sky's so blue it looks fake. There's a lot to like about today.

"Maybe someone found the treasure and erected those stones as a monument to it," he says. "Maybe the island grew them from pebbles. Doesn't matter, Bart. You're asking the wrong questions. It's not who or how, but what those stones say."

They whispered to me a month ago when Bishop brought me to the island to mark landmarks with a mysterious symbol. It's not actually mysterious to us—it's straight from Bishop's brain—but he's hoping it will be to treasure hunters. I carved it right into one of the Star Stones, which was *not* the right thing to do. Bishop went on and on about them being super old and maybe important.

"They talk about the truth," I say. "But what truth?"

He shakes his head. "Isn't that the question?"

Captain Thirwall has glued his hand to the Race 'Round the Island chalice.

He was worried about the cup getting lost or stolen. That's what he says, anyway. More like he was worried people would stop asking him to reenact the race. And then he'd have to stop talking about it so much.

Now whenever a little kid tries to steal the trophy, the captain screams.

It's hilarious.

I make a move for it, but Bishop yanks me away.

"Sometimes you act like you're six," he says.

"Maybe I am."

"Maybe you're immature for your age."

"*You're* immature for your age," I say, stopping in front of Hank Windsor's stall. It should smell like the morning's catch, but the barrel fire nearby masks the scent.

Bishop explains the barrels to me as we wait in line. Goes back almost four hundred years.

French missionaries and Native Americans lived out on Gray Wolf Island at the start of the seventeenth century. When the English came to the island a few decades later, they claimed the land. Slaughtered French and Native Americans alike. Burned the bodies.

Some people whispered that the bodies weren't burned. They'd been thrown in a pile. One on top of the other. Mixed with all that sorrow, it was too much for the land to bear. It crumbled. They fell.

There's an endless hole marking their grave.

Not long after the first excavation of the Gray Wolf Island treasure pit got under way, the people of Wildewell started dying. Everyone thought the two were connected.

They were convinced it was an epidemic of angry spirits looking for revenge.

The treasure hunters wanted to stop. Wanted to not die.

But they wanted that treasure more.

So the people of Wildewell crafted big metal barrels. Created giant fires inside them.

It scared away the angry spirits.

That's what they said, anyway. Bishop says it was a cholera epidemic all along.

"The English takeover on the mainland wasn't quite as devastating," he says.

Charlie Francis doesn't think so. He huffs from behind us in line and says, "They graciously didn't kill the indigenous people and allowed my ancestors plots for crops on their own land as long as they fought in a war for the revolutionaries' freedom."

But Wildewell likes a party, so once a year, during the Festival of Souls, the town sets out fat steel barrels. Lights their insides on fire.

They smell amazing, even if they mask the scent of my lobster roll.

Bishop and I meander through the crowded streets. His dark fingers are white with frosting from his cupcake. I devour squiggles of dough fried in oil and dusted with powdered sugar.

It's the best thing I've ever eaten. I don't need to know my past to know that.

"Bishop Rollins," a voice squawks. "Get that fine ass of yours over here this instant."

"Don't curse, Doris," he says with a smile.

Doris Lansing is Bishop's closest friend and something like a billion years old. Bishop is old, but Doris is old enough to be his mother. Doris doesn't seem to care about that, though.

"Look, it's your girlfriend!" I laugh. Powdered sugar puffs in the air.

It's not like that with them. Everybody knows this. But everybody agrees it's more hilarious to watch Bishop get red-faced and tongue-tied than to stop Doris's flirting.

I stick around for a bit, but the whole thing stops being funny and starts being pretty gross.

I wander the art stalls. This guy is whittling these amazing animal figurines—bears, snakes, birds, deer—all with so much detail they could be alive. He's using wood that might be Indian laurel, so I buy a carved wolf to remind me of myself.

I join a crowd gathering by the waterfront. A man decked out in traditional tribal regalia stands on a bench. He gives us a rakish smile—he's old, but *rakish* is the best word for how he looks. It's a good word.

He introduces a group of drummers and dancers. They're from the reservation an hour northwest of Wildewell. Came down with the other artists and crafters for the Festival of Souls.

Doris used to be one of the dancers. Lived on the reservation and everything. But Gray Wolf Island called to her husband, so loud that he had to come to Wildewell and he had to join Bishop's dig.

Well, she says that's why she stopped dancing. I'm pretty sure she's just too old for it.

The drummers and dancers don't come to celebrate the English's triumph over the souls of the slaughtered. I asked Doris.

They come to celebrate the undying spirit of their people. I like that a lot more.

The man with the rakish smile beats a drum. Someone else joins. Soon it's all drumbeats and dancing and voices. It's the coolest thing I've ever seen.

I see my first ghost at ten o'clock. Bishop went home a half hour ago. He was falling asleep at a picnic table.

He's really old.

I'm sitting outside the bookshop, eating blueberry pie on a stick, when one shuffles toward me.

"Oh!" I jump. Blueberry pie filling plops onto my white shirt.

"Right to be scared of that one," Sal Caine says. He's sitting beside me, demolishing his third piece of angel food cake. A stray cat sits on his other side, trying to knock his plate over like an absolute jerk.

The ghost stares right at him. Like he knows Sal's giving me a warning.

"Lady gets pregnant without a man. Nobody knows what the kid is." He licks his fingers. "That one's something evil. I can feel it."

"When'd he die?"

The ghost drifts closer, and I realize he's about my age. I can't imagine he's any more evil than an adult ghost.

"Die?" Sal's brows cross. "That boy's as alive as you and me. Though I plan on staying that way. Take my advice and go home."

"I don't get it."

"You wouldn't. You're a tourist, Cooper."

That stings.

Sal stands. Takes a shuddering look at the boy. "At the very least, don't look into his eyes. Seven years' bad luck."

I don't move.

The boy approaches the bench. He solidifies as he nears the light.

I look away, just in case Sal's right. Figure with my past erased, I've had all the bad luck I need.

He sits at the far end of the bench. Out of the corner of my eye, I catch him staring at me.

"You spilled," he says.

I follow his gaze to my shirt. With a flick of my finger, I toss the blueberry filling to the ground.

A napkin lands on my leg. I rub at the stain.

"You really should wet it. Then dab."

"How do you know that?"

He shrugs. "Mr. Caine told you I was a demon, didn't he?"

I dab at my shirt. "I thought you were a ghost."

The boy laughs. "No one's ever thought that before."

"Aww, Gabriella's got a boyfriend." A tall kid with a buzz cut walks out of the shadows. Two others follow.

The boy's spine stiffens.

Buzz Cut laughs. It's sharp. Cuts the boy right open.

I see his insides as plain as day, and they look like hurt.

"Nah, he was just telling me about the girl he kissed on the Ferris wheel."

"Please," Buzz Cut says. "Gabe's more likely to turn into a girl than kiss one."

Gabe's fists clench. "Screw you."

"Looks like Gabriella's getting upset," Buzz Cut says. "Let's go get Ash's brother to buy us candy."

They leave. Smack Gabe's head into the hard bench before they do.

I won't embarrass him by asking if he's all right. So we sit there. Don't speak.

After a long while, Gabe says, "Hey, you know any girls?"

TWENTY-TWO

RUBY

"The wolves," Anne repeats. "Where are they?"

The forest is silent except for the rattle of wind in the trees.

"There aren't any wolves on Gray Wolf Island," Charlie says. "Not anymore at least."

Elliot releases an almost predatory snarl. "Where the hell did they go?"

"How should I know? It's not like I lived with the wolves until they accepted me into their pack and divulged their travel plans. I just know they're not here." Charlie crunches through the forest, tearing leaf and limb from trees as he goes. He swats Elliot with a thin branch. "I thought your family knew everything about the island."

"Charlie," Elliot says, snatching the branch from him, "where'd you hear this?"

"Where'd you hear there's a treasure down the pit?" Charlie scales a nearby tree, all grace and agility and hidden power. "I've known it for so long I forget not knowing."

Elliot rakes his hands back and forth over the shorter hair on the sides of his head. "Maybe this is something you could have mentioned during one of the dozens of meetings we had about the poem!"

Charlie shrugs. "I didn't think I was coming, so I wasn't paying attention."

Elliot launches off the ground. His hands grasp for Charlie's foot, but Charlie jumps to a higher branch. He's got the moves of a mountain lion.

Elliot has the roar. "I'm going to kill you. That's how you're going to die."

He latches on to a low branch. That's when I see it. Peeking from beneath the hem of his T-shirt, down by his hip. Two paws with sharp claws. And suddenly I know why Elliot's chasing Charlie up a tree. "The wolves."

"Exactly!" Elliot drops to the ground. "We're supposed to see wolves!"

I say it again even though we all know the words. "'Go down to go up, pay no heed to the dead. If you're on the right track, you'll see gray wolves ahead.'"

"How are we supposed to see wolves if there are no wolves on the island? How are we going to beat the other treasure hunter when we haven't even figured out the map?" Elliot growls. "I spent a week analyzing the poem, but of all the instructions, that one never—"

"How is it that smart people are so dumb?" Charlie sniggers. "What'd you expect? A wolf to stay in the same spot as a marker?"

Well, now that he mentions it.

Anne tosses Charlie a water bottle so he won't have to leave the tree and face Elliot's wrath, which I find amusing but also pointless since Elliot's staring into space. Which is what Gabe's been doing all morning, only now he's mumbling to himself, too.

"All right, fine. It's not a real wolf," Elliot says. He has this delightfully wild look about him that makes me think of riding a roller coaster for the first time. "But it could be carved into a tree or . . . the Star Stones."

"Is one of the runes in the shape of a wolf?"

Elliot gives an aggravated sigh. "They're not runes. If they were runes, my mom and I could have translated them. And if they were pictures, they'd be hieroglyphs."

"I honestly don't care," I say. "All we need to know is whether the stone could have a wolf on it."

"I saw the photos—there's no wolf on that one." Elliot's pinched lips blossom into a smile. "But I bet it's carved into one of the others. Which means you were right: down into the valley, up to the Star Stones."

"Let's do this," Charlie says, clapping his hands together. He drops from the tree and falls into step with Anne. They scurry after Gabe, who's wandered deeper into the forest.

I don't know where we are, but Elliot—who doesn't even try to hide his Boy Scout past beneath his attempt at bad boy—has a compass, so we have a direction.

"Ruby?" His fingers whisper against my bare shoulder.

Somewhere, in some universe, a girl is getting a kiss that feels a whole lot like this touch.

I lower my gaze to the three fingers on my skin.

He jerks them away. "We'll find the thief and get the book back."

"Yes!" Charlie shouts from a few feet ahead. "I'm adding that to my bucket list: Take down evil treasure hunter dude."

"Or woman," Anne says, but she's giggling. It's a wonder how a moment can feel so light when there's such heaviness to this day.

After three hours of walking and a quick lunch, the woods thin and the trees shrink until they're gone and there's nothing but a grassy hill and a sea of green. In the distance, two rounded mountains meet to form what resembles the humps of a camel.

"They look like boobs," Charlie says. "Hey, Gabe, don't the mountains look like . . . Oh, right. You're busy with the self-loathing." Charlie shrugs. "I'm just saying, those are very breastlike mountains."

Sadie would have loved that. She'd have said it first. "You would have liked my sister."

"I kinda did. Not because of her—" Charlie points to the mountains. "Not that they weren't nice. They totally were. Oh, this is awkward, isn't it? Because of the twin thing?" He peeks at my chest.

Elliot smashes his fist into Charlie's shoulder. "What the hell's wrong with you?"

He points to the base of the leftmost mountain. If we had

followed the map as intended, cut west from the cliffs, we'd have an almost-straight walk down the hill, across the valley, and up to the Star Stones. Coming from the pit, we're taking a southwesterly route. "That's where we need to be."

For a minute nobody speaks, and in the silence the island sings and it sounds exactly like Sadie. It's somehow in my head and all around me. It's as raspy as my Marine Band playing the blues.

> *Ruby Caine whose heart went sour*
> *took her sister to the highest tower.*
> *Said her heart was full of love,*
> *then gave her sister a hard, hard shove.*

"Let's go," I say to stop the song. I clench my jaw and tell myself I'm not that girl.

It's a lie, of course.

I thunder down the hill, thighs shaking with the weight of my pack and the strain of maintaining a slow march. Charlie gives up on it, letting his legs carry him as fast as gravity likes before face-planting in the tall grass. Elliot kicks Charlie's pack as he passes. Anne and I attempt to lift Charlie to his feet, but his skinny body's heavier than it looks and he's not trying very hard to get up.

I leave them there, hurrying after Elliot and nearly running into Gabe, who appears to be having a conversation with himself. His words don't wander far from his lips, but though I can't hear what he's saying, I can tell he's passionate about it. His hand rakes through his hair, tugs at it tragically.

"Gabe? Are you okay?"

He closes his eyes, squeezes tight. "Do you hear it, too?"

"Hear what?" I speak like I'm testing a field for land mines.

"The voice. The island. I don't know." But I do know. I heard it, too. A million different sounds of the island—the *shhh* of waves against its shores; the scuttling, slithering, stomping through the forests; the roar of the wind; the rattling leaves; and the absolute silence of secrets—all of it swirling around in my mind. All of it sounding a lot like Sadie.

Gabe shakes his head. "I think it wants the truth from us, Ruby."

My stomach drops. "What truth?"

Panic ghosts across his face, and I wonder whose voice he heard on the wind. "All of it," he says.

I must look like he does: white as winter with wide and wild eyes. We walk in silence as we enter the valley, slowing our steps to lag behind the others. "It can't have mine," I say when we're finally alone. "Any of it."

We're halfway across the valley, following a path worn into the earth by long-ago tires, when the wind begins its assault. It roars across the empty plain, beating red into our cheeks. If it weren't for my backpack, I'd worry a gust might lift me straight into the air.

"You know what'd be real useful right now?" Elliot shouts over the wind.

"A truck," Anne says. If we were ever going to find a truck, it'd be at the end of this overgrown path, worn into the island by excavation equipment years ago. That's why we decided to follow its haphazard route across the valley in the first place.

"That, too. But I'm thinking we'd definitely beat the thief with *Star Trek*–style teleportation."

I try to shake my head, but the gale holds me steady. "If you get any nerdier your tattoos are going to wash off."

"Ahem!" Anne shouts the word so it's not swallowed by the wind. "I meant to say that I see a truck. Over there."

I follow her gaze to a pickup with rust bleeding down its sides and grass climbing its back. I imagine it must have been blue at some point, before the island began devouring it.

"Here's your wolf." Charlie grins at Elliot. I circle the truck until I'm also staring at the driver's side. Disappearing letters spell ROLLINS CORP. And below that, half hidden by grime and weathered by time, is the silhouette of two wolves.

We give in to glee. Jump around as much as our heavy packs will allow. Whoop and holler with all the breath in us.

After a few minutes, Elliot tugs the door open with a creak, slides behind the wheel. He flips down the visor, rifles through the glove compartment.

"I can't find any keys," he says, bending to the floor. I expect him to search beneath the carpet, but he whips out a Swiss Army knife and uses the screwdriver to remove the plastic panels around the steering column. They land on the passenger's seat with a clatter.

He switches to the blade to carefully cut through two red wires. He removes part of the covering, then twists the exposed wires together. The process takes much longer than it does in the movies. No ripping wires in one hasty motion. No careless cutting. Only steady hands and cautious movements and one hundred percent Elliot Thorne.

He catches me staring and smirks. "What was that about me not being a badass?"

"Please. You wouldn't steal even your own car."

Another two wires are snipped and stripped. Elliot touches the wires together. We're waiting for a spark, a coughing to life of the engine. He tries again.

"It's dead," Gabe says, and though the wind's still whistling through the valley and his voice isn't raised in the least, he might as well have spoken thunder for the way Elliot jolts.

"It's dead!" Elliot slaps a palm against the hood. " 'Pay no heed to the dead.' The poem. *This* is the dead."

He holds my gaze, a wide grin creeping across his face. "You were right. It must be taking us to the Star Stones."

"Aw, look how happy you've made him," Charlie says, wrapping his skinny arms around my shoulders from behind. "You have a beautiful brain, Ruby Caine."

"Excellent rhyme," Anne says.

Elliot cranes his neck to find a stoic Gabe gazing at the cloudless sky. "Gabe, man, what the hell are you doing?"

Gabe blinks at Elliot. "It's all going to come out, Elliot. All of it." He turns and walks in the direction of the Star Stones. Elliot races to catch up. Charlie and Anne stare at each other with equally bewildered expressions before following. I hurry to their side.

"Have you kissed a boy before, Ruby?" Anne asks as we trek through a field of purple lupines so tall their tips brush Anne's thighs. "Before Gabe?"

I wish for the wind to swallow my words, but in this moment the fierce gale that was terrorizing the valley quiets to a breeze. I release a hard laugh. "Sadie kissed enough boys for the both of us."

"Yeah, Elliot figured. He yelled at Gabe for ruining your first kiss," Charlie says. He uses his shovel as a walking stick as we hike out of the valley. Jams it hard against the ground. "I don't think you have to count it. Right, Anne?"

"Oh, that doesn't much matter. I'm curious, though, whether your lips are venomous." She tilts her head and regards me through slitted eyes. "I'd ask you to kiss Charlie, but then he might go mad, too."

"I'm not kissing Charlie," I say. "No offense, Charlie. And my lips aren't venomous."

"Then how do you explain Gabriel?"

I don't mention the voice or the way Gabe answered it back. I don't talk about the truth he's adamant must come out. But I don't lie. "I think the island's tormenting him. I don't think it wants us to find the treasure."

Anne bites her lip. "That makes sense," she says. "The island wouldn't keep the treasure hidden if it wanted the treasure found."

TWENTY-THREE

RUBY

FIND HEAVEN ON EARTH—
a sign you will see.
Then let go the lie
and set the truth free.

Elliot and Gabe are leaning against a stone slab that juts from the ground like an oversized tombstone when Anne, Charlie, and I stumble into the grassy clearing. Five more stones, as tall and deteriorated as the first, surround us. The air snaps with energy, raising the fine hairs on my arms.

"There's something here, isn't there?" Anne stretches her arms wide and twirls around, her loose tank catching air and swirling around her. "There's nothing, but there's *something*."

I can't help but agree. There's an otherness to this place,

though I can't tell whether it's been here all along or if our excitement coaxed it into being.

I wander to the center of the stone formation, where the meadow is balding of its grass. The ground buckles around knuckles of rock that at one time must have connected in a single fist. It's the hole that stops me, though.

Anne finds me digging through my bag for my flashlight and calls for the others. Soon we're gathered around the rocks, beams pointed downward.

Blackness and rock, nothing else.

Elliot bumps his shoulder against mine. "This might be heaven on earth."

"That sounds like one of Gabe's lines."

"Oh. Um." His eyes flit to mine, then back to the hole. "I was talking about the poem. Stars are in the heavens, and the Star Stones are on earth. Whatever's down the hole could be the sign we're supposed to see."

"Think I can fit through there?" Anne asks, pulling a line of rope from her bag. She knots it around her waist. "Someone hold the other end."

"And somehow I'm the one who's going to die." Charlie unties Anne. He pulls a handful of fancy ropes from his bag. Seems to be pretty much all he packed. He jangles a couple of carabiners and says, "Never know when you'll need to rappel down something."

Elliot rolls his eyes. "That's not actually something real people consider."

"What do you think, Anna Banana? Up for some exploring?"

And that's how Anne ends up in an elaborate harness and helmet, feet dangling over a mysterious nothingness. She looks like a child playing in her father's gear, small head in a too-big helmet with hair shooting in every direction. She's attached to a bunch of nylon ropes that run through the three anchors Charlie has set into cracks in the rocks. I expect him to push her off the ledge in an attempt at adventure, but Charlie, it appears, is all caution when it comes to everyone but himself. He guides her forward. Feet, calves, knees, and thighs. It's the hips that do her in.

"A shove might be nice," she says, rocking her body side to side in an attempt to slide farther through the hole. Elliot presses on her shoulders, but she doesn't budge. She flops backward, rests the back of her helmet on the stone. "Everyone's always teasing me for being tiny, and just when I thought it might finally come in handy, I'm too big. What cruel irony."

"That's not irony."

"Don't lecture me, Elliot," Anne says. "I'm half in the ground and possibly stuck."

I crouch behind her. Tug her by the armpits until she's able to wiggle the rest of the way out of the hole. She jumps to her feet, throws off the helmet, and wrestles with her harness. "Failure makes me hungry."

It makes me hungry, too. I'm completely ravenous for the treasure.

"We can still look for the sign," I say. "Let's focus on that. Let's check the Star Stones."

"Give before you get," Gabe says, voice low and hypnotic. "There's nothing here for us. Not yet."

"Are we waiting for something?" Anne squats beside him, rests a hand on his shoulder.

Gabe flinches.

"He's not right. And he's getting more and more not-right the longer we're on the island." Anne's eyes are wide and worried. She whispers, "We should leave."

The suggestion wraps around my chest and tightens. I can barely breathe at the thought of giving up this hunt. Of giving up on Sadie. "I can't." My voice croaks. I try again. "I can't, not until I find the treasure. But you can leave me here. I'll call for a boat pickup when I'm done."

Elliot stares at Gabe. "I'm staying," he says, and it sounds like an apology. "I've been waiting for this since before I was born."

"Gabe?" Anne's hands flutter in the space between her body and his.

"We're not leaving without the treasure. Gotta tell the truth to get the truth," he says. He pushes off the ground and hurries to a stone on the far side of the clearing. Anne starts after him, but Elliot calls her back.

"Let him be." Elliot bites his lip ring with such force I'm afraid he'll tear it out. He stares after his friend, a mournful expression on his face. "You two make dinner. Ruby and I are going to inspect the stones."

Warm hand firm around my fingers, Elliot leads me to a towering slab of granite, far enough from Gabe that we're not intruding but close enough for Elliot to keep watch. He presses his forehead against the cool rock. "I'm the one who's supposed to lose my mind," he whispers.

"It's the island." I'm not talking in excuses like poisoned lips. I know with strange certainty that this place is tormenting Gabe. It's tormenting me, too. "It's telling him things."

"Why would the island talk to Gabe?"

"Maybe it's sick of Thornes."

Elliot stares at me a moment longer, then turns his gaze to the stone. It's nearly a head taller than Elliot, as wide as both of us side by side. The top right corner has long since crumbled. "Same symbols my mother spent years trying to translate," he says, running a hand over the etched stone. "No clues."

We circle to the other side, which is free of any markings. It's the same for the next four stones. Elliot and I approach the final monolith with lowered shoulders and little hope. We start at the back, prolonging the suspense. I whirl around the slab to find Elliot punching the rock.

"Idiot." Without thinking, I catch his hand in both of mine. If Sadie were here, I'd be six steps behind her, watching as my sister's lips met raw knuckle. I feel six steps behind right now as my thumbs brush away blood.

Elliot takes a long breath, gaze fixed on my fingers. Then he lifts his head. It's only now that I realize how close we're standing, how easy it would be to press my forehead into his.

But I don't.

I drop Elliot's hand and turn to the stone. Like the others, it's free of the thick grooves that marked the first. A blot of blood stains the stone at shoulder height, a smudge of Thorne forever tied to the island. I'm sure Elliot will be absurdly pleased by that fact just as soon as he's finished sulking.

"We'll check again," I say. "We'll—"

"No." Elliot is kneeling in front of the stone, hands laced behind his head.

There, carved into the rough stone, is a wide square slashed through with a lopsided line. It's sloppy, but it's our sign.

Elliot greets the stone like it's an old friend, at once excited and restrained as he traces the shallow grooves. "We're going to find the treasure," he says. There's a hint of a smile in his voice, but it's mostly serious, like Elliot. We stand in stunned silence for a few seconds, staring at each other without really seeing.

I shake my daze and take a last look at the symbol. It doesn't hold the answer to all my questions, but on an island that can sedate a smooth talker like Gabe, during a quest for unfathomable treasure, it seems a single answer is good enough. For now.

TWENTY-FOUR

RUBY

"I WANT YOU TO REMEMBER THAT I RAISED YOU FOR SEVENTEEN years. All those clothes, all that food . . ." Though I can't see him, I know my dad's grinning. "I distinctly remember paying for your baby teeth."

"Are you saying the Tooth Fairy isn't real?"

"That I am," he says. "Neither is Santa. Those presents were from me. I want you to remember that when you're rich with pirate treasure."

"Elliot says we'll have to give the treasure to the Smithsonian."

"What a buzzkill." He repeats the conversation to my mom, who's washing dishes and pestering him for details. "Your mom says he's a good boy."

"Um, okay." I don't actually enjoy talking about boys with my parents. "So I should go. Can't hog the phone."

"She can't hog the phone," he tells my mom. It's like the speaker feature doesn't exist. "Mom says she loves you and expects you to have fun." He pauses, but only for a second. "But good, wholesome fun."

I'm smiling as I walk back to camp. The air is heavy with the scent of smoke and fire when I reach the meadow. Gabe's slouching against one of the ruins, mumbling, " 'Let go the lie and set the truth free.' "

I've read it a thousand times while studying the map, but I always imagined we'd skip that step and head straight to the next clue. And I know I should stop and ask him what it means, how it'll lead us to the treasure, but I want nothing to do with revelations of truth. So I hurry away.

At the opposite end of the field, Elliot's reading and Charlie and Anne crouch over an open flame, squabbling like siblings over a pot of something green.

"I've fallen in platonic love with you, Charles Kim, but no, I do not trust your judgment. Not on a boat. And not in the kitchen." Anne tilts her head. "Or the outdoor equivalent."

Charlie spoons what appears to be green mashed potatoes into five bowls. Elliot and I exchange a glance, and I know we're thinking the same thing because he whips his head around and yells, "Gabe! Anne and Charlie are going to poison us if you don't snap out of it."

Gabe stands up slowly, like the wind that beat down the valley has taken up residence directly in front of him. His feet shuffle through the grass until he's standing over the fire. Anne hands him a bowl of green potatoes, which he looks at with a fleetingly curious expression before squeezing between Elliot and Charlie.

I'm assaulted by pungent oregano as I stir my mashed potatoes, revealing small chunks of hard brown. "So dinner . . ."

"Oregano," Elliot coughs. "First used in the late seventeen hundreds. From the Spanish *orégano*. Wild marjoram. From Latin: *origanum*."

Gabe takes a bird bite. Lets the rest plop back into his bowl. He eyes Charlie, who doesn't seem bothered by the obscene greenness of the potatoes.

Anne delivers a smug smile—a particular arrangement of features that looks out of place on her face—and says, "Told you we should have gone with the cinnamon."

Gabe chokes on his water. I narrow my eyes and watch as Anne and Charlie exchange a knowing glance. "My mom always puts cinnamon in sweet potato pie." She taps a finger to her chin. "And mini marshmallows, but we don't have any of those. I have jelly beans, though."

Gabe slams his bowl to the ground. "If you bothered to read the front of the box, you'd know these are instant cheddar mashed potatoes. You don't put cinnamon in cheddar potatoes, Anne. You just don't." He swings his head to Charlie. "And even though oregano is the better option, it's only slightly better than putting garlic powder on Lucky Charms, especially when you dump the entire bag of oregano in a single pot. I'm not even going to comment on the bits of beef jerky that appear like rat turds throughout this green mess of a meal."

At that, Anne and Charlie lose it. I mean, they just let go with laughter that causes tears and the occasional snort. I catch Anne's eye and she delivers a clumsy wink that has her other lid partially dropping, too. I stare in wonder at these two people who would cook a terrible meal on the off chance it could fix

170

their friend, and I know with sudden sureness that I'd eat green potatoes for a month straight if it meant my friends were okay.

The lightness lasts until the sun disappears and the fire snaps against the black sky. Gabe becomes increasingly agitated as we clean the dishes and set up tents. So I pull out my harmonica and play a fast and folksy tune. My pulse keeps the beat. Something more me than air pushes from my lungs, through these reeds, and into the night. The song's the sound of me—hope, love, desperation—and I wish it were enough to bring Gabe back.

His hands twist in his hair. His head shakes side to side to side to side. "Just do it," he says under his breath, and I only hear because I've paused for a drink of water. " 'Let go the lie and set the truth free.' Let go the lie. Let go the lie."

Elliot stops Gabe's babble with a punch to his bicep. "You're freaking me out. What the hell's going on with you?"

"I did something last winter." Gabe stares around the fire, crazed eyes scanning each of our faces. He flinches when he meets my stare. "You'll hate me. You'll all hate me."

"As your best friends, we're legally obligated to like you," Charlie says.

Gabe rakes shaking fingers through his knotted hair. "The island's in my head. Or . . . I don't know. But it wants the truth." He scrubs his face with the heel of his hand.

He speaks low, almost too low to hear over the crack of the flames. He seems to gather his strength—deep breath, squeezed eyes—and then in a wobbly voice he says, "I did something terrible."

TWENTY-FIVE

RUBY

The island seems to hold its breath, greedy for Gabe's confession.

"Remember Hodge's party over winter break? Charlie, you lit fireworks in the backyard and burned off that freshman's right eyebrow. Elliot, you were there, but you weren't."

"There were too many annoying people there," Elliot says. "I locked myself in Hodge's little sister's room and read."

"That's not important," Gabe says. Flames dance in his pupils as he stares into the fire. "Here's what's important: That bastard Ronnie Lansing—sorry, Anne—was there, and he started talking shit about my mom and how without a dad, I can't have a Y chromosome so there's no way I can be a guy. And, I mean, I was drunk. And I drank more, telling Ronnie and those guys to go to hell. But they just kept at it, you know?"

"They're losers," Elliot says. "They deserve whatever beating you gave them."

Gabe shakes his head. "I should have. I should have laid into Ronnie and busted his nose, but I was out-of-my-mind drunk and for some reason that didn't cross my mind. I just kept thinking about what they said and how maybe no one really believed I was a man.

"And there she was. I'm not going to tell you her name because I promised I'd keep her secret, but she was there and she was gorgeous. She wanted me. She kissed me first, you know? It was like, I don't know . . ." He laughs, but there's no humor in it. "It was like she could disprove everything everyone said about me."

My stomach sinks. Part of me wants him to continue, but most of me doesn't.

"I didn't do it on purpose. You have to believe me."

Anne's hand snaps to her mouth and she whispers through shaking fingers, "What did you do?"

Gabe's eyes are glassy when they meet hers. "We were in this room. I don't know what room, but it was dark and we were kissing. And she was into it. At first. But then I heard this voice in my head that sounded like Ronnie and then I thought I'd show him I was a man."

If I still have a heart, it's not doing its job. It's a stone in my chest, heavy like the rest of me.

Gabe takes a shuddering breath, and with his exhale releases fat tears. His fist pounds his head. "I thought she was into it, you know? I was kissing her so hard, pushing her so hard against the wall. And when I put my hand up her shirt I thought—I don't know. I was so drunk on beer and anger that I convinced myself she jumped because my hands were so cold.

"Then she said no." As Gabe talks, the fire whimpers and ducks, then dies. He looks at me now, stooped with shame. "She said no, and I didn't listen."

Anne takes a ragged breath. "Did you . . ."

"No," Gabe says, and it's the strongest his voice has been all night. "No, not that. But I may as well have. I lifted her shirt, and she said no again. She pushed against my chest, but I was stronger."

He shakes his head. Releases a harsh laugh wet with tears. "I pressed her harder against the wall and I heard her say, 'Please, stop.' And you know what I thought for a split second? I thought, 'I'm a fucking man.'"

"Gabe." There's a jagged edge to Elliot's voice. "Did you rape that girl?"

Gabe buries his head in his hands. His shoulders shake with sobs. "No!" he cries. "Thank God, no. She was so afraid of me. Her face—I see it every time I shut my eyes. I ran. I ran out of the room and out of the house and out of the neighborhood, and I didn't stop running until I was under the docks on the east bay. I beat the shit out of myself, but it didn't make me hate myself any less."

No one speaks for a very long time. It's impossible to make sense of my emotions. Disgust marries pity, and I can't seem to feel one without the other. This horrifies me. "And everything went back to normal?"

Gabe flinches at my words. "It had to. That Monday I went to school and apologized. I told her to tell someone. I wanted to be punished. I wanted anything but pretending it never happened. She didn't want anyone to know. I couldn't— After everything, I owed her that."

"Dude." It's as far as Charlie gets. His mouth makes an O and he shakes his head like he's shaking the story from his mind.

"Why do you listen to those shitheads?" Elliot shoots to his feet. "You've heard Ronnie tell me to blow my brains out. 'Like father, like son.' You hear that, but you don't think I'm going to stick a gun in my face, do you?"

"I know!" Gabe pulls his knees to his chest. "I knew it then, too. That's what makes me so horrible."

Elliot runs a hand through his hair. "You say that. You say you're horrible, Gabe. Well, if you felt so bad about it, why the hell did you keep flirting with every girl in Wildewell? Why have you been hitting on Ruby this entire trip? Why didn't you try to be better?"

"Because!" Gabe's voice is sharp. "You wouldn't get it, Elliot, because everyone sees you as this tough guy. They don't wonder if you're a man. What do you think they'd say if I took a break from hooking up?"

"I don't . . . I mean, what do you want me to say, Gabe? I'm trying to understand, but—"

"I don't want your understanding," Gabe says. "Do you have any idea what it's like letting everyone see someone good and worthy when you're a monster inside?"

"Yes." The whisper's out before I realize it. Gabe's watery gaze meets mine. "I've done things I'm not proud of. Everyone has secrets."

"It's not the same," Gabe says, standing. "It's not the same."

He disappears into his tent, leaving shock and silence

behind. No one's in the mood to talk, so we wordlessly work to snuff out the fire and get ready for bed.

❖

Overhead, insects beat against the top of the tent, dark smudges against the dark night. Soft fingers rest over mine. I stare at Anne's hand, and I know she's not Sadie and she's strange, but I hold tight and squeeze.

"When I was little, Bishop Rollins told me Gabe was an angel." Even in the dark, I can see her blush. "I don't even believe in angels, but for the longest time I believed that."

A rustling of nylon. Anne's face appears less than a foot from mine. She lowers her voice. "I fell in love with him that day. Never talked to him before this summer, but I knew him in my mind and I loved him. That's my secret, Ruby."

My stomach clenches. Hasn't the island had enough truth for the night?

"I don't hate him," I say. I can't—I'm as wicked as he is. Still, I hate myself a bit for that piece of truth.

"I loved him this morning. And this afternoon. But he's not the boy I built in my head. And he's not the same person he was before dinner." Anne shakes her head, and out pour a few more tears. Down the side of her face, into her hair with the others. "But of course all of this happened months ago, so he's exactly the same person he's been since we first became friends."

"I'm not sure that boy ever really existed." I close my eyes and see Gabe's easy smile, see him flirting not because he wanted to but because that's who Gabe Nash was six months ago so that's who Gabe Nash had to be.

"Can you really know someone without knowing the one horrible thing that defines who they are or who they become?" Anne's watery eyes search my face, and I feel such a connection to this girl who's so unlike Sadie. Is this what friendship feels like when blood doesn't tie you together?

I think about the warmth of Charlie's arm over my shoulders, the way my chest tightens then gets really loose when Elliot smiles, and the feeling of Anne's fingers wrapped around mine. But most of all I think about Gabe's words.

It's not the same. It's not the same.

No, it isn't the same. Because what I did? It was much, much worse.

I've kept that horror hidden somewhere dark and deep, but they know me. I might be more me than I've ever been, here on the island with these new friends. "Yes." I squeeze Anne's hand. "People can be real, even if they're not being honest."

Anne brushes the wet from her cheek. Her gaze returns to the ceiling. "Ruby?"

"Yeah?"

She squeezes my hand. "You can be honest with me."

"Thanks." I turn on my side, my back to her. What would happen if she knew that evil hid behind a friendly face?

I can't tell her. I can never tell.

TWENTY-SIX

COOPER

BISHOP MAKES ONE MORE TRIP TO THE ISLAND. HE DOESN'T take me with him this time. Says he has stuff to do alone. I try telling him he's too old to go around spray-painting and carving the symbol all over the island. That isn't my best idea.

A week later, Bishop's back, and Doris Lansing is at his door. She brings along a girl who looks more fairy than human. We follow Bishop to the patio. It's warm out, a little too hot to be comfortable. Bishop and Doris don't seem to mind. Old people are constantly cold.

Bishop places a plate of cookies on the table. I give Doris a look.

"I'm old, not blind," he says. "You can stop trading glances. I didn't make the cookies. Got them from that angel boy."

"He's really an angel?" Doris's Lilliputian great-granddaughter regards Bishop with huge eyes. She's been attached to Doris since Doris's daughter died a few months back.

"What do you think, Annie girl? Could a mere mortal bake like this?"

"No," she whispers. Shoves the whole cookie in her mouth.

"How's the treasure hunt, Bishop?" Doris asks. She's braiding grass into a basket, which she'll send to the museum. Bishop has some of these baskets hanging in his house even though they're not as fancy as his other stuff, like the sword he won't let me play with. "Find my Fountain of Youth yet?"

"Wouldn't that be scary? Bet you'd be up to all sorts of trouble if you were young again."

If Doris had any eyebrows left, she'd be hiking one up her forehead right now.

Bishop laughs.

The old-people-flirting thing. I just can't.

"As a matter of fact . . ." His eyes dart to mine. Only for a second. "I have a theory."

I stare at him. Eyes narrowed. Mouth tight. "About the treasure?"

Doris slaps the back of my head. "Don't look so excited."

"I wish you'd told me when you got back." This is a severe understatement of my emotions.

Bishop runs a hand over his hair. There's not much left. "I knew you'd have questions."

"Obviously."

"You're not ready for it."

"I'm ready."

179

"Me too," Doris says.

"Me too," Anne repeats, crunching on a butterscotch cookie.

"I'm sorry, Bart." Bishop *looks* sorry. For some reason, that makes me angrier. "Time's coming when you'll be ready to know about it. When it's here, you'll feel it."

I shoot to my feet. My chair hits the ground.

"This was our thing."

"It's still our thing."

For the first time in four months, I'm Nameless Boy again.

"Go to Hellmann's, Bishop."

"Don't be sad." Anne holds out a cookie.

I take a bite. Doris is right. No human could make these.

"When I'm upset, I think about things that make me happy."

I slouch against the living room couch. It's expensive and fancy and very uncomfortable. "The treasure hunt makes me happy."

"Treasure hunting with Mr. Rollins makes you happy."

She lies on her stomach. Head in her hands. She looks somewhere between six and sixty.

"Fine. I like working on it with him."

More things I've learned about myself: I like research. I like puzzling out a mystery. I like both better when Bishop's by my side.

Anne kicks her feet in the air. "Riding my horse makes me happy. Do you know how to ride a horse?"

"I don't know."

"Well, did anyone ever teach you?"

"I don't remember."

"Your childhood?"

I laugh. "I don't remember *anything.*"

"Not even yesterday?"

"No, I remember that." I snatch a cookie from the plate on the floor. Of the eight Anne brought into the living room, she's eaten all but two. I have no idea where she puts it. She's the size of my forearm. "I don't remember anything before I came to Wildewell."

"That's sad."

"I'm happy now."

Turns out, that's the truth. I can't stay mad at Bishop for too long.

He found me. Taught me. Trusted me.

Gave me a job. Made me somebody.

"Do you have a lot of friends?"

"Just the one."

"I don't have any." She eyes the last cookie. "My brother, Ronnie, says I'm only good for my time."

"Then Ronnie's a spithead." I unclasp the braided leather bracelet on my left wrist. Bishop bought it for me at the Festival of Souls. I wrap it around her wrist. "You're supposed to give it away when you meet a true friend."

She traces the braid. "So we're friends?"

I nod.

"Do you miss your mom and dad?" Anne asks.

"Sometimes."

I don't miss Mom and Dad. I miss the idea of a mom and a dad.

I glance at her, real fast. "Sometimes I don't even want to remember."

"Because you're happy with Bishop," Anne says, and I nod. A breeze blows her hair in the air. It's shiny like silk. "Don't try to remember, but don't try to forget. Then maybe you'll stumble upon your memories when you're supposed to."

She snatches the last cookie and bites it in half. "Gotta trust the gut, babe."

"Did your mom say that?"

"No, my great-grandmother."

That makes sense.

"Okay, I'll trust my gut."

"Yeah, and when it tells you to pay attention, listen."

TWENTY-SEVEN

RUBY

*INTO THE DEPTHS
is your eventual demise.
Part the water instead
for the ultimate prize.*

First there's a swish, then a rustle and a hiss. I open my eyes.

"Let's go."

I shimmy halfway out of my sleeping bag, shake my hair from my face. "What happened? What's wrong?"

A crease forms between Elliot's brows. "Nothing's wrong. I figured it out." His expression is hard to read in the dark, but I hear the impatience in his voice. He ducks out of the tent.

"Impossible," I say, frozen in place.

"Most possible things used to be impossible," Anne says.

I turn to find her sitting cross-legged on top of her sleeping bag, small flashlight held close to a book.

Elliot's head pokes through the tent door. "Hurry up."

I glance at Anne. "You coming?"

Her eyes jump between the space Elliot just occupied and me. "I think I'll finish this chapter."

I shrug. Crouch through the tent and into the humid air. The night's a chorus of buzzing insects and crunching leaves, the snap of a branch and hoot of an owl. Elliot walks with purpose, as if he discovered this island ages ago and is only now sharing its secrets.

We leave the Star Stones in our wake, diving into a forest of thin trunks that go white under our flashlights' glare. Two minutes later, we enter a small clearing circled by towering birch. Elliot tosses a brown cylinder to his feet, then settles onto the mossy ground. I kick off my sandals and sit beside him, digging my toes into the spongy earth.

"This can't wait until morning—not if we want to beat the other treasure hunter." Elliot's wide eyes make him look younger than usual. "This is it, Ruby."

"What'd you find?"

He crosses his legs. Rests his elbows on his knees and leans forward. "I couldn't sleep because . . ." He gazes in the direction of camp. "Because I couldn't sleep. Anyway, I was thinking about wolves and how they named this island after an animal that doesn't even live here, and how that's really ridiculous. And then I wondered if maybe they were overhunted or something. So naturally I started thinking about decoys."

"Naturally."

"I'm talking about those fake animals they use to attract

wolves and birds and deer. Which really has nothing to do with our search since we already found the gray wolves, except that *decoy* comes from the Dutch *de kooi.* You probably know where this is going."

"Surprisingly, I don't."

"De kooi," he says again. "It comes from the Medieval Latin *cavea,* which means 'hollow.'"

"Like a cave."

Elliot grins. "Exactly. Trace both words back far enough and you'll land on *cavea.*"

I raise an eyebrow. I wonder if I look as much like Sadie as I feel.

"Yeah, I know, my nerd is showing. But it got me thinking about the caves again. What if we're wrong about the Star Stones? What if they're not the stone that stabs at the sky? Before I came for you, I dangled a piece of rope down the hole in the center of the Star Stones. It didn't even hit the bottom. There could be a huge cave below us. A cave with stalagmites."

"What about the square on the Star Stone? Or the poem? It all fits, Elliot."

"But the poem says 'part the water,'" he says. "And I know what that means."

Elliot uncaps the cylindrical container and coaxes a thick piece of paper from it. Gentle fingers lay it on the ground. I hold the flashlight over the map. Unlike the gift shop version we've been using since we first met in Elliot's bedroom, this map is detailed and old, curling at the edges and smudged with dirt. "Isn't this part of the Gray Wolf Island exhibit in the museum?"

"Not anymore." He presses a finger to a point on the western side of the island.

I lean closer, see a lagoon and a waterfall. "The island's sur-rounded by water. What makes you think that's the spot?"

"What other body of water can you part?" Elliot rolls the map, slides it into the carrier. "I bet there's a cave behind it. Maybe it connects to the one beneath the Star Stones."

"It's not like we have time for more strategizing. The other treasure hunter could be close to finding the treasure by now." I lie on the cool ground. "Besides, it'll be nice to bathe after today's hike."

He leans close, so close I can almost taste the metal of his lip ring. So close I wonder if maybe . . .

And I'm hoping for it. That's the most surprising thing of all.

But no, he just sniffs my hair. "Yeah, a bath would be nice."

I try to punch him, but he dodges. I give up and turn my face to the glimpse of sky circled by the tops of tall trees. Against an inky backdrop, thousands of stars appear like dust. But that's not what makes me gasp. It's the amber and purple scar that arches across the sky. "It can't be."

"The Milky Way." Elliot lies beside me, hands clasped over his stomach. "I heard it was dark enough out here to see it, but I never thought . . . It's amazing, right?"

More than that. As I stare at the spot where the sky marbles, the trees overhead seem to shrink. Everything shrinks, even me. I'm unimaginably small beneath the band of light and stars. "It looks like magic."

We stay like that for what feels like half the night. Time seems to stretch out, as if it's waiting for us to finish this mo-ment before a second goes back to being a second and a minute no longer lasts an hour.

"Ruby?"

I turn my head, breathing in the earthy scent of the moss. Elliot's closer than I remember, so close I can see the lightness of his eyes.

"What do I do about Gabe?"

I absently pick at the fraying hem of my pajama shorts, which used to be Sadie's and therefore will never be thrown away. "I have no idea."

Elliot turns back to the sky. "I made fun of him. Not to be mean or anything, but I called him Gabriella to get a rise. I knew it pissed him off, but I didn't realize . . . It's partially my fault, you know?"

I know Gabe was built, word by cruel word.

But everybody can be made into a monster. Not everybody embraces it.

"It's nobody's fault but Gabe's," I say.

"Would it be so terrible if I wasn't ready to forgive him?" Elliot's voice is a plea.

I don't answer right away. I need to get this right, so if Elliot ever learns my secret, he'll remember the mercy he showed Gabe and maybe extend it to me. "It's never okay to force a girl, no matter how far you let it go," I say. "But I'd like to hope good people who do bad things can be redeemed."

Elliot rolls his head in my direction. "Sometimes I wonder if one day I'll wake up and feel all the bad stuff in me, too."

"We're all a little bad." I'm a lot bad, but I don't tell him that.

I can't look at him, not after that, so I stare at the sky until I see flashes of the moon when I blink.

"My dad," Elliot whispers.

Everything I know about Patrick Thorne I learned from

Doris Lansing, and it's not much: He enlisted in the army when he couldn't find the treasure because when you're a Thorne, war's preferable to failure.

"I read my mom's journal. I didn't even know she kept a journal until I found it two years ago and read that unforgivable thing."

I finally turn my head. Elliot's teeth are worrying at his lip ring. Hands plucking moss from the soft earth. He takes a deep breath and says, "My dad didn't kill himself."

My head and heart float somewhere far above me, maybe in the trees or clouds or up with the stars. It's not the secret making me dizzy but the fact that Gray Wolf Island seems to be coaxing the truth out of all of us. But it can't have mine.

Elliot stares at me, all wide-eyed and worked up. "You want to know the truth, Ruby?"

"Is the island making you say it?"

"No, not the island."

I'm not as relieved as I should be. Deep down I know—and it feels like tempting fate to even think it—the truth doesn't die or disappear just because you will it to.

Elliot's hand slides down my arm. His fingers lace with mine, hold tight. "My mom did it. She killed him. Blew his face right off."

"Elliot."

"Everyone always says my name like I'm standing on the edge of a cliff, getting ready to jump. Like maybe I have some of my dad's sickness in me." He squeezes my hand tighter and tighter. "What if I have hers?"

We stare at the stars and hold on tight, fingers crushing fingers.

"My brother died that day," he says. "Maybe my mom might have seen him wandering into the water if she hadn't been so busy killing my dad."

"Why'd she do it?"

"She won't tell me. Won't talk about that day. But does it really matter why someone murders someone else?" He doesn't say *murder* the way I do, holding it in until the very last minute. He says it like the word will sting his tongue if he doesn't spit it out fast enough.

I try my hardest to hold his gaze, but it's impossible with his twisted expression and the memory of Sadie's scratchy voice whispering "Murder" on that Sunday afternoon. "No. There's never a good reason."

I wake in the middle of the night to the sound of my name on the wind. I turn to face Anne, but when the call comes again, her lips aren't moving. She's so engrossed in her book, she doesn't object when I tell her I'm going to the bathroom alone.

The grass is cool and slightly damp beneath my bare feet. The wind is as wild as my sister was, pushing and pushing until I'm right where it wants me. I'm standing in the center of the Star Stone formation, static zinging across my skin, when I hear her. Scratchy voice barely a whisper.

Ruby, she says. *Oh, Ruby, what have you done?*

"Something terrible," I say before I realize I'm speaking to the wind.

Tell them, it rasps in my sister's sick voice. *Tell them everything.*

TWENTY-EIGHT

RUBY

"I SHOULD HAVE STOLEN THE DAGGER," ELLIOT SAYS THE NEXT morning as we're tramping through yet another forest. There's a certain sense of peace among the spindly trunks, but I can't seem to touch it. Instead of chasing away darkness, the morning light seems to have brought it to the surface. Every silent space still shouts Gabe's secret. Sadie's voice still plays in my mind. And there's still someone else on the island.

And so, the dagger.

Elliot growls. "It was right there. I should have taken it."

"What do you imagine doing with that knife that you can't do with your pocketknife? Engaging in a knife fight?" Anne shoots me a look that says these boys are bizarre.

"As a matter of fact, yes," Elliot says. "Who knows what this guy will do if we get to the treasure first?"

"*If* there's another person on the island." Gabe shuffles to a stop beside a thin birch. He's no longer lost to the island's taunts, all empty-eyed and filled with fog. But he's also not the same oil-slick and shimmery boy who hopped a boat to Gray Wolf Island. He's human in a way he's never been before.

And he's absolutely drenched in relief.

"I think . . ." For the first time today, Gabe raises his eyes higher than our knees. He looks like a thing with wings that's been let out of a cage but still needs permission to fly. "I think the island can make us see what's not there. Maybe it can make us not see what's there, too."

"Maybe the island took the book. Maybe some treasure-hunting dude did. The point is," Charlie says, "you promised a waterfall today, Elliot. And all I see are trees."

Elliot's sigh is so deep it nearly creates a breeze. He glances at his compass. Without a word, he heads farther into the forest.

Trees. Ferns. Grass. More trees. An hour becomes two, and the scenery blurs until I can't tell the difference between where I am and where I came from. I'm starting to hate the forest, but not nearly as much as I hate my hiking boots.

I'm not the only one cursing this godforsaken island and the thief forcing us into a frantic pace. Charlie slaps at a fat fly. "How far to the waterfall, Elliot?"

"Do I look like a member of the Gray Wolf Island tourism board? It's out there, somewhere closer than it was the last time you asked."

And then it's there, a white curtain of rumbling water and a pool of dark blue.

We trudge over rugged shoreline, a jumble of rock, mud,

and the occasional tuft of grass. Thick tree trunks climb out of the lagoon almost horizontally, their long branches skimming the water's surface and creating shady caves beneath their emerald leaves. At the opposite end of the lagoon, tall boulders covered in moss and lichen nip at the sides of frothy white water. It tips over an opening in the rock twenty feet above.

Charlie is the first to break from the trance, shucking all but his swim trunks and diving into the clear pool. I strip down to my bikini, toss my filthy clothes on a nearby rock, and jump.

I hold my breath and let myself sink, let the water rake its fingers through my loose hair and kiss goose bumps onto my skin. Down here, the weight of everything that's happened and everything that still needs to happen floats away. Too soon, I'm pushing for the surface, wiping the wet from my eyes.

"I was looking for you," Charlie says from a rock jutting into the lagoon. I clasp the hand he offers. "Time to jump."

"Jump?" I shake my head in an attempt to get the water from my ear.

"Yes, jump." He grins. "From there."

I follow his gaze to the towering boulder to the left of the waterfall. "No way. We'll crash into the rocks below."

When Charlie rolls his eyes, his whole head follows. "I don't die in or near water. See? Safe."

"Yeah, for you. But I don't get glimpses of my death."

Charlie grabs my shoulders. "Ruby. This is where you start to live."

This is the year you finally live, Rubes.

That's what Sadie said before she died. She'd want me to do this. So I square my shoulders. Nod. Follow Charlie from one baked rock to the next until we're at the top of the leftmost boulder, the sound of pounding water loud in our ears.

"I've already checked the area below. You can only land there," he says, pointing to a dark spot in the water below. "I mean, you *can* land where it's more shallow, but you'll probably get maimed or at least go brain-dead or something."

I'm shaking, gaze hooked on the thundering water. This should be Sadie, standing atop a slimy green rock with a boy who looks death in the face with a wink and a dare.

Palms to my cheeks, Charlie forces my gaze to him. Staring into Charlie's eyes is like staring at a beating heart. He's so intensely and perfectly alive. "See you down below."

He releases me. Backs up as far as the rock will allow. And then he's running running flying over water and air. He's pencil-thin and piercing the glassy surface. He's under and gone.

My heart's somewhere between my lungs and my lips. I peer over the edge of the rock. No Charlie. I call his name, but it's lost in the crash of the waterfall.

A lifetime later, he surfaces with a whoop. "Ruby Caine! Get down here!"

I shuffle backward, blistered feet over slick rock. I take a breath. Three more.

I run.

I jump.

TWENTY-NINE

RUBY

THERE'S NOTHING BUT AIR AND THE SPRAY OF COLD WATER. Something like euphoria rushes me, and I release a shout that's part laugh. As I go down, my heart goes up, up, up. I swallow a lungful of air a second before my feet slice through the surface.

The force of the falling water spins me around until up looks like down. I open my eyes to bubbles and blue, but as I swim toward stiller water, a face forms. It's indistinct at first, clearing as I near. She has auburn hair that floats around her like a veil. Blue eyes blink at me. Bow-shaped lips part, but she doesn't speak. Somehow I know this isn't me even though it's as if I'm staring into a murky mirror.

My fingers reach for her, float right through her face. I'm greedy for any glimpse of my sister, so I ignore my screaming lungs.

"I'm sorry," I say, filling my mouth with water and blowing out my remaining air with a burst of bubbles. There's so much more I have to say, but an arm grabs me from behind and tugs me up. I gulp a few breaths before searching the lagoon. Three people stare at me, and not one of them shares my face.

"Hey, you're alive," Charlie says.

"We were mostly certain you were dead." Anne's perched on a rock, filling our water bottles.

"I saw . . ." But now it sounds silly. I look up to find Gabe's gaze on me. I hold his stare and say, "I saw Sadie."

"You probably saw your reflection." Elliot's voice is loud in my ear, and for the first time, I realize his arm's holding my back tight to his front even though we're now in the shallows. I wiggle from his hold. "Or lack of oxygen made you hallucinate it."

"No, you saw her," Gabe says. "The island wanted you to see her."

Elliot shoots him an annoyed look. "Since when do you know what the island wants?"

Gabe shrugs, which seems to annoy Elliot even more. He refocuses on me. "You're okay, right?"

I grin. "Charlie was right. That was amazing."

"You hear that? She said I was right." Charlie turns to Elliot. "*You* never tell me I'm right."

"That's because you never are."

Charlie responds, but his voice sounds immeasurably far with Elliot looking like a picture I might pin to my wall.

"You sure you're okay? After, you know, your sister?"

Oh. So this is about . . . oh. I shrug. Drop my eyes to the tattoo over his heart. Semicircles in shades of blue and white fill the bottom half of the circular image. A black cross rises from the waves, dark against an azure sky. "What does your tattoo mean?"

He shrugs. "Told the guy to pick one for me."

I do a really fantastic job of staying silent even though that's the dumbest thing I've heard all week.

He glances down, hesitates, and then says, "No, that's a lie. I do know what it means. But if I tell you, you'll think I'm a dork."

"I already think you're a dork."

"Ruby," he says sternly, then smiles. It's a spectacular thing.

We drift toward a flat rock half dunked in the lagoon. Elliot climbs onto it. I pull myself up beside him.

"All right," Elliot says. "It's from a recurring dream. Me and my mom are on the beach having a picnic and this fawn steals our dinner. My mom is so mad. She has this big umbrella and keeps trying to shoo the deer away with it. You know how dreams cut from scene to scene but it doesn't seem weird? Well, one second the deer is eating our dinner and the next it's dead. It was shot in the head. And I don't know why, but it's so sad."

"So you went out and tattooed its gravestone on you?"

"It's dumb, I know." The wind kicks up, flapping the ends of his swim shorts.

"No, I like the idea of preserving dreams like that." I wonder if once I'm gone anyone will think of me the way Elliot thinks of his deer. "Sometimes I think I've existed for so long only because Sadie was there to remind everyone there was another of us. And now that she's gone, I'll just fade away, not even a memory of me left behind."

Elliot's eyes snap to mine. "You'd haunt me, Ruby. Even

if you faded to nothing and everyone forgot." He opens his mouth to say something else, but the wind stops him with a deafening roar. It sprays us with water and pine needles that stick to my wet skin.

We stare at each other for a long minute. Finally, I say, "I should call my parents."

"Yeah. We need to get going anyway." Elliot hauls himself out of the water. I follow him to the bank of the lagoon, dig around in Charlie's pack for the satellite phone, then call home.

"Tell me you're safe," my mom says as I stand atop a boulder overlooking the lagoon.

"We're fine, Mom. They're just planning to use me as a virgin sacrifice."

She heaves a dramatic sigh. "Well, that's a relief."

"That they're going to kill me?"

"That you're still a virgin."

"You need to get your priorities straight." My voice is stern, but I'm smiling. I lucked out. I could have Elliot's mom, and then I wouldn't have a dad, either.

My mom says something else, but the wind swallows her words. From my perch on the tall rock, I see an angry current of air battering the trees. Each blow sends them into a backbend, trunks arched at the top, leaves thrashing.

I hurry off the phone as I hurry down the rock. "Pack up!" I yell when I reach the ground. "There's a storm coming!"

The wind howls, and everyone springs to their feet. They're shoving food and dirty clothes into their packs when I reach them.

"It's trying to kick us out," Gabe says. "Blow us straight to the other side of the island. Maybe even into the ocean."

"Because the island doesn't want us to find the treasure?" My words seem to shake the trees. Spindly branches reach for us, strike our skin with territorial rage.

"Why would the island talk to *Gabe*?" Elliot's voice is crisp and condescending even over the howling gale. "It's about high- and low-pressure systems, and how hot air is less dense than cold air, so—"

"No," Gabe says to Elliot, but he's looking at me. "No, it's the island. It won't let us at the treasure until it has the truth. All of it."

"Let's look for the cave," I say, searching for my bag to give my eyes something to do other than stare at Gabe's stupid face with those stupid eyes that are trying to tell me something I think I already know. We've decided to leave the tents behind—they add bulk and we won't need them in the cave—so I toss mine beside the boys'. Elliot adds the large shovels to the pile.

We follow the curve of the lagoon, Charlie in the lead. I pinwheel my arms as a particularly strong gust of wind tries to knock me into the water. Gabe holds my pack steady as I regain my footing. I try to see him as I always have, but it's impossible. Everything he's done is right there on his face.

I give him a terse thanks and hurry after the others. A minute later, when a mouthful of air has me gasping for breath, I know I'm choking on my own hypocrisy.

There's a gap between the lichen-covered boulder and the curtain of water, but not even Anne could squeeze through and stay dry. Charlie leaves his pack with Elliot, then pushes through the water. He disappears in bits and pieces, the way I was disappearing until these people put me back together.

I hold my breath and hope and hope and hope this isn't how Charlie dies.

And then he's there, all shiny skin and hair sticking to his face. His smile's a mile wide, and Elliot's pushing for the water like the cave will vanish if he's not quick.

Anne follows on his heels, and then it's my turn. The wind's wild now, sending rocks sliding from far above. The air smells like threats and promises.

"Ruby."

I twist around, and when I see Gabe's face I know he's going to say something I don't want to hear. "I don't know what it is or why I know it's even there—"

"Stop it."

He does, for a moment. Pine needles rain from the sky and tangle in our hair. Then he says, "You have to tell."

He's lit from above, a splash of sunlight turning his skin fiery gold. In the rumble of water and whistle of wind, I hear Sadie's voice. Or maybe it's the island.

Tell the truth, Ruby. Tell him what you did.

I part the water instead.

THIRTY

RUBY

Night descends quickly and
dark is made near.
It cloaks you in shadows,
but strangle your fear.

So the cave's a letdown. And it's not because I'm in a mood, which is what Elliot says as I'm squeezing water from my hair. "Oh no, Ruby's in a mood."

My hiking boots squelch as I walk farther into the cave. It feels more like a tunnel, really. Wet stone walls curve on either side of us like parentheses. The ceiling's so low everyone but Anne has to hunch. "I'm not in a mood, Elliot. I'm sick of this island telling me what to do."

Elliot sighs, a long, laborious thing. "The island is not talking to you."

I don't have to turn around to know Gabe's expression is telling me just the opposite. I change the subject. "I thought it'd be bigger."

Charlie snickers. "Careful, you'll ruin Elliot's self-esteem."

Elliot aims a punch at Charlie's gut, but Charlie swivels out of the way. "I bet the cave gets bigger as we go farther in."

I strap on my headlamp and make for an opening at the back of the cave. We're forced to squeeze single file through the crevice, and I'm amazed we can fit at all with our massive backpacks. It doesn't take long for the air to cool and the dim light from the cave entrance to fade. Soon we're walking through blackness so black it seems to swallow light. The beam from my headlamp illuminates less than five feet in front of me.

My mind creates the sound of dragging claws. Of hot breath on my face. Of a rock-rumbling roar.

How have none of us considered that this cave might belong to something other than ourselves? "Animals," I say with a full-body shudder. "We didn't consider what animals might live in here."

"I researched Gray Wolf Island wildlife last week. Because I actually have a sense of self-preservation." I can't see him from here, but I just know Elliot's rolling his eyes. "Aside from the pit, this is the most trafficked area of the island. There's been so much human disturbance from excavations over the years that bears and foxes have stopped turning its entrance into their dens. It's mostly small animals, like mice and spiders."

Charlie sucks in a breath. "And bats?"

"There used to be brown bats in these caves, but they abandoned it. They relocated to an old mine in Waldo County." Elliot pauses. "And your bedroom."

"Don't even joke."

"Is an animal going to kill you, Charlie?" There's something to Anne's words, a deep scratching sound, that makes me think of strong fingers around a beating heart. Squeeze. Squeeze. Squeeze.

I think Charlie hears it, too, because he doesn't speak for a long while, and when he finally does, it's with a smile in his voice I can tell doesn't belong there. "Nothing's going to kill me," he says. "I'm wearing your bracelet, remember?"

In the silence and in the dark, with Charlie's phony voice chasing us like an echo, the path seems endless. I follow the curve of the cave left, then right, then right again. That's when I hear the song.

It's beautiful and haunting. I imagine long draws on my harmonica, lazy chords meandering through the air. I imagine the sort of mind-blowing throat vibrato I've yet to master, and it twists its way into the tune.

The voice ruins it all.

Ruby, Ruby, what have you done?

I breathe out, and with it comes a strangled "No."

"Ruby?"

I don't answer Anne. My boots scrape across the rough ground. The scrape gets louder and the scrape gets human.

Ruby, Ruby, what have you done?

I cough to break the sound. For a minute it's like I simply lost my mind. Like the dark was taking up so much space in this cave it had nowhere to go but in through my ear, making me hear things that aren't really here.

For a minute.

But it's back with fingers of a breeze that walk their way down my spine. *Oh, Ruby,* she says, and I'm suddenly not sure: Is the island taunting me or has it summoned Sadie's ghost?

The air hums a melody I want to forget. The voice that might be Sadie's croons.

> *Ruby Caine's tears did make*
> *a dark and deep and ice-cold lake.*
> *Gave her sister one more breath,*
> *then held her down to meet her death.*

My body moves as if it knows where to go. My muscles predict this twist, that turn, the dips and rises in the earth.

"Slow down," Elliot says from somewhere behind me. But I can't, not when Sadie could be here somewhere, turning half-truths into nursery rhymes. If I can catch her, I'll set her straight. Remind her of my fingers on her nose. Remind her that she asked, knowing full well I've never refused her anything.

"You made me a monster," I whisper. My breath's ragged from my run. Ragged from shame. Ragged from finally saying aloud what I've hidden since Sadie begged me that day.

The cave winds this way and that, a maze of low ceilings and tight walkways. I only stop when there's nowhere left to run. My anger's gone, replaced with the guilt I know so well. I rest my forehead against the cool cave wall, waiting for Sadie's voice to tell more lies. But this part of the cave is silent.

The others arrive with a scuffing of shoes and a slurry of curses. Gabe hurries to me. "Stop this."

"I'm not doing anything!"

"Ruby," he says with a shake of his head. "You can't out-run it."

"I just did." But even I know that's just another one of my lies. And this time it doesn't drive the pain into that deep, dark part of me. That's the problem with lies: They're only comforting in the beginning. They'll cut you if you wear them too long.

"What was that?" Elliot says, flinging his arm toward the entrance to this tunnel. As if I've dropped the wretched rhyming verses behind me. "Are you okay?"

I shake my head. No no no. I'm not okay.

He moves toward me, and I think there's going to be a hug involved, but I can't let that happen. Not with that rhyme in my head. "Let's focus on the treasure."

"I thought there were supposed to be cave spikes," Charlie says. He's removed a pocketknife and is carving his initials into the stone wall.

Elliot regards me for a few more seconds, then turns to Charlie. "Stalagmites. Let's try a different route."

He leads us through the cave, and I don't even care that he's usurped control again. I can barely think, let alone follow a treasure map. My mind's a swirling mess of childlike voices singing, *"Gave her sister one more breath, then held her down to meet her death."*

A warm hand clasps my elbow. I jump at the contact, nearly smashing Anne with my backpack as I swing around. "Sorry." My voice is a little too shaky, but for a split second I really thought . . . It was dumb, because Sadie's gone.

"Sorry," I say again. "I wasn't really here."

She walks beside me—while I was blind with that poem, the cave must have doubled in width—and clasps my hand. "I've decided to forgive Gabe."

"That was fast."

Anne nods. "I'll be taking back my crush, of course. He's not the Gabe I had in my head."

I think of my new friends and say, "Nobody's ever who you imagine them to be."

The boys are so far ahead of us that they're nothing but shadows in the bright of our bobbing flashlight beams. I tug Anne's hand, and we speed up. "Aren't you curious why I forgave him?"

"I think you're about to make a point."

"I am! My point is that everyone who's truly sorry deserves a second chance. *Everyone,* Ruby."

And people can say that her head's full of clouds or her feet never touch the ground, but they don't know. They don't know her at all, and that's a shame because Anne may be the best person of all.

THIRTY-ONE

COOPER

IT'S AN AMBUSH.

One captures my right hand. The other gets my left.

"Do you want I Eat Mainely Lobster or Green-wich Village?"

Even without knowing my past, I know I'm not the kind of guy who wears nail polish.

But there's this girl. Rosy cheeks. Auburn hair. All sorts of bossy.

"I don't think he wants a manicure, Sadie." That's the other girl I'm hanging out with. Exactly like the first but quieter.

I've got an hour with these two while Bishop sits inside with their lawyer dad and updates his will. I'm trying not to think about that.

"He's a boy," Sadie says. "He doesn't know what he wants."

I try to tug my hand out of hers. She tightens her grip.

I flop back onto the grass. Their backyard is a carpet of green, and it's sort of relaxing. "Fine," I say. "But you have to take it off before I go home."

"It's a deal." Sadie shoves two bottles of nail polish in my face. "So?"

"I like this one," her sister says. "It matches his eyes."

And that's how I end up with green nails. They look slightly fungal.

We're all hungry, but the girls won't let me grab lunch with wet nails. The quiet one, Ruby, runs inside for snacks, which Sadie says they'll feed me while I'm drying. This isn't a half-bad deal.

"You don't say much," she says.

"You say a lot."

"I have a lot on my mind." She pokes my forehead. "What's going on in there?"

"I'm thinking about a treasure I'm burying on Gray Wolf Island."

I'm not sure if Bishop would want me to talk about this, but it seems harmless enough. She's just a girl.

"Treasure!" Sadie edges closer to me. "What kind of treasure? Where are you going to bury it?"

Obviously I haven't spent much time around girls.

"It's a secret."

"Down the hole, right?" She pokes my shoulder. I swat her away. "Hey, you'll ruin your manicure. So, am I right? It's down the hole?"

"Maybe. Or maybe I'm burying it near some random tree."

"Is there a map?"

"I'm making one." I open one eye.

She's looking toward the ocean with a dreamy expression. "Can I have a clue? Just one. I promise I won't tell anyone."

"You'll tell your sister the minute I leave."

"Please?" She clasps my hand. No regard for my wet nails. "I promise I won't tell. Not even Ruby."

I sit up with a groan. I don't want to share, but now I feel guilty. Should have kept my mouth shut.

"One clue," I say. She leans closer. "The map is a poem."

Sadie's reading a book of poetry beneath the oak tree in the backyard. She found it in her parents' study.

I almost reminded her that I'm still writing the poem, so there's no use searching for it. But reading is quiet. And I could use a break from her nonstop chatter.

Girls are exhausting.

I wander to the garden. There's a small greenhouse in the back. Glass body, metal bones.

Ruby's bent over the hose, drenching her hair. She straightens to her full height. Her personality is too small for such a lanky body, and Sadie's is too big for hers.

"It's hot as Hellmann's out here." I gesture to the hose.

"You're supposed to keep mayonnaise in the fridge."

"Um, okay. Mind if I borrow the hose?"

"That way it doesn't get hot." Ruby hands me the hose. It's still on. Now it looks like I peed myself.

I spray my hair with water. "Much better."

"You shouldn't eat hot mayonnaise."

I turn the water off. "Why are you so hung up on mayonnaise?"

"You said it's hot as Hellmann's."

"Oh, right. I'm trying not to swear."

"Because I'm a girl?"

"Because of Bishop."

"Okay." She wipes water from her eyes, heads farther into the garden. She keeps stopping in front of flowers and telling me how she'd paint them. It started off annoying, but now it's funny.

"This one's all wrong," she says. "It's a peony."

It's pink. "What color should it be?"

"You know when the sun's setting and it's really red so you know it's going to be a good beach day tomorrow? I'd paint peonies that color."

"Sunset Boulevard Red."

Ruby crinkles her nose. "That wasn't very good."

"Despite what my green nails are telling you, I'm not a nail polish aficionado."

"Sadie's a nail polish aficionado."

"Technically *aficionada*. She's a girl."

Ruby sends me a chastising look. "Fine. Sadie's a nail polish *aficionada*."

I peek at her nails. Bare.

"How'd I get roped into wearing Fungus Among Us polish and you don't have any?"

"That was a good one!" Her face dimples in a smile. "And Sadie thinks you're cute."

"I have Indian laurel hair."

Ruby shrugs. Wanders to a cement birdbath at the center of the garden.

"C'mon!" She bounces on her toes.

"It's hot as—"

"Mayonnaise, I know. But there's been an injury."

Ruby pokes at something in the birdbath. I bend down.

Floundering in the shallow water is a butterfly. Amber-colored wings with black veins. White polka dots along the edges. Its left wing is torn in half.

The real issue, though, is its middle. It's almost completely smushed.

"Think we can save it?" Ruby pulls the insect from the water with gentle fingers.

I pluck it from her cupped hands. Lay it on the edge of the birdbath. Pick up a small rock.

Stone against stone, and the butterfly's dead.

"Why would you do that?"

I look at her wide eyes, and I say, "Mercy."

THIRTY-TWO

RUBY

"How strange," Anne says in her floaty voice. "Charles Kim standing completely still."

I follow her gaze. At the end of the long tunnel, the guys are rooted beneath a doorway of arching rock, as if they've been magicked into stone statues.

"Ruby." Elliot holds a hand out behind him. I take it, squeezing between him and Charlie, then finally turn to the expanse of cave before us. Late-afternoon sun streams through a crack in the rock, lending dim light to a ceiling dripping stone. The cavern stretches for miles and miles, seeming endless as the faint light tapers into dark. It's an absurd thought, but I can't help wondering whether the cave is bigger than the island itself.

We're standing on a cliff. To my left, aged wood forms

the top of a man-made staircase. Everywhere else, it's bumpy ground—until it drops a hundred feet to earth studded with spikes.

"Hello!" The cave sends Anne's voice back to us again and again. With each echo, my smile widens.

Elliot squeezes my hand. "We're going to find it. We're really going to find it."

"No, we're not." Gabe glares at me. "The island won't give up the treasure until Ruby tells the truth."

"It's not staying invisible just because Ruby's keeping a secret. Either it's here or it's not. And it's here. I can feel it."

"You can feel the treasure, but I can't hear the island? Whatever, Elliot." Gabe's shoulder slams into Elliot as he moves farther into the cavern.

"Fine, you're right. The island only shares its plans with guys who sexually assault girls."

Gabe shoves Elliot against the wall. He stands tall, a full inch taller since shaking off his secret.

"Get out of my face."

I expect Charlie to jump in—he's always good for some pointless recklessness—but he's standing motionless at the threshold.

"You're jealous," Gabe says. "That's what this is, right? You think the island should speak to you, not some piece of shit like me." He swings for the face, but Elliot shifts and Gabe's fist smashes into Elliot's shoulder instead.

"It's in my blood!" Elliot's arm shoots out, fast. Gabe doubles over, clutching his stomach.

They're so focused on each other, the boys don't notice how near they've wandered to the edge of the cliff. This seems to snap Charlie out of his stupor. "Okay, wow, you both are so tough. The girls are puddles of hormones on the floor. *I* can hardly stand it. But maybe don't be tough and dead? Which is what you're going to be if you take one step to the left."

But the boys aren't listening, or they don't care.

If Sadie were here, she'd shove herself between those two beautiful boys and say something like "Let's make love, not war."

For the first time in forever, though, I think maybe I don't need Sadie to speak for me. I tip back my head, release a guttural cry. The acoustics in the cave and the echoes it creates give my scream a songlike quality. It's the raw stuff you hear when it's just you and the harmonica sitting around a fire—fear and hope all mixed up together.

Gabe and Elliot freeze. Charlie shoots me a puzzled look. Anne winks.

"There's a thief with the map and you two are wasting time fighting. If you don't mind, there's a treasure I'd like to find."

"Excellent rhyme," Anne says, linking her arm with mine and leading us to the side of the cliff. We tug on our headlamps, then descend.

Charlie hurries after us, leaving Elliot and Gabe to either follow or kill each other. A minute later, they add their footsteps to the clatter against the rickety stairs.

"Think we're below the waterfall?" Charlie asks.

"According to my compass, we've been heading north," Elliot says, his voice a rumbling remnant of his earlier anger. "We're probably headed into the belly of the southernmost mountain."

"Into the breast." Charlie erupts into giggles. It's true what my mother says: Boys can get taller, but they never really mature, not even when they start calling themselves men.

I hold tight to the railing even though the rough wood stings me with splinters. I don't even let go when I spot a ginormous bug with hundreds of legs scuttling inches from my hand.

Our descent feels endless. There's fire in my thighs, in my butt, in nearly every muscle in my body. My sister would use this as proof that my aversion to team sports and people in general is harming my health.

Elliot pauses on the last step, surveying the land in front of us. Judging from his smile, you'd think we'd discovered Shangri-La. "Ruby," he says, walking backward toward the center of the cave, "we're going to make Sadie proud."

Then he tips right over.

He's on his back, stuck in his backpack and laid out like a turtle turned upside down, when we reach his side. Charlie kicks his hip. "I think you really impressed her," he says.

"He didn't even stumble," Anne says. "Just went straight down."

Elliot rolls his eyes, but his mouth's twitching to smile. In a swift move, he tugs Anne off her feet. She teeters, but her balance is no match for her backpack, and she falls with an *oomph* on top of Elliot. "You're supposed to be tiny," he says, a bit out of breath. "How is it that you weigh five hundred pounds?"

She throws off her pack, rolls onto her back. She laughs, all light and tinkling bells like you'd expect to come out of Anne. Then Elliot joins in, a sound that's rocks rumbling down cave walls. It's a laugh he doesn't let free too often, which makes it feel like a special sort of gift.

Charlie and I ditch our bags, sit cross-legged on the rocky ground. I flick on my headlamp to cut through the gloom.

Anne kicks Gabe's calf, but he's a statue above us: jaw tight, arms crossed over his chest, gaze stuck on a stalactite overhead. "I'm not rolling around in the dirt."

"What's a drop of rain in the middle of a downpour?" Anne says.

"What's she talking about?" Gabe asks Charlie.

"It's a thing my great-grandmother says, Gabriel. And it means this: You're already filthy, so sit down." She tugs the hem of his shorts, and he crumples to the cave floor. "To think I ever liked such a pigheaded boy."

Gabe's eyes are huge and fixed on Anne. His cheeks are red red red. "Me?"

Anne waves him off. "I thought you were adorable. That's not really the point. The point is you're also a complete idiot."

"She's right," Elliot says. "There was that one time you trusted Charlie's rope swing."

"I trusted my friend not to try to kill me."

"Or what about when you baked Mrs. Kim a casserole because Charlie told you Stella died?"

"How was I supposed to know Stella was her car?"

Elliot grins. "And there was the time you took Mia Stein to see that horror movie even though everyone knows Mia Stein has that thing about blood and blacking out."

"That's because Charlie told me she'd been dying to see it!" Gabe laughs. "Maybe I'm an idiot, but can we agree Charlie is a bastard?"

"I'm right here."

I watch them all, and I'm amazed. How is it that after a

purposefully solitary year so much of my own happiness is wrapped up in theirs? But solitude is a crafty devil, deceiving you into thinking you're alone by choice. Only when you meet people who make you feel a part of something real does he whisper in your ear, "You see, I've been loneliness all along."

I lean back, shut my eyes.

It's a perfect moment. Like untroubled waves that lap at the shore just before the ocean turns violent.

"Hello, Gabriella."

And just like that, the storm descends.

THIRTY-THREE

RUBY

AND IN THE BLACK
you'll find the star
to guide your way,
to take you far.

Ronnie Lansing is a tower of hard muscle. Hard smile, hard stare, hard words. Even the spikes of his hair look sharp enough to draw blood.

He's emerging through an opening tucked behind the staircase we descended earlier. "I think they're after our treasure," he tells the freakishly pale boy who follows him. I don't know his name—like Ronnie, he's two years older than me—but with his ice-blond hair and almost-colorless eyes, he's like a ghost drifting behind Ronnie wherever he goes.

"Ronnie?" Anne's forehead crinkles. She blinks a couple of times. "*You* stole our map?"

He ducks his head as he passes beneath a low-hanging stalactite, heading in our direction. "Just looking out for you."

"You said you were camping," Anne says, her voice growing in strength and certainty as she speaks. "We were here first. It's our treasure."

Ronnie stops his thunderous approach. Spreads his arms out to his sides. "What treasure, Anne? Me and Ash followed the map. We checked that pointless hole. We've been all over this cave—and yes, we knew the poem was talking about someplace underground because I overheard Mr. Rollins telling Great-Grandma about it years ago—and found nothing. It's time to head home."

Elliot rolls his eyes. "Yeah, I don't think so. You lied to your sister and stole our map. Also, you're a colossal douchebag."

Ronnie's mouth cuts a harsh line across his face. He runs for Elliot, feet pounding anger into the ground. I half expect the earth to quake from the force of it. Elliot rises, fists at his side and ready to swing. And that's when Ronnie screams.

Time goes topsy-turvy. It's slow enough for me to note the puff of dirt Elliot kicks up in a run, the look of horror on Anne's face, the burn of my muscles as I launch off the ground. But it's fast, too. So fast that Ronnie goes from there to gone with nothing in between.

We stop at the foot of the staircase. There's no time to gape at the hole in the ground. No time to discuss the fact that Ronnie's dangling by his fingertips. No time to mention the stakes studding the base of the pit. I wrap an arm around Anne, and she collapses into my side.

"You can have the treasure," Ronnie pants. Beads of sweat dot his hairline. "I don't give a shit about this cave. Just pull me up."

The boys drop to their knees and help Ash haul Ronnie out of the hole. They grunt and groan and curse like a shipful of sailors, but they drag him onto the ground. His eyes are wide, his body trembling. It's a Ronnie Lansing that I'm certain didn't exist before this very moment.

"I was positive you were going to fall," Anne says, flinging herself at her brother and squeezing tight. His whole body sags at her touch, and for the briefest second he soaks up her comfort. But only for a second. Only until Gabe speaks.

"You all right?"

Ronnie disentangles from Anne. "You crying for me, Gabriella?" His hands run through his hair, adding height to the spikes. "That's adorable."

"Careful," Anne says. "Venomous words have a way of poisoning more lives than you intend."

Ronnie ignores her.

Ash steps between the boys. "Let's just go, man. I'm not killing myself for a treasure we both know isn't here."

Ronnie's gaze flits to the hole that nearly swallowed him. "Yeah, okay. At least as a consolation prize Gabriella won't be walking out of here any richer, either. C'mon, Anne."

Her hands flutter at her sides. "Oh. I think I'll stay with my friends."

"Friends?" Ronnie grins with teeth that could cut diamonds. "You think they look at you and see a friend? They see free hours. 'Cept Gabriella. He sees free hours and someone to giggle about boys with."

Elliot shoots to his feet. Charlie is right behind him. I wish they'd hurry up and put a fist in Ronnie's face, but they seem to be waiting for Gabe's go-ahead.

"I don't have a father," Gabe says, rising. "But you know what?" Gabe's less than a foot from Ronnie. He leans in and whispers, "I'm still twice the man you are."

There's a moment when I'm sure Ronnie's going to lurch forward and pummel Gabe. His knuckles go white as he squeezes his fist. But then he's backing away. Laughing like he's in on a joke we're all too stupid to catch. "You losers have fun searching for something that doesn't exist."

Ronnie picks his way toward the staircase, Ash following behind like a bleached shadow. My heart's still hammering a wild beat when Ronnie whirls around. Hurls *Treasure Island* at Gabe. "Enjoy the story, Gabriella. There'll be one about you circling Wildewell by the time you get home."

"Honestly, Ronnie," Gabe says with a sigh. "Who the hell cares?"

While Ronnie and Ash climb out of the cave, we inspect the hole. It's cut from the stone ground, a gaping mouth opening to sharp metal teeth. A catch on the side seems to have broken beneath Ronnie's weight. With a firm push, the time-rotted wood hinged to the top swings down to reveal the fifteen-foot pit. Only luck saved us from plummeting through when we stepped off the stairs.

It takes forever for Ronnie and Ash to leave the cave, so long that guilt drops from Anne's face and pride lulls Gabe to sleep. After a half hour, Elliot gets antsy for the hunt. "Recite the directions, will you, Ruby?"

" 'Night descends quickly and dark is made near. It cloaks you in shadows, but strangle your fear.' "

"Right. We're in a dark cave. What's next?"

" 'And in the black you'll find the star to guide your way, to take you far,' " I say. "Seems like we have to wait out the night here. Maybe see a star through the crack in the ceiling."

"And then?"

" 'Take caution, dear friend. Do not be misled. If trickle turns torrent, you'll soon end up dead.' "

"There has to be a river down here," Elliot says. "What else could trickle and become a torrent?"

"Blood," Charlie says.

Elliot screws up his face. "Way to be morbid."

"I *am* going to die here."

"Stop saying that or I'll punch you in the face."

Charlie grins. "I'd like to see you try."

"I really will, Charlie. I mean it."

Anne kicks my foot. "Let's search this cave for a treasure. If we wait for these boys, we'll never get anything done."

We heave ourselves off the cool earth, leaving our packs behind.

"Wait," Elliot says, tugging on the hem of my shorts. "You shouldn't go by yourselves."

"Elliot," I say through clenched teeth. "We're girls, not toddlers. We will be no worse at spotting trapdoors in the floor than you."

I stomp away, Anne at my heels. "He's such a Thorne. Can't let anyone else make the discovery."

221

"I think he wanted to spend time with you," Anne says, panting to catch up.

"Oh."

"It's okay. Your speech was still very good."

"Really?"

"Oh yeah," she says. "I'll probably save it for later."

Neither of us wants to explore the cave behind the staircase yet, so we head for the far reaches of this cavern. It seems entirely possible that we could walk in this direction for miles and miles. That the cave might extend all the way to the bottom of the pit.

"I had a thought," Anne announces as if her head's not full of them. "Whoever wrote the poem wanted the treasure found, even if the island doesn't. So we can't possibly be waiting for the stars."

"The next clue?"

She nods. "Though it would be romantic, holding our breath for a special star."

It takes me some time to untangle that. To realize each of our clues came with tangible markers—rough-carved symbols, wolves howling on hot metal, the cool rush of a waterfall. Anne's right: The night sky's too changeable to signal our next step. "The slashed square is our star. We should be looking for that."

"Precisely." She smiles. "Aren't we a fantastic team?"

I like the sound of that, and as I swing my flashlight in search of the symbol, I say it again. "A *fantastic* team."

We pick our way around pointed pillars, over a ground littered with cracked rocks. The air's at least twenty degrees cooler than at the surface, and I wish I'd tugged on a sweatshirt before venturing farther into the cave.

"Ruby?" Anne says after a short while. "Do you remember that day in fifth grade when the park ranger spoke to our class about wilderness safety?"

"No." I wish I did, considering we're in the mouth of a cave that, if we're not careful, might swallow us whole.

"He asked the class what we'd need to survive. He called on this girl who said food and water. And he called on this boy who said fire and shelter. When he called on me, I said hope and love." She pauses, flicks her eyes to me. "I told him hope gives you the will to survive and love makes survival worth it. He said I was too dreamy."

Shadows swallow the sunlight as we move farther into the cave, and my body's almost tired enough to believe we've walked our way into nighttime. Something cracks underfoot, brittle like old bones.

"I had friends back then. This was right before I started charging for my hours and they stopped asking me to hang out because they only ever wanted my time. That day, I overheard them saying the ranger was right. I was too happy. Too short and wispy and dreamy. They found that hilarious because I don't dream." Anne stumbles over a rock, grips my hand to steady herself. I squeeze it, hard. Even when she's steady, I hold tight. "I remember sitting behind these two girls with the same face, and the shorter one leaning into the tall one. She said, 'Imagine being stuck in the wilderness with Anne Lansing.' I remember the taller one leaning into the short one. I remember this because she said the nicest thing anyone's ever said about me. She said, 'I'd rather be stranded with her and her hope than the rest of them.'"

"Proof I was a smart kid," I say, but I mean the opposite. I should have talked to her, should have been her friend. Shouldn't have let Sadie's words mean so, so much.

We curve around a low-hanging shower of stalactites. Water drips off the ends and puddles on the ground. On the other side of the formation, the air is stale with the faint whiff of death. "Ruby!"

I follow Anne's voice to the left. My headlamp shines on her hunched form in front of a flat rock. She leans back, and the slashed square symbol is startlingly black in the bright beam. In my mind, I use its point to draw our star.

We've found the next clue.

THIRTY-FOUR

RUBY

TAKE CAUTION, DEAR FRIEND.
Do not be misled.
If trickle turns torrent,
you'll soon end up dead.

We return to find Elliot standing on a stone slab, lit up like a god. The beam of light spilling from the crack in the ceiling is dust-specked and murky, like a veil that separates Elliot from the rest of us. *Just like a Thorne,* I think, though I think it mostly affectionately.

"Catch a star yet, Elliot?"

His eyes find mine, but his gaze quickly returns to the gap in the stones above. The hollows of his cheeks are pink going red. "Won't know till night."

Anne gives me a look that says *End his embarrassment,* so I do. I climb the stone, legs quaking as I push myself up. He pretends not to see me, but his swallows are hard to miss with his neck arched back. I slide my hand into his. "I thought you wanted to be the one who discovered the star. That's why . . . before."

"Is that an apology?"

"Yes?"

He bites back a smile. "It was really awful."

I groan. "I've never had to apologize to anyone but Sadie before!"

Elliot shifts closer. Our shoulders kiss. "That's because you didn't ever talk to anyone."

"I bet you're good at apologies," I say.

"Because authority figures are constantly asking me to make reparations?"

I roll my eyes. "People who use terms like *authority figures* and *reparations* generally aren't the kinds of people authority figures ask to make reparations. Just so you know."

"Oh my God," Charlie groans. "This is going to go on forever. Either kiss or let's explore the cave."

My face feels as red as Elliot's looks. He jumps off the stone, wallops Charlie in the bicep. "You're a good friend."

Charlie holds his arm out to Anne. "Massage me, Anna Banana. I need full strength if I'm going to find the star thing before my enemy, Elliot."

"Nobody needs any strength to find it. Ruby and I already did."

"You should have led with that," Elliot says, shouldering his pack. "It's better than your apology."

"Send Anne, she's pocket-sized."

"I'm five feet, Gabriel. And I'm standing right here." She glares at him, then drops to the ground. The crevice between the cave wall and the stone with the slashed square looks even smaller next to her hulking backpack. She inches between the rock, making it as far as her shoulders before she's stuck. She tries to back out so we can take off the pack she forgot to ditch, but she barely budges. "Gimme a push, boys."

Gabe's eyes flit to Anne's butt. He jerks around to face me. "What's the point if Ruby won't tell the truth?"

Charlie kneels behind Anne. "The point is we get to explore a cool tunnel."

"Take your time." Anne's voice is muffled from inside the cave. "I'm sure there are no snakes or other creatures hiding in this pitch-black tunnel."

"Snakes?" Charlie's eyes go wide. "You didn't mention snakes, Elliot."

Anne kicks wildly. "Push me through or I'll be the one killing you, Charles Kim."

It's slow going. Charlie pushes while Elliot and I smash down the top of her pack. Anne worms forward on her stomach, and Gabe alternates between ogling Anne's legs and staring at the cave floor with a guilt-ridden expression. Anne's pack disappears through the hole, and the rest of her follows behind it.

The boys and I crowd around the opening. "Anne?" Gabe sticks his head through the hole. "You still alive in there?"

A small hand reaches through the crack. Pokes Gabe in the eye. "Headlamp."

I toss her mine. It disappears through the hole.

"Getting in is the hardest part!" she says from inside the tunnel. "It opens after a few feet. It's tight, but I can stand."

"Which is like sitting to the rest of us," Gabe says.

"I heard that!" Her head appears at the mouth of the tunnel, blinding us with her lamp. "It'd be easiest if you didn't squeeze through with your packs."

Gabe scowls. "We can't leave my bag behind. It has all the food."

"God must have made you so beautiful to atone for making you so stupid," Anne says. "Shove your backpack through before you."

Gabe shrugs off his pack. Kicks it through the opening. He shimmies through the crack, twisting at the waist to fit his broad shoulders. His words are muffled by a wall of rock when he says, "You really think I'm beautiful?"

Charlie, Elliot, and I follow, slithering through the tight crevice and emerging into blackness broken by halos of light. Even with all our headlamps on, the tunnel is dark, gray-brown walls painted with our inky shadows. It's high enough for Anne to stand, but just barely. I try hunching, but my heavy pack pitches me forward, so I get into a crawl instead.

Anne moves at a quick pace until Charlie whines about his knees and Elliot yells at her to slow down. She retaliates by telling Charlie there's a bat colony ahead, which only makes the next hour more excruciating for everyone else.

The tunnel winds northwest toward the ocean, gaining a few feet of height as it goes. It comes to a stop before two entryways: a stone slab and a rusted metal door connected to a pulley.

"We'll try the door first," Elliot says, then turns to me. "If that's okay with you."

"Thank you," I say like the words could light the cave. "And yes, it's okay with me."

"I feel like I've entered a Hallmark movie. Can we get back to the adventure now?" Charlie tugs on the rusted chain, but the door doesn't budge. "I think it's broken."

"I think you're weak." Gabe elbows him out of the way. His muscles bulge as he tugs on the rusted chain. The door creaks but doesn't lift.

"Ha. Told you it was broken."

Gabe whips off his shirt, wraps it around his hands, and tries again. His voice is more groan than words when he yells, "Come on!"

The door rises, a slow yawn that rattles the metal. The chug of metal rollers on their tracks starts to echo once the door hits the halfway mark. And then it's not an echo but a high-pitched screech.

I point my headlamp at the opening. It's black as death in there, but light glints against metal a few feet back. "It's lifting a second door," I say. "They must be attached to the same pulley system."

"Feels like I'm lifting fifty doors," Gabe says. Sweat trickles from beneath his headlamp and into his eye. He repositions his hunched form—there are only so many ways to grip the chain in the cramped tunnel—and heaves again. The door gives one last shudder, then slides all the way open.

This time, a rumble swims beneath the rattle and squeal. The musty cave fills with the scent of salt and fish.

We don't say what we all know. The sea is coming.

THIRTY-FIVE

RUBY

When narrow opens
up to wide,
take a deep breath
and step inside.

Gabe springs for the metal chains. Tugs and tugs and tugs. Elliot and Charlie pull with him, putting their body weight behind the movement. The doors don't move.

Elliot punches the wall. "It's a trap."

Water rushes from the new tunnel. Flows over our feet. Climbs to our ankles.

Gabe darts toward the stone slab. His hands flatten against the rock, and it's as if time stills. I see the swell of his back muscles as he pushes. Hear the splash of Charlie and Elliot racing to his sides. Feel the cold water inch up my calves and to my knees.

I glance behind us. Miles of tunnel. A ready grave.

Anne and I join the boys, pleading, cursing, grunting with effort. Our words weave a spell, and the stone inches forward. Water soaks our shorts and makes it hard to stand, but panic grows our muscles and we move the stone again.

Inch by inch by excruciating inch.

There's a two-foot-wide gap when the water hits my hips. I taste salt, and I'm not sure if it's from my sweat or the sea. Anne slips through. I follow.

This tunnel is larger than the last, and I stand with ease. I back up, making room for Charlie and Elliot.

"Hurry!" Charlie shouts as water spills through the cracked doorway. In response, a backpack squeezes through.

"Screw that," Elliot says, tossing the bag behind him. "Get in here, Gabe. Right now!"

Another bag. Another.

I twist my hands in my shirt as Gabe pushes a fourth back-pack through. In here, the ground is wet, but not puddling—we're at an incline, so the water's flowing downhill to the rest of the tunnel—but it has to be at least chest-high out there. Anne grips my hand.

Elliot fists his hands in his hair. When the edge of the final backpack appears in the opening, he yanks it through with a growl.

A hand. A shoulder.

Elliot wrenches Gabe through the doorway. With barely a pause, we push the stone back in place. When it's done, the magic that gave me strength disappears in a wave of exhaustion. I bend forward, hands on knees, gulping the briny air.

"You have got to be an entirely new breed of idiot," Elliot says, and though his voice is low and contained, it sounds like a roar. "Between you and Charlie . . . God, it's like you're determined to die."

"I got the bags. I got out. What's your problem?"

Elliot gives Gabe a look that would be truly menacing if he weren't still wearing a headlamp. He spins on his heel and hurries farther into the tunnel.

There's no fire tonight.

"You strike me as a top-notch Boy Scout, Elliot." I gobble my second protein bar. By the time we reached this cavern—at least an hour east of the flooded tunnel and, Elliot guesses, somewhere deep below the mountains—we were too hungry to wait for a hot meal. That, and while Elliot saved our lighter from the flood, the kindling we collected on our way to the waterfall is still wet from it.

Still, I could really go for one of Gabe's pizzas. "How is it that you don't know how to start a fire with something other than wood?"

With shadows slashing it to pieces, Elliot's grin looks downright feral. "They kicked me out before I got to that lesson."

"They kicked you out because you kept correcting the troop leader," Charlie says. "No one likes a know-it-all."

"Well, obviously I *didn't* know it all or else I'd know how to light a fire without sticks." Elliot nudges Charlie's thigh. "What's your excuse?"

Charlie grins. "I sucked at it."

I glance at Gabe. "I don't see you as an upstanding Eagle Scout, either."

He hangs his head. "Yeah," he says so softly it's more breath than word. "I'm not so upstanding."

"I didn't mean it like that." I really didn't, even though it's true. But that doesn't matter because I've already soured the mood of the group.

"It'll take time for everyone to forgive you for your secret, Gabriel," Anne says. "Are you planning to wallow in self-pity until then? I can hardly take another minute."

"You wouldn't understand, Anne. You're too good." His lips rise into a half smile, not smirky and flirty but a sad little thing. "You're the best of all of us."

"Everyone's a little bit bad, even the good." Her gaze flicks to the ground. "I told Ronnie about the treasure."

My spine stiffens.

"I'm sorry." She's talking to the ground still. "I never get invited anywhere, and I was . . . I was over the moon and into outer space."

"The ranger was right," I whisper. "You *are* too dreamy."

Her shoulders tremble, and it's worse than tears because it means she's crying and wants to do it alone. That drains all the fight from me. I slump forward. "I don't really mean that."

"It's true." Dark hair swings against her chin as she shakes her head. "I thought . . . It's just that Ronnie's always telling me how people look at me and see hours and minutes and seconds. The way my old friends look at me. The way my aunt and uncle do. I wanted to show him, you know? And he didn't say it that time. Didn't say you were all after my extra time. He listened and asked questions, and I never thought— Not even when they showed up on the island that night."

"Wait, you knew Ronnie and Ash were on the island?" Elliot tugs at his hair. "And you didn't tell us?"

"They came at night. The captain of the fishing boat they took would only come so close to the island, so they rowed the rest of the way. They said they hid the boat, which should have raised suspicion. But it didn't because Ronnie is my brother." She pauses, shudders. Charlie wraps an arm around her shoulders and tugs her close. "They said they were getting an early start on a camping trip, which should have raised suspicion. But it didn't because Ronnie is my brother. We sat on the dock so we wouldn't wake you. At one point, Ronnie walked far down the beach, down by our tent, to go to the bathroom, which should have raised suspicion. But it didn't because he's my brother. And I'm a fool."

Charlie wipes the tears from Anne's face, leaving behind finger-sized smears of dirt. "Don't cry, Anna Banana."

"It's just— You know what he once told me? He said, 'The world you see and the world out there aren't the same, Anne. Someone's going to walk all over you, and you won't even know it.' But I didn't think it'd be him."

"I like that you see the good in people," Gabe says, coaxing a grin out of Anne.

"Ronnie Lansing is a jackass," Elliot says. "Besides, he didn't find our treasure."

Anne casts a nervous glance my way. "Can you forgive me?"

I'm still a little annoyed that her blind trust threatened my promise to Sadie. But if we're comparing crimes, hopeless optimism has nothing on murder.

"Already done," I say, edging closer to her. She rests her head on my shoulder.

I've only ever belonged to Sadie, but for the moment—as my cheek meets Anne's head and she tells a tall tale about a kleptomaniac named Hortense who once stole all the magic from Wildewell—I'm part of these people. I think Sadie would have liked that a lot.

"I think 'narrow' opened 'up to wide' when we left the flooding tunnel and entered this cave," Elliot says, because his mind is always partly on the treasure. "Tomorrow we'll 'look for the place where stone stabs at sky.' I say we travel northeast first."

He's talking about the four entrances to this cave. We flooded the tunnel to the west, which leaves us caverns to the northwest, northeast, and south. We're betting one of those leads to another slashed square.

"Who knows?" he says, turning to Charlie. "Maybe we'll end up at the pit after all. Then you can climb up the hole instead of down it."

Charlie shakes his head. "I'm done climbing."

"What do you mean you're done climbing?"

"You're supposed to be the smart one. It means I'm not climbing anymore." Charlie's face dares Elliot to argue.

"Charlie?" My voice is unsure even though I'm not. "Is this where you die?"

He drops his head into his hands. "I think so."

"Let's go!" Anne zips up her pack. "You can wait for us by the waterfall. You're not dying, Charles Kim."

He tugs her to his side. "'S'okay, Anna Banana. I can't be certain this is the exact spot."

"You need to tell us how you die," Gabe says. "How can we stop it if we don't know anything?"

Charlie hesitates, but only for a second. "That's how I felt when I was little. I'd get flashes—close-up of my head, a huge gash, lots of blood. I didn't know if someone was going to bash my skull with a brick or the basement was going to cave in on me. Nothing.

"I got a little more in middle school: I'm facedown on a rocky ground. My fingers are swollen. Nails dirty." He glances at his nails, releases the kind of soft laugh that's not actually a laugh. "Freshman year, the vision started coming with the knowledge that this was Gray Wolf Island. I don't know everything—not where it happens or what hits me. But I know I'm on the island."

"That's horrible," Anne says.

"That's not the worst of it. A year ago, I got the emotions. There's, like, this overwhelming relief, then joy, then worry. Then I'm going out of my mind with fear. It's—" He runs a shaky hand down his face. "It's probably the worst I've ever felt."

"And then?"

Charlie swallows hard and says, "And then I'm dead."

THIRTY-SIX

COOPER

BISHOP DIED ON A WEDNESDAY AFTERNOON. IT HAD BEEN SUNNY all morning. The kind of clear blue that makes sailors weep.

I was in the study, finishing my poem. Lit by the piercing sunlight.

In an instant, it went dark.

The rain came hard. Not a shower. A torrential downpour.

I peered out the window. The sky was clouded over and charcoal gray for a five-mile radius. Just enough to drench the hill and the cliff and Bishop's house.

Beyond that was blue and light.

I ran to Bishop's room. Pounded on the door.

Walked in.

Sat on the floor.

I haven't moved since.

It's been raining nonstop since Bishop died yesterday. After the first day, visitors coming to pay their respects wised up and started wearing raincoats and toting umbrellas. Not Miller Gravis, though.

"Salty as tears," he says, wiping rain from his face. "How you holding up?"

"Fine."

That word never means what it means.

"Good, good. Listen, this burial thing's not going to work."

Bishop's will said he wanted to be buried in his backyard at the edge of the cliff. Wanted to watch the island into eternity.

"It'll work."

"You telling me you were a gravedigger in your mysterious past? Because if you were, have at it." His clothes drip water onto the floor. I should have talked to him in the garage. "My guys have been digging all day. Six different holes and it's always the same."

"Mud."

"Mud, yeah. But the blasted roots keep clutching their legs. Trying to tug them under." He shakes his head. "No, we can't bury him, Coop."

The next day, I'm standing on the beach. A rowboat bobs in the water.

Bishop is inside.

"Of all the days for the rain to stop," I mutter.

"Not a dry eye in town." Doris squeezes my elbow. "It's okay if you cry."

"That's not what I meant."

She hums under her breath.

"It's not!" I wipe at my eyes with the heels of my hands. "Okay, maybe it was. But I'm only crying because I'm mad. It's not fair he's gone."

"Nobody said anything about fair."

"Whatever, Doris." I grab a stick from the pile on the beach. Light it in the bonfire.

They let me go first. I didn't know him as long as everyone else, but it doesn't matter. They all know I belonged to Bishop and Bishop belonged to me.

I toss my torch into the boat. Move farther down the beach. Smoke from the bonfire makes my lungs ache.

Doris throws her lit branch into the boat, joins me by the water. "He would have thought this was so fancy."

It was her idea to give him a traditional Viking send-off.

Bishop had African, not Viking, ancestors, but he had Viking artifacts. Plus, he'd think this was cool.

Jud Erlich was sure it was illegal or something. Might be.

Everyone decided that if there is a law, we're bending it for Bishop.

One by one, they pay their respects in fire. Little kids hold thin twigs. Mrs. Gupta lights a spray of eucalyptus, and it scents the whole beach.

The sky's dark when four men push the boat from the shore. Pants rolled to the knees and soggy with seawater.

I watch the boat for a long, long time. It's a speck on the horizon when a hand slips into mine.

"It doesn't seem so bad," says Ruby Caine. Firelight dances in her eyes.

"It seems the worst of all."

"No," she says softly. "Being left behind would be worse."

I get Bishop's letter two hours after his funeral. His lawyer, Mr. Caine, says Bishop wanted it that way.

It's no longer raining a circle around the house, but the ground is soggy. I squelch my way to the garden. Sit in Bishop's chair, the one overlooking the cliff and ocean below.

Rip open the envelope.

The letter's on heavy paper. It's handwritten. Bishop was an infuriatingly slow typer.

> *I won't beat around the bush, Bart. I'm dead.*
>
> *This isn't very shocking to me since I've been working my way up to dead for the past eighty-six years. You're probably shocked, though. I did my best to hide all of that from you, and I hope I did the right thing.*
>
> *I never had kids, Bart.*
>
> *(You're rolling your eyes and telling me you've heard this before, but let me talk. It's the least you can do considering I'm dead.)*
>
> *I never had kids, Bart, so I never know if I'm helping you or doing the exact opposite. Would it be better if you knew I was sick? Would it make my death a little less hard? I don't know. It's nine at night and I'm tired and I just don't know.*

The first page ends there. A splotch of ink and nothing else. I flip to the second page.

Good morning, Bart. I'm all rested up and won't fall asleep while writing your letter this time. I was just getting to the good part, too.

I have had three great possessions in my life. I have hundreds of possessions—you know that. But only three have been truly great.

I found the first in 1942. I was just a kid at the time but got it in my head I'd found a real treasure. This wasn't a real treasure, Bart. It was a metal sailboat from a Cracker Jack box. (Do you remember what those are?) This is one of my greatest possessions because it was my first.

The second has to do with the discovery I mentioned the other day. I know you're still sore I kept it a secret. I think it's time I explained myself.

I went to Gray Wolf Island to say goodbye. I spent thirty years of my life there, supervising digs and searching the land. Wildewell is my home, but Gray Wolf Island is my soul.

It called to me, Bart. The week before my last trip to the island, it called my name on the wind. I'd given up on the treasure by then. I figured I was too close to death to hope I'd find it in my lifetime. But I set foot on that beach and I felt it out there.

I dragged this old sack of bones across the island. Call it magic or intuition, but when I finally came to a stop, I knew I had discovered where the treasure was hidden.

It wasn't there, Bart. I know you're skimming ahead for this, so there you go. I found the spot, and it was empty.

The island hasn't had its murder. For all my hunting, I'll never see the treasure. I don't know if you will, Bart. Can't say I wish it one way or another, not when someone's life's on the line.

Which brings me back to my second-greatest possession.

Contentment, Bart. That's what I found on that island.

Thirty years digging up that island and I finally solved the riddle. That might not sound like much of a gift, but it is. Trust me, it is.

I'm sorry I didn't tell you this earlier. I'm sorry I'm not there to tell it to you now.

There on the island I realized four things:

You're meant to leave Wildewell.

You're meant to know the truth.

You're going to be okay.

And this is probably the most important of all: You're my greatest possession.

Your friend,
Bishop

P.S. I had left you my home. This hill, this estate, it was all yours. I think you would have liked it like that. I had left you my belongings, all the items I've collected over the years. You would have liked that, too. That was before I returned to the island. I can't leave you that stuff, Bart.

You're not meant to be the young Mr. Rollins high on the hill (though I had left you my name, too). So I leave you three things: the red backpack in my closet, directions to the treasure on the back of this letter, and symbols to guide your way. And my eternal friendship, Bart. I leave you that, too.

THIRTY-SEVEN

RUBY

AGAIN ELLIOT COMES FOR ME. AGAIN ANNE STAYS BEHIND, curled up with a flashlight and a book.

He leads me across the cave, into a smaller tunnel that reeks of mustiness and brushes both shoulders as we walk. "This doesn't seem safe. Where are we going?"

"We'll be fine," Elliot says. He doesn't sound too certain, though. "And I don't know where we're going—I've never been here."

That doesn't make me feel better. We walk for a few more minutes until we hit what appears to be a large cavern, though it's impossible to determine its size with a single flashlight. Elliot finds an alcove, and we sit with our backs to the cold stone.

He presses the base of the flashlight, and we're in the dark.

"Do you think we can change our destiny, Ruby?" he asks, sliding his fingers between mine. He turns the flashlight on me.

"I want to believe."

"Yeah."

He clicks the flashlight off again. My imagination conjures images of a thousand creepy-crawlies. I force myself to focus on Elliot's fingers, the way his thumb runs back and forth over my thumb.

"When Sadie . . ." He squeezes my hand. "Knowing it was coming, did you prepare yourself?"

"I tried. You can't really— I mean, you still fall apart."

"It's just, with Toby it was so sudden and horrible. I thought maybe with Charlie . . ." He releases a sad laugh. "I thought maybe it'd be easier after because I spent so much time saying goodbye before."

"No matter how many times you say goodbye, it's not nearly enough." I've never talked about Sadie's death this way, and a part of me wants to stop. But the darkness wraps around me like a security blanket. "It didn't get easier until I found my poem," I say, though I really mean it didn't get easier until I found these friends.

"If Charlie goes, help me find *my* poem." Elliot turns on the flashlight. He stands, extends a hand.

I make a show of brushing off my shorts because I'm not quite ready to go. It's just that Elliot's smile is so sweet and his hair's doing that swoopy thing it does when he's tired and he's so scared for Charlie.

"I followed you once," I blurt. "Sadie had this thing about you, like you were really independent and could teach me how to be. So one day when you skipped class I followed just to see what kind of immoral or illegal things you did when you weren't in school."

"But I snuck into a college lecture instead?"

Embarrassment burns my cheeks, and I'm thankful for the dim lighting. "You knew?"

He laughs. "You were kind of hard to miss."

If I wander long enough, can I find a sharp stalagmite to impale myself on? "You must have thought I was creepy. Or a stalker."

"I thought . . ." Elliot runs a hand through his hair. "I don't know what I thought. I just know I thought about you."

I've never really wanted anything of my own, not when Sadie was always there wanting enough for both of us. But then I look at Elliot in the almost-dark, forearms flexing as he squeezes the base of the flashlight. *Light, dark. Light dark light. Dark.*

I boldly press a finger to his collarbone. He jumps at my touch. *Light.*

I'm lit from above when I step into his space, and it's too late to go back now. My lips brush his, the barest of touches.

"Oh," he says against my mouth. A clatter of metal against stone. *Dark.*

Elliot's hands are in my hair, mine traveling up, up, up his arms, over his shoulders, to the back of his neck, where baby hairs prickle my fingertips.

And it's dark, so dark in this sunken alcove. We're nothing but lips and breath and hands.

Elliot pulls away and says, "You're so beautiful."

"You can't even see me," I tell him. But of course he can. He's been seeing me all along.

His fingers trace the lines of my face. Part of me wants to stop him because it's blacker than black down here and I'm afraid he's going to poke me in the eye, but I don't move because I like the feel of his rough fingers on my face and the sound of his voice when he says he can feel how pretty I am.

Then I can't take it anymore, the not kissing. I want my lips on his, but I get his eye instead, which is exactly as sexy as it sounds.

"Missed," he says, and I can hear the smile in his voice. "Try again."

I take my time. Maybe people who've had a thousand kisses can anticipate where lips hide in the dark, but I'm lost like a treasure. My hands find the sides of his face. He smiles under my palms.

I don't have to wonder whether my lips are in the right spot because when my nose gets close enough to brush his, Elliot says my name, and his breath on my lips tells me I'm right where I want to be. I kiss him, feeling the cold metal of his lip ring press into me. Like I wanted it to that night in the clearing when he showed me the scar in the sky. And I think I might know a bit about how it feels, filled up with stars and ripping across the universe.

A long while later, I rest my forehead against Elliot's and I breathe in the scents of lavender and insect repellent clinging to his T-shirt. He searches for the flashlight. Clicks it on. We squint at each other through the brightness.

We're staring and we're grinning and we're absolutely drunk on each other.

THIRTY-EIGHT

RUBY

Look for the place
where stone stabs at sky
and the earth sings a mourning song
for your echo to reply.

There are a lot of stalagmites. *A lot.*

"I'd like to punch the jackhole who wrote this map." Elliot's lost the giddy glow he woke up with, back when we were both still high off our kiss and hopeful about the day.

Before we spent hours looking for "the place where stone stabs at sky" and finding about a billion of them.

"Or you could ask him where the treasure's buried," Anne says with a sigh. Her endless optimism is dying a slow death.

"Maybe we're not even looking for another slashed square,"

Gabe says, exiting the cavern through a cramped tunnel. It's single-file shuffling from here on out. "Maybe we'll know we've found it when the island sings."

"Don't be an idiot," Elliot says.

I punch his back. "Don't be a jerk."

"How about a scary story, Anne?" Gabe asks as he leads us through the tunnel. We're meandering all over, though Elliot's doing his best to keep us pointed northeast so we have a chance of finding our way back.

"I'll tell you a story, but it's not scary." She clears her throat. I think it's more to announce her impending narration than anything else. Anne does like to be listened to. "My great-grandmother used to tell me about Wildewell Boy when my brother was asleep because I loved the part where he cries out a rosebush, but Ronnie was always scared when the boy turned to dust."

"What do you mean he turns to dust?"

"Charlie, man, that obviously comes later on," Gabe says. "Start at the start, Anne."

"It starts on the island, when the sun's risen but the morning's still murky. The fog was thick, so thick that the Truth-Seeker couldn't see the bottomless pit. So thick he couldn't see his fingers in front of his eyes. But he watched the spot where the pit should've been—maybe three feet to the right, where the mist seemed thinnest. Or a few yards to the left, where a black smudge marred the white fog.

"The Truth-Seeker was staring somewhere in between the two when the ground rumbled and the fog dripped from the sky like wet paint on a tilting canvas. When the fog cleared, the Truth-Seeker saw a boy curled at the edge of the pit. His hair was made of dirt and his feet were rooted to the earth like the trunks of a tree, and when he looked at the Truth-Seeker his eyes were young buds.

"As the boy rose from the ground, his legs became muscle and skin. He was a boy—close to being a man—but his head was as empty as the fog. The Truth-Seeker found the boy could understand him, could even communicate with him. He understood *home* and *identity*, even though he couldn't remember his own.

"So the Truth-Seeker took the boy from the island, from the pit that spit him out without a past, and gave him a room in his palace. The boy had a soft bed to sleep on and clothes more comfortable than the moss and leaves that clung to his body when he appeared on the island. The boy had a friend who quickly became a father, and he had the townspeople, who loved strangeness if they loved anything at all. And the boy was strange. He had no name, so they fondly called him Wildewell Boy."

"It would have been easier to give him a real name," Charlie says. "Like Bob."

"Charlie." I imagine Anne pinching the bridge of her nose, high between her eyes. "I can't conceivably tell a story about a boy named Bob and still have it sound magical. It's really not possible."

"Keep going," Gabe says. "I can tell you're getting to a good part."

"I am." She clears her throat again. "Days became weeks, and weeks became months, and Wildewell Boy's roots dug into the earth and sang that Wildewell was home. The Truth-Seeker trained him as he would his own son, teaching him about the mysterious island with the infinite hole and buried treasure. When the Truth-Seeker took his afternoon nap, Wildewell Boy would walk the path from the palace to town. There he'd listen to stories of heartache and pain. And like plants guzzle water to grow tall and strong, Wildewell Boy drank up their sorrows.

"At night he'd visit the palace gardens and bury his long fingers in the ground. He'd weep for the townspeople, spilling their sadness into the dirt, and in the morning the gardener would find a new rosebush, as tall as a man and in full bloom. Then one day the Truth-Seeker took his last breath, and Wildewell Boy sobbed out his own grief. The garden withered and the dirt turned to dust, and the boy knew he had to leave."

"But what about the treasure?" Charlie asks. "Did the Truth-Seeker tell him where it was before he died?"

"He did," Anne says. "The Truth-Seeker's spirit found the broken-down Wildewell Boy and with phantom fingers led him to a grand study. In the middle of the room sat an oak desk and on that desk sat an envelope and in that envelope were instructions for the boy. He read them, folded the note, and left the palace."

"What'd it say, though?"

"Charlie," Elliot snarls. "Shut the hell up and let her tell the story."

"But she didn't tell us what it said."

"No more interruptions," Anne huffs. "So, as I was saying, the boy left the palace. He took with him the Truth-Seeker's bag and nothing else. He paddled a boat to Gray Wolf Island, which seemed to whisper his name on the wind. He paid no attention to it; he was Wildewell Boy and no one else.

"When he arrived at the pit, the air sang with crickets and glowed with flashing fireflies. Wildewell Boy stood at the edge of the pit, and his body began to tickle. Quickly, he unwrapped the Truth-Seeker's bag and tossed gems the size of baseballs and gold as thick as bricks down the hole. He worked fast, because the longer he stood, the more his body prickled. His clothes thinned and turned to dust. Roots grew from his feet, from his tree-trunk legs. His hair became thick as mud, and his eyes were green bulbs waiting to bloom. His body became the island, breaking apart and disintegrating into dust."

Nobody speaks for a long moment; then Charlie says, "It was a good story, Anne. Even if it wasn't scary."

"I like how he was created out of nothing but he was so important to the townspeople." Gabe shoots Anne a smile over his shoulder. "And I like the way you told it. Like you were reading from a book."

Elliot pauses, turns around. "Did he ever learn the truth?"

"He was never searching for the truth," Anne says, holding his gaze. "But yeah, he found it. That's why he was able to disappear."

The air is stale.

It's the first thing I notice when we enter the small cavern, and I can't help but think we're the first people to stand in this chamber in a long, long while. Something about that makes me feel impossibly small.

"Magic," Anne whispers, body swaying into Charlie.

I feel it, too. It's the same otherness I felt in the center of the Star Stones, only this time I'm light and floaty.

We fan out, searching for the slashed square. The whole while, I'm listening. For a mourning song. For an echo. For the island to whisper we're in the right place. But beneath the scuffling of feet, there's a whole lot of silence.

In the center of the chamber stand two stalagmites, squat structures with pointed heads. They look less like rock than columns made of dripped candle wax. I check and recheck, but neither is marked by the symbol.

I press my palm against the cool surface of the taller column. Let the cave's dizzying magic course through my body. I'm light enough to float to the ceiling, to the sky, to space.

"You okay there, Anna Banana?"

That snaps me out of my daze. I turn to find Charlie leading Anne to the center of the cave. "Too much magic," she says.

"Or low blood sugar," Elliot says, rolling his eyes. "How about those cookies, Gabe?"

Gabe stumbles his way to the group, digs around in his pack. He tosses each of us a cookie, flinging Charlie's so far off the mark it lands in a cloud of dirt. We laugh like it's the funniest thing we've ever seen, and it really is.

Charlie wipes it on his shirt before taking a bite.

"When you're rich on pirate treasure, you should open a bakery," Elliot says, catching a string of caramel before it sticks to his chin. "Or maybe I'll use my share to hire you as my personal chef."

"Like you could afford me." Gabe laughs so long it turns into a cough.

"What'll you do with the treasure, Ruby?" Anne lowers her head to Charlie's shoulder.

I open my mouth, but I have no answer. For all I've thought about the treasure in the past week and a half, I've never considered what I might do with it. My mind was stuck on the finding, on Sadie's final wish. "I have no idea."

"My aunt and uncle need money to send my cousins to college," Charlie says from beside me. Or maybe he's on the ground. It's so hard to tell with the magic swirling my mind. "I want you to give my share to them."

"Shut up, Charlie," Elliot growls. "Give it to them yourself."

No one wants to think longer about Charlie being too dead to deliver the treasure, so we start imagining the most ludicrous ways to spend our money. "I'm going to buy a candy store. Not for me. For Ronnie," Anne says, and we all groan. "He loves candy, so I'll buy a store full of it and never let him in." I can tell she's proud of herself, so I grin extra wide.

"I'm going to buy a motorcycle." To his credit, Elliot says it with a straight face.

"Stop trying to make the bad-boy thing happen." I try to punch his shoulder, but I'm too tired from our endless hours of stalagmite exploration to really commit. Elliot captures my hand in his, opens my fist, and slides his fingers between mine.

"I'll buy you a black leather jacket with my portion," Gabe says. This sends him into another fit of laugh-coughing.

Charlie's heavy-lidded eyes fix on Elliot. "I'll use some of mine to bail you out of jail."

"I hate you all," Elliot says with real menace, then kisses the top of my head.

If I could record this moment, I'd save it somewhere safe so I could watch it on repeat again and again. So I could forever feel like this—like I've swallowed the sky and everything in it.

But that all changes in an instant. In a breath.

Between the time Anne inhales and stops breathing altogether.

THIRTY-NINE

RUBY

THERE'S A TIGHTNESS IN MY CHEST, AND IT FEELS A LOT LIKE panic. If the room would stop spinning, I could double-check. Make sure Anne's chest is rising. Make sure she's just asleep.

But the cavern's still a swirl.

And Anne doesn't sleep.

"Anne." My voice is a low rasp, but it's enough for Charlie. He shakes her, hard, then harder. I can't stand to look at the terror on his face, so I grip her hand and tug. Her body slides down Charlie's and onto the ground.

"You guys get the backpacks," I say, pulling Anne from his grasp. He barely puts up a fight.

My steps are shaky. My hands slick with sweat.

I worry about stones on the ground scraping Anne's bare

skin. I worry about thunking her skull into a stalagmite. But more than that, I worry about being too slow.

My mind's a muzzy mess, brain sliding all over the place. Still, I don't stop. I drag her across the cave, out through the small opening, into the dark tunnel. I drag her another few yards just to be safe.

Then I drop to the ground. My body's beating humming-bird fast. I suck lungfuls of air, and it tastes like the cool spray of water on a sweltering day.

I drag myself to Anne. My first instinct is to do CPR, but I doubt whatever's in my lungs will revive her. "Breathe," I say. My lungs scream, but I say it again. *"Breathe."*

A scuffing of shoes. The sound of labored breathing. And then the boys spill out of the cave. They crawl down the tunnel until they're by my side, a riot of sounds: coughing, wheezing, gasping for air.

They're sick and they're hurt but they're so blatantly alive.

We huddle around Anne. I try not to play What If, but *what if?* What if all I'll ever get with Anne is a week? What if I never get to tell her that she's all the things she fears about herself and that they make her extraordinary? What if we never get the chance for a forever friendship?

But then Charlie is shaking me. He's pressing my palm to Anne's chest, right where his was resting. And it's shallow, so shallow, but her chest is rising.

I rest her head in my lap, knock the pebbles and dirt from her hair. And I wait.

As I do, I catch a sound, faint beneath our raspy breaths.

Rushing water.

The humming wind.

There's something about the sound . . .

"It wasn't magic," Elliot says, shattering my concentration. He's lying with his head on his backpack. "I'd bet anything that was some sort of noxious gas. That chamber's pretty closed off aside from the small entrance. It's not absurd to think it got trapped in there."

"Yes, it is," Gabe says. "It'd escape and you know it. This was the island. And it's going to kill us if Ruby doesn't tell the truth."

"This isn't her fault," Elliot says.

"Thanks," I say. "But could we not do the fighting while I'm trying to have a breakthrough?"

That's when Anne decides to have her own sort of breakthrough. With a whimper, she's awake.

The four of us jerk our heads in Anne's direction. She heaves herself off my lap and presses her back to the tunnel wall. She releases a round of dry, wheezy coughs.

"I'm really, really glad you're alive." It's about all I can say right now. Even Charlie is lost for words, staring at her like she's the dead come back to life.

"So, what's the breakthrough?" The look on Elliot's face is so eager I'm almost afraid he's going to shake the words out of me.

Anne turns to Charlie. "It's like I didn't almost die."

I grit my teeth. "I said I was *trying* to have a breakthrough, and aside from that you're being very rude to Anne."

"It would have been ruder to care about the breakthrough before we knew she was alive." Elliot's wearing a very self-satisfied smile. It's my least favorite of all his faces.

I close my eyes and listen for the sounds. There—like low notes from a flute and brushes on a drum.

It's a windblown melody.

It's a watery lament.

"Oh." I draw out the wait as I draw out my smile. "It's musical."

Elliot's a gash of light against dark as he listens to the sound coming from the end of the tunnel. He leans around Charlie, lays a loud kiss on my cheek. "You're a genius." His gaze lifts, and his grin grows impossibly wide. "We've seen a million places where 'stone stabs at sky.' And now the earth's singing a mourning song."

"We need an echo." Elliot's standing atop a tall rock, hands on his hips like some kind of superhero. His chest heaves, and sweat runs down the side of his face.

What we assumed was a straight shot west to the source of the sound turned out to be a straight shot west with miles and miles of tunnel in between. The trek would have been tiring enough with oxygen-starved lungs, never mind at a jog. But slowing Elliot Thorne when he's on a mission is a little like stopping a cave-in after the ceiling has crumbled to the floor.

I bend over my knees, gulping salty air. It's breezing in through an arched opening in the far wall, which offers a glimpse of the northwestern coast and an aggressively gray sky. Water rockets through the opening, thrashing and throwing itself against the hard stone. Though the ocean has probably hurtled in and out of this cave for centuries upon centuries, it's done nothing to blunt the sharp edges.

As we raced after the music, I was amazed at what acoustics could do—drift a bit of nature for miles. But now I know that's only half of it. This cave rumbles with sound.

As does Elliot. "I'm coming for you!"

Hundreds of rectangular rocks hold fast to the ceiling. It's like the inside of an organ. And it sounds like an organ when the cave replies, *I'm coming for you. I'm coming for you. I'm coming for . . .*

"Well, that wasn't ominous," Charlie says, searching for someplace to sit. But the ground is a riot of rock—short rocks, tall rocks, rocks the size of stairs stepping up the walls, rocks with flat faces and sharp corners that'll slice you if you take a wrong step.

He finds a small clearing among the stones, and I sit beside him. Elliot squeezes next to me, distracting me with that mussed-up hair and those light, bright eyes and that neck. I'm not sure how I'm expected to do anything but stare at that long neck with the beauty mark at one end and the tease of a tattoo on the other. I look away.

Even though we're positive the poem is talking about this cavern and even though our lungs are tired, Anne and I test our music on the cave. From her mouth comes a sound as breathy as the wind, as strong as the ocean, as high as the ceiling in this cathedral of a cave. I jump in with my harmonica. It's a strange and wonderful thing, her singing between my riffs, her words dipping and curling around the notes.

I play a final chord, let her voice finish the piece. We're left with echoes of a song that plays to crashing waves and howling wind. Gabe stares at Anne as if she sang the universe into existence. "I'm . . ." He steps toward her but jerks to a halt at the last minute. "I'm making dinner, so you losers can set up camp."

Charlie muffles a laugh. "Anna Banana, you siren."

"If that were true, I'd never sing, so my voice wouldn't lure you to a rocky death." She blinks again and again. "Not that you're going to die today."

"No, he's not." Elliot's expression is fierce. "He's going to die as wrinkled and bald as the day he was born."

"Hey, this hair isn't going anywhere." Charlie runs a hand over his head "My *harabeoji*'s hair grew three inches on his deathbed and another four after he died. My dad says it runs in the family."

Anne loops her arm through his. "My great-grandmother was bald until she was four. You'd make very normal babies together."

"*Annnnnee,*" Charlie groans. "That is the one hundred per-cent last thing I ever want to think about."

They traverse the cave, disappearing into a small alcove. Elliot pauses, but I don't move. "Meet you there," I say.

He glances at Gabe, nods, then follows Anne and Charlie to the alcove.

By now, Gabe has gathered twigs from near the cave's oceanside entrance—most likely blown in during a storm or carried by water to the rocky shore—and built a small fire. He bends over a pot of boiling water. Shadows stretch across his face, but I can see his pinched mouth clearly enough to know he doesn't want company. I sit down anyway. "Can I help?"

"I've got it," he says. Fat noodles go into the pot. Dehy-drated veggies follow. We stare at them until the noodles soften and slide underwater. I'm sure Sadie would have something smart and funny and life-changing to say, but I don't, so I stay quiet. He looks up, and in the fire his face is red as wrath. "Do you ever just hate yourself?"

"I'm a work in progress."

He releases a low laugh, more breath than anything else. "In the valley, the grass whispered that truth brought freedom. The other day, after I told you guys what I did and the island stopped attacking me, I felt so much lighter. For the first time in forever, I thought I might one day forgive myself." His eyes dart to the far end of the cave, where the others are setting up camp. "And then Anne sang that song and . . ."

"You wanted to make out with her."

"Ruby! I'm trying to be all deep and stuff and—" He pours a powdery mixture into the boiling water, which turns creamy yellow. "And I'm trying to talk about beauty and worth and, yes, I wanted to kiss her."

"But you don't feel worthy of her."

"I'm not."

"Not yet," I say. "Become the kind of guy who is."

I wrap him in a hug. He squeezes tight, and I think maybe I'm getting this friendship thing. Maybe wickedness tears holes in our hearts, like it did for me the day Sadie died. But maybe we fill those hollows with the people we love, and they make us better, stronger.

FORTY

RUBY

Search for the six,
sturdy, solid, and true.
For centuries they've been waiting,
waiting for you.

A slap to the face, and I'm awake.

"Ruby!" Anne's eyes are wild, her hair hanging around her face like a lion's mane. "Wake up, Ruby. Wake up!"

I startle to my knees. Blink into the blackness. "Charlie!"

"He's fine. For now." Anne rouses Gabe with an elbow to the gut. "Get up, Gabe. We have to hurry."

He's quicker to rise. He fumbles with his bag; then another light clicks on. "What's going on?"

Anne pauses. "I don't . . . I don't know. I felt this rumbling, like the island was growling with hunger and we were lying on its stomach. It was so strong, but none of you woke up, so maybe I imagined it." She shakes Elliot's shoulder. "It doesn't matter, though. I have a feeling."

"A bad one?" Gabe tugs his shoes on.

Anne's face is white above her flashlight's beam. "Worse."

"So let's get out of here. Wake up!" Gabe yells, smacking Charlie awake. "C'mon, you idiot."

When my shoes are on, I help Anne with Elliot, who can apparently sleep through a pummeling. He finally blinks awake, swatting my hand from his sleeping bag. With a hard yank, I pull the bag back, leaving him shirtless and shivering.

"Too cold," he mumbles before Charlie douses him with water. He jumps to his feet. "You are so dead."

"We're trying to prevent that," Anne says with a huff. "We have to go."

A low rumble builds in the cave, as if the island is clearing its throat in preparation for a big announcement. And then the announcement comes, a sound like a stampede of angry cattle. Rock crashes into rock. Dust chokes the air, coats our skin, our nostrils, inside our mouths.

Elliot shoves on shoes. Shoulders his pack. It's half open and spilling its contents on the ground, but there's no time to care. Our sleeping bags and any other items strewn around the cave are left in our wake.

The tunnel that led us to this cave crumples. We race for the far wall, the only slab of rock not cracked and crumbling. I don't know what's on the other side, but it has to be better than this.

"Charlie!" Anne yells without glancing back.

"I'm okay!" He's bookended by Elliot and Gabe, who scan the cave for the rock that'll steal Charlie from us. "Just get us out of here."

And she does, her nimble body dodging falling rock as she leads us as far from the destruction as possible. But we don't avoid it for long. The cave's two sides curve inward, putting us in the middle of two rockslides. Something slices my head, knocks me sideways. My hip crashes into a felled stalactite. The ache radiates to my leg, the whole way to my feet, but I shake it off and hurry after the others.

It's as if the island's trying to eat us whole. I lift my face to the ceiling, where a wrecking thunder sounds behind a cloud of dust. Where a jagged rock the size of my head is hurtling toward— "Charlie! It's going to hit Charlie!"

Elliot and Gabe wrap him in a hug with their hands clasped over Charlie's head. I hold my breath and count the seconds, but I don't stop running. I nearly collide with the boys, who release Charlie from their embrace. He propels us forward, races toward the black hole at the end of the cave, and I don't know if he's hurt, but at least he's not dead.

He's not dead.

He's not dead.

He's not dead.

I say it over and over again as I follow the boys across the cave and through the rockslide and into the darkness. A rock crashes into Elliot's face, but we don't stop. Never stop. We run through the pitch-blackness for minutes or hours or years. Nothing exists but the rough earth beneath our feet and the inky air over, above, around, and beyond.

Long after the earth's stopped crumbling, we emerge into a

large cave. We're a circle of heaving, huffing bodies, slick with sweat and covered in dirt.

"Charlie." Anne lurches for him, and he catches her in his arms. "Please tell me you're okay. Please."

"I'm fine." He grins. "I think I'll hire Elliot and Gabe as my bodyguards when I get my share of the treasure."

"Is everyone else okay?" Anne scans our faces, stops on Gabe. She rubs the dark streak of wet trying to sneak into his eye. "Just a scratch."

I wipe away my own blood, press my fingers to my forehead. The cut's shallow.

Elliot touches a finger to his lip, winces. His gaze flicks to my head, but only for a short second. Then he's pulling me closer, palm hot against the back of my neck. As if he didn't take a blow to the mouth, his lips crash into mine. This kiss is hard, almost frantic. It's the rumble of falling rocks. It's gasping and aching and running for your life. It's want and worry all mixed up. And I have to pull away. I have to do it because if I don't, I might miss the whole world crumbling down.

"We're safe," I tell Elliot or maybe myself. "This cave's safe."

"It's strange," Elliot says. "When we ran through that dark tunnel, the walls didn't even shake. Not even a little."

"Because the island didn't care if we were in there," Anne says. "As long as we're not where we used to be, it's okay where we are."

"Which is . . ." He examines the room. "I have no idea where we are."

"I do," Charlie says. He's sitting with his back against a stalagmite in the center of the cave. He taps the rock once, twice, three times. We huddle in close, the beams from our headlamps overlapping so it's impossible to miss the CHARLIE carved into the stone.

Elliot straightens. "When did you . . ."

"I found it when you were devouring Ruby's face."

I bury my head in my hands.

Elliot smacks the back of Charlie's head. "No, when did you carve that?"

Charlie leans his head against the stalagmite. "The night after the booby trap. I just . . . I wanted to stay around, somehow."

"Pointless—you're not dying," Elliot says. "But at least now we know where to go. The west exit leads to a booby-trapped tunnel filled with water. The northeastern exit leads to the gas-filled cave. We just came from the northwest, so south it is."

I know it's the right choice. It's not just that it's the path least likely to kill us. I still suspect the map will lead us to the Star Stones. And that's exactly the direction we're headed in.

It takes an hour of walking south until the twisting, turning network of tunnels opens into a large cavern. Through a crack in the ceiling, night paints moonlight on the ground.

We survey the cave before setting foot inside. No rocks hanging by their toes on the ceiling. No spikes on the ground. The entire cave is empty, except for a handful of towering stones.

"Not even a murmur," Anne says.

"What does she . . ." Gabe yawns. "What, Elliot, is the meaning of what she said?"

"The island says it's okay for us to go back to bed," Elliot says with a laugh. We settle onto the ground, too tired to unload our packs. Too anxious about another avalanche of rocks.

"This reminds me of the Star Stones," Anne says. She stretches her arms out beside her. "It has the same skin-prickling feeling."

"It makes my arm not move," Gabe says. "I think it's magic."

For me it's a buzz of energy racing my blood up my arm and back again. It's exactly like the air inside the Star Stones, a bit thicker than air's supposed to be. I gasp. "We're there. We're still within the Star Stones."

I point my flashlight at each of the monoliths scattered about the cave in a not-so-random pattern. They're formed from the ground and shoot up through the ceiling, single slabs of stone. Elliot squints at the ceiling, where the moon squeezes through the rock.

"A snake," Gabe says, erupting in a fit of giggles. "It's a rope-snake lasso like Indiana Jones's."

"Dude, that made no sense. And Indiana Jones hated snakes." Charlie kicks Gabe's foot. "Go back to bed."

"He's right," Elliot says, words slurring as he removes his lip ring. The corner of his mouth has already started to swell. "That's the rope I left hanging through the crack. So we're really beneath the Star Stones. That's why the slashed square led us here."

"It seems," I say, "that this treasure hunt would have been a whole lot easier if the map had taken us straight south."

"Obviously," Elliot says. "But there's probably no direct route. Plus, what kind of treasure hunt would it be if they gave us all the answers? The hunt's only fun because it's convoluted."

"And because of the treasure," Charlie says.

Treasure.

I close my eyes because this feels like a moment. Like one of those life events that come with a label for anyone telling our story when we're gone. *In Which They Discover the Treasure,* this one would say. " 'Search for the six, sturdy, solid, and true.' " My voice is low and husky from dirt. " 'For centuries they've been waiting, waiting for you.' "

"Tell the truth to get the treat, treater, trees . . . treaties?" Gabe laughs. "You're so pretty, Anne." He reaches for her hair but misses. This sets him off with deep, wall-shaking belly laughs.

"Gabe." Elliot kneels in front of him. "Gabe, look at me."

Gabe lifts his face, and there's a line of blood from his nose to his chin. "I like to look at her." He blinks against Elliot's flashlight. "Nooooo. I was not being a creepiness, Anne. It was not what I was."

"Do you remember hitting your head during the rockslide?" Elliot's hands run over Gabe's head. "Dammit."

Elliot rips off his shirt, presses it to the back of Gabe's head. "Gabe? Hey, Gabe, let's not go to sleep."

"Yellow," Gabe says. "Yellow and they said so."

Gabe's eyes slide closed but flutter open in time for him to lean away from Elliot and throw up. "Not on Anne."

"Thank you, Gabe. Now sit up and talk to me." Anne's hands grasp Gabe's face, slap him lightly. "Hey, wake up."

"Oh, hi." He grins. "I hoped it was you."

Gabe shrugs Anne off. He pushes to his feet, his left arm hanging at his side like a sewed-on appendage. "Gotta go," he says, wiping at his bloody nose. "Make Anne's eyelashes closes, okay? Don't watch, Anne."

He throws up.

"Sit down," Elliot says, rising to his knees. He reaches for Gabe's T-shirt but misses. "No one cares about your puke, Gabe. Just sit down."

Gabe's legs wobble as he makes his way back to us. His eyes are slits if they're open at all. And then they're open, wide and clear. "I never told you, Anne," he says with a slur to his speech.

He blinks. Again.

Gabe pitches forward, and time holds its breath. I live three lifetimes like this, knees to rocky earth, mouth full of a scream I can't seem to let out. I watch the ground beneath Elliot's feet slowly erode. I watch Anne's hair grow so long it starts snaking its way through the cave, past the waterfall, and off the island. I watch Charlie's fingernails claw at his bracelet for decades and centuries. For that long, Gabe hangs over the ground like a phantom, eyes rolled up into his head and nose watering the rock red.

It takes forever and no time at all for Gabe Nash to fall to earth.

FORTY-ONE

COOPER

I haven't been back in Bishop's room since the sky stopped crying. It smells stale and lonely.

The backpack's at the edge of the closet.

Red as hurt.

Red as pain.

Red as blood.

Bishop would say it's red with potential. Like a red sky at night. Sailor's delight.

I pick it up. It's not huge, but it's heavy.

Unzip it. Peek in.

Holy sheet.

I dump the backpack onto the bed. Heavy coins bounce on the mattress.

Stones clump where the quilt puckers at its seams. Diamonds. Rubies. Emeralds. The blue ones, too.

There are some other artifacts from Bishop's collection mixed in with the coins and gems. A small bronze figurine. A wooden ax. An agate cameo.

I don't study the treasure for long. It's not mine anyway.

When it's back in the bag, I leave Bishop's room. Close his door. I think it'll stay closed for a long while.

The doorbell chimes, so I hide the backpack in the hall closet. I race down the stairs. Skid across the slick marble foyer.

Sheriff March seems surprised to see me. Like sometime between getting out of his car and ringing the bell he forgot Bishop was gone. "How're you doing, Coop?"

"I've been better."

He winces. "Listen, I hate to do this to you. Wouldn't do it if I didn't have to."

"You're the sheriff. You don't have to do anything you don't want to."

"Tried that once. They just sent down another sheriff to police me into policing everyone else. No, I have to do this."

"Whatever it is, just get it over with."

"We've been lenient letting you stay here since Bishop died. But it's been four days, and now you've got to go." He scratches his neck. "This isn't your home."

"I'll be out in a few days."

"Listen, Coop, I hate to do this. I really do. But I need you out today." He stares at the sea instead of me. The crash of waves against rock is loud this afternoon. "This place is Wildewell's now, and Captain Thirwall is in a tizzy over possible theft and vandalism what with Mr. Rollins gone."

"I'd like to vandalize his face."

"That's not how vandalism works," he says. "And you really shouldn't say stuff like that to me. I'm the sheriff. I don't want to arrest you for threatening assault."

I sigh. "If you arrest me, at least I'll have a place to sleep tonight."

"You have a place to sleep tonight. My sister is waiting for you."

He says it like that settles things. I guess it does.

I gather my belongings in a small bag. Steal a few of Bishop's books. He'd be okay with that, I think.

In his bedroom I find my treasure. A small metal sailboat. I pluck it from Bishop's dresser, shove it in the red backpack.

When I'm done, I enter his study. Of all the rooms in his house, this one misses him the most.

I sit behind his desk. Run my hand over the polished wood. Indian laurel.

My finished poem is on the desk. So is the last book Bishop ever read. He thought it'd be hilarious to hide the poem in *Treasure Island.* Got a real laugh out of that idea.

I pick up the book. Flip to the last page.

The old man would want me to finish this thing.

I write the poem, making my letters old-fashioned and fancy. When I'm done, I snap the book shut.

Two bags wait for me by the door. I head for the library first.

I have a book to hide, then a treasure to bury.

I end up in the back of a police cruiser, wedged between a door with disabled handles and a heavy red backpack. I keep thinking Sheriff March is going to look in the bag and arrest me for theft now that Captain Thirwall put the idea in his head.

We near an old house. Gray shingles. White trim. These arched windows that make me think of Bishop's history books.

The sheriff strides to the front door. A towering woman with wild eyes answers it.

They disappear into the house.

The sun disappears over the horizon.

I'm disappearing, too.

Bart's gone. Left with Bishop.

Cooper's on his way out. Not sure where he's headed, but it's not here.

Soon I'll just be Nameless Boy, and even that will vanish.

One day I'll be a hint of a memory. Or maybe Wildewell won't remember me at all. Minds wiped clean as mine was that morning on Gray Wolf Island.

A quiet *tap, tap, tap* on the window.

I turn my head. Standing beside the car is a skinny kid. He's young, maybe nine or ten.

"Open the door," I say.

He tugs it open. Cool September air chills the sweat at the base of my neck.

I stand on drowsy legs. They prickle as I walk.

"What're you doing?" The boy follows me to a stone wall. It connects to more stones that connect to a rocky cliff.

"Guess I'm staying for a bit." I stretch the ache out of my legs. "Where's your uncle?"

"Helping Dad. He's having a bad week."

The sky darkens, revealing a slice of moon. The beach fades in the darkness. Nothing down there but the crashing waves.

"Did you know he has post-traumatic stress disorder from the war?" The boy works a stone loose from the wall. "Mom says *trauma* comes from the Greek word for 'wound.'" He shakes his head but doesn't glance at me. "I hear what they say about him in town. That he should stop being so sad and angry. He doesn't *try* to be sad and angry."

I nod. "It's like a wound. You can't tell someone to stop bleeding so much."

I'm tipping over the edge of drowsy when a strange sensation jolts me awake.

Someone's watching me.

Hairs on the back of my neck reach for the ceiling.

I lie real still. Keep my eyes shut.

Deep breaths of sheets scented with Mrs. Thorne's home-made lavender detergent.

Then, a creak.

I shoot upright. The couch squeaks beneath me.

The dark's a solid form filling every inch of the room. I

blink and blink. My eyes are slow to adjust, but when they do they snag on a chair in the corner of the room.

In the chair is a man.

And he's staring at me.

"We hurt the children," he says.

I don't reply.

"We hurt the children."

I clench my blankets in a fist.

The tall shadow leans forward. "You think they're in heaven?"

"I don't know."

"Head shot. Them's the orders."

His voice is low. Almost too low for a human. It sends a chill through the room.

"You think they're in heaven?"

"Sure," I say. "They were only kids."

"Yeah." The man leans back against the chair. "Better to go when they're still innocent enough to get in."

The man stands. Pauses before leaving the room.

"Don't grow up," he says over his shoulder. "It'll turn you into a monster."

FORTY-TWO

RUBY

BONE ON STONE. THAT'S THE SOUND OF DYING ON GRAY WOLF Island.

Gabe's nose presses sideways against the stone. A river of blood clots in the dirt. "Charlie."

"I'm here." Charlie stands above us, hands fisting his hair. He blinks and blinks and blinks. "I'm right here."

"Tell Charlie," Gabe says, his voice a muffled gurgle. He winces. "Hurts."

"I know it hurts, man."

Gabe's eyes meet mine, and I want to look away. I did this. Holding on to my secret so tight, that's what's really killing Gabe. But I won't turn away. I rest a hand against his cheek. "You're almost there, Gabe." I swallow back everything waiting

278

to release. "Can you see it? All that treasure? It's miles and miles of gold and every bit of it is perfect."

He swallows hard. "Tell Charlie it's better like this."

Then he blinks, one last time.

"Stop this," Elliot says to Gabe, though I think he's really talking to the island. He kneels by Gabe's head. Covered in blood and lit by only a sliver of moonlight, Gabe's sandy brown hair looks raven black. Strands stick out in every direction, some shooting skyward, others plastered to his forehead. The back is wet and matted. He'd hate that. With gentle fingers, Elliot smooths it down, over the divot of skull cracked in the rockslide. Then he gently flips Gabe onto his back.

Elliot stares at his hand, trembling and crimson. "This isn't real." Elliot wipes his hand against the ground. He rubs harder, as if resurrecting Gabe is as simple as wiping away his blood.

"This—" Elliot stares at his palm, a dirty mess of pebbles and blood. "It's not here. *We're* not here."

I wrap my arms around him, trapping his arms at his sides. "Elliot," I say, voice froggy from the sadness caught in my throat. "He's gone, Elliot."

My secret did this. I can see it now, like a backward premonition. Crisp in the way understanding gets only when you're viewing the past.

I held on to the truth, and now Gabe is gone.

My chest aches with guilt and grief. I'm not fifty feet

underwater like I was when Sadie died, but I'm still in the middle of the ocean, coughing salt from my lungs.

We stare at him for a long while, long enough for blood to run down the back of his head, down his neck, down to his shoulder blades. Long enough for the blood to wing out on either side. Elliot stumbles back before it hits his knees. Anne doesn't care. She lets Gabe's blood feather against her skin, then she leans forward and sprinkles his body with sadness.

The cave cries with her, dripping tears from the tips of stalactites. They're liquid light in the hazy gloom. Where they wet the earth, white flowers push through the rock. They cradle Gabe's body, shoving so close to his skin that his fingers are forced to spread. White buds hug his sides. Petals kiss his cheeks.

They grow and grow until Gabe is covered, and it's the most awful and awesome thing I've ever seen.

The island croons. It's the whistle of wind through the crack in the ceiling. It's the rush of the ocean, somewhere outside this cave. It's a low and lovely melody, and I find myself humming along. Anne gives the song words, tear-drenched things that tell the story of a broken boy who sought a treasure but found his way. Of a boy with broken bones who had never been so whole.

Charlie's body shakes with silent sobs. "It was supposed to be me," he says. "He saved me and I never even tried to save him. Not tonight, and not any of the days before."

Nobody says anything but we all know: It's a particular kind of cruelty to get a glimpse of destiny's cards and still lose the game.

"I should have known!"

"Stop," Anne says. "It was an easy mistake."

Charlie barks a laugh. "I'm Korean, Anne. *Korean.* Gabe and I look nothing alike."

"You got flashes." I draw a ragged breath. "His hair was black with blood. And it was dark. Dark enough to mistake the back of his head for yours."

"The fingers," Charlie says, staring at his hands. "It always seemed wrong how much thicker they were than mine are now, but I thought . . . Well, they were coated in dirt and blood and I thought they were swollen from a fight or whatever awful event killed me."

Charlie's shoulders droop under the weight of solid sorrow. I imagine if we try to bring it on the boat, we'll sink straight to the bottom of the ocean. "The thing is, all of Wildewell's expecting my death. They've been saying goodbye for almost my whole life."

I lay a hand over Charlie's. "It shouldn't have been Gabe. But it shouldn't have been you, either."

White flowers flatten against rock as Elliot stalks to the opposite side of the small cave. His hands fist at his sides. "It didn't happen," he says to one of the tall stones. He punches the rock, leaving behind a red smear. He punches again. And again. "It's not real."

FORTY-THREE

COOPER

The fog rolls in, white and heavy. It hides half of the beach and the ocean beyond.

"Advection fog," the boy, Toby, says.

I'm lying on the stone wall, partway between Thorne Manor and the drop to the ocean. Directly below, a powerboat clunks against a dock.

Toby sits in the grass, tying his shoes. His dad's taking him fishing, just the two of them.

I don't like fishing. Bishop took me once, but it was a whole lot of doing nothing.

I swing a leg off the edge of the wall. "Is that a special kind of fog?"

From the looks of the stuff, it could be.

"I thought you were smart."

"I'm smart—not a meteorologist."

He sighs. "Mom says it forms when warm, moist air flows over a cool surface, like the water. The water vapor condenses and forms a fog."

His words kick the otherworldly out of the atmosphere.

"You should use your brain a little less and your imagination a little more."

"Mom says you don't need imagination when you know the answer."

But it's cooler to pretend the fog is a veil between our world and the next. Or a sign of something big to come.

The back door squeaks. Slams against its frame.

The shadow man from last night stands on the deck. His face is more frightening in the light than the dark. Sharp angles and handsome features layered over darkness.

He walks down the driveway. "Toby, let's go!"

The boy watches his dad jangle the keys as he walks to the car. Before he runs off to his father, he looks up at me and says, "It's a good day today."

"Elliot Thorne, you better not be sitting on that wall again."

I've yet to determine if Wendy Thorne objects to everyone sitting up here or just her sons.

I slide to the ground.

Her body follows her voice, rounding the side of the house and heading straight for me. She stops short when she sees me. Her eyes dart from me to the wall to the drop beyond.

"This was built with Thorne Manor," she says. "That makes it old. Very old."

I nod. "You'd have to be an idiot to sit up there."

Her eyes narrow. "How wonderful your shorts aren't damp from sitting in the wet grass."

"It's a miracle."

She opens her mouth to reply, but a thunderous clap cuts her off.

The world is frozen.

The breeze stills. The ocean stops crashing against the cliff. I don't breathe.

And then the world unfreezes.

"Was that a gun?"

"Did it come from the beach?"

"Where's Toby?"

We don't waste time with answers.

My feet collect raindrops as I speed across the lawn. They collect broken shells as we cross the garden path. They collect sand on the way to the beach. Then they stop.

Left, right, front, back. It's all the same in this fecking fog.

A scream.

"Toby!" Wendy yells.

At first all I see is the red. Inside the fog, that's about all there is.

White, white, white, red.

"Turn around," the fog whispers. Wispy coils twist around our ankles.

We push forward.

The fog sighs, then thins.

We have to get real close. Almost toe to toe with him.

"Oh God." Wendy stares at the crimson sand. Not at Toby's body, though.

"He's in heaven now," the man's voice says on the other side of the fog. His hulking shadow follows.

Wendy flinches. "Who did this?"

The man doesn't answer.

"No." Wendy's head shakes back and forth. And back and forth. "No, Patrick. You didn't, love. Tell me you didn't. It's not real, is it?"

"Had to," he says.

Her eyes lock on the gun in his hand. Won't look away. She whispers, "What have you done?"

"Head shot. Them's the orders."

She stares at her son. Back at the man.

He raises the gun to my head. "I'm helping, you see?"

My heartbeat can't decide between speeding and stopping.

The man mops his sweaty forehead with his sleeve. Wendy and I snatch those few seconds when his eyes are obscured and we run.

Wendy calls my name, and it sounds like it's been ripped straight from her soul.

And then he's on me. Knocking me to the ground, knee across my stomach. I yell for help, words made of sand and fear.

That's when I notice the rock. Dark against Wendy's pale hand. She's less than ten feet from where the man now stands.

He's not looking at her. Hasn't noticed her.

She's made of fog, moving like mist across the beach. Closer, closer.

"They made me do it. Came down from above. And I just can't—" The gun wobbles in his shaky hand, but it doesn't stray from my forehead. "I can't live with that anymore."

"Don't," I say, and it must be magic making my voice so strong and sure. "Don't do it. Please."

"They'll make a monster of you. Like they did with me."

Wendy wears the fog like a cloak. Invisible until she's an inch away.

"I'm going to send you to heaven."

The man's staring at me. Doesn't notice Wendy's knuckles gone white around the stone. Doesn't see her smash the rock's sharp edge into his head.

He cries out. Stumbles. He's on all fours, blinking.

She hits him again, hard. The man goes down. She snatches up his gun.

I'm shivering, teeth chattering. It's the youngest I've ever felt.

"He killed him," I say. "He . . . he shot Toby."

"Elliot," Wendy says. "Elliot, listen to me. You're confused. You climbed the sourwood tree. The one in the center of town with droopy sprays of bell-shaped flowers. And when you came down, you had three branches of flowers in your fist, and you gave me two because you thought they were so pretty. And I loved them so very much."

Her eyes are intensely green, her voice so earnest I begin to see ivory flowers scattered in the sand. "We walked home, down to the foggy beach. And I didn't know. I didn't know you'd eaten the flowers until too late. And Toby, he wanted that treasure like Patrick always has. He thought he'd walk across the ocean for it, but he couldn't swim. You know he couldn't swim.

"And Patrick, he'd been hunting. There was a deer on the shore. Deer from his hunt. You thought something else, but it was the flower's magic making you see horrible things. It was just a deer."

And because she says it, it becomes true.

"It was just a deer."

And because I say it, it becomes true.

Wendy begs me not to tell.

She does it after washing Toby's body in tears. She does it while staring at her unconscious husband with a terrible kind of love. She does it while holding the gun in her hands, and that's the only reason I agree.

He will not go free.

"Go on ahead," she says.

I step into the fog. I don't look back.

Not when I hear Wendy wail.

Not when I hear the second gunshot of the day.

FORTY-FOUR

RUBY

THE TRUTH IS ALL THAT REMAINS.

It's been locked up for so long I hardly know how to get it out. But I will. I won't be the reason anyone else dies.

"I need to tell you," I say. "I need to tell you now before the island takes someone else away."

Charlie and Anne huddle against one of the Star Stones. She's crying without sound, the kind of heart-crushing grief that makes you think you'll never not be leaking a bit of your soul from your eyes. Elliot drops down beside them, raw knuckles sprinkling the ground with red.

I squeeze my hands around my knees. My fingernails dig into my skin. I press harder.

"I . . ." My throat closes. I don't know why it's so hard to get it out. There's nothing to the truth but four little words. "I murdered my sister."

"What does that mean?" Elliot asks, as if the word *murdered* is fluid. As if today it might mean "lost" or "injured" or maybe even "loved."

"It means she was dying," I say with a little too much bite. "It means she was so close to the edge of dead she could have seen Death himself."

Elliot reaches for me, but I flinch and his hand ends up in his lap. "That's not your fault."

"No, that was the cancer. But there was this day—God, it was the perfect day. The sky looked like it had been painted on, and the air was salty-crisp like it gets after a storm. Leave it to Sadie to go on a day so absolutely beautiful." They stare at me—I can feel it, like a million ants crawling over my skin—but I focus on my hands clenched around my knees. "Sadie's coughs were red, which was maybe the only colorful thing about her at that point. She asked—"

My mouth puckers around the truth. Lemons to Sadie's lemonade. She once told me that a little bit of sour makes sugar taste extra sweet, and that's why Sadie was everyone's favorite twin, even mine. I stare at my knees, at the half-moon indents climbing my skin. "Well, you have to know that I never said no to Sadie. Not ever."

"Oh, Ruby." Anne's voice is muffled by the hand over her mouth.

"She begged me. It was the most awful thing in the world, the way her eyes looked at me when she asked." My words are wet. They splash around in my brain before I pour them out.

"I said no. At first I said no, and I meant it. I swear I meant it. But then she looked at me and she said, 'It hurts.' I couldn't—"

I wipe at my cheeks, though there's really no point. It doesn't stop the tears. "I couldn't let her suffer. We all knew she was going soon. She had a few days, maybe a week. But she was never not in pain."

"So you—"

"I did," I say, interrupting Elliot before he can say the word. It sounds like screaming vultures when I say it, and it would sound even worse coming from his mouth. I still remember what he said that night in the clearing when his fingers clasped mine. *Does it really matter why someone murders someone else?*

I should feel worse with my secret exposed, but I'm numb. That's the thing: The truth isn't sharp or cutting. It's not the opposite of comfort. It's the absence of it.

Charlie nudges me with an elbow. "It doesn't change the way I see you. You're still my best girl friend."

"Charles Kim . . ."

"Nah, Anna Banana, you're my platonic soul mate. So Ruby can be my best girl friend."

I smile at him, then glance at Anne. She's staring at me with watery eyes and an expression I can't decipher. "Come on," she says, snatching a flashlight and dragging me to the back of the cave. It's far enough and black enough that I can't see Gabe's body, and for that I'm thankful. We press against the far wall, where thin rocks fuse together so tightly it's impossible to tell whether time's in the process of joining or separating the stones.

"Remember when you asked me which sister I was?" I look Anne in the eyes as I say, "I'm the one with evil inside."

Continents shift and stars wink out as Anne holds my gaze.

"Ruby," she finally says, moving toward me as if I'm a spooked horse. She wraps her arms around me. I'm stiff and still, a straight line of shock and hope as Anne tightens her hold. "I think you're the sister who cared too much," she says, and I break. Back bends. Forehead crashes to her shoulder.

"I'm sorry your sister got sick. I'm sorry you had to watch her die. I'm sorry she asked you to do that. I'm sorry you had to make that tough choice, and I'm sorry you hate yourself for it." Anne pulls away, but she doesn't release me. "Don't hate yourself, Ruby. I don't hate you."

"Even after all that?"

"You're my friend," Anne says as if that's enough. I don't know how to say what I want to say, so I hug her extra tight.

After, I run my fingers over the fused stone wall, tracing its dents and ridges. It looks like a mosaic. "How'd you know about this?" I ask.

Anne blinks at the wall as if she's just now noticing the collage of stones. "I didn't. But all the best things are discovered when you're not trying to discover them at all."

She smiles, and I sense she's talking about more than this secluded spot in this magical cave. She's talking about her arms holding me up as I break into pieces. She's talking about Charlie's sense of adventure and Gabe's culinary skills. She's talking about Elliot's endless knowledge, his trust with his secrets, his mouth on mine.

She's talking about searching for buried treasure and stumbling upon friendship. And even if we do find the treasure, I know it won't be this—buckets of guilt and despair lifted out. Hope and happiness hurled at me.

So maybe I'm not empty, not even a little.

Anne and I sit on the ground, backs to cold stone. I'm telling her a story about twelve-year-old Sadie, who sucked venom from my veins when I was bitten by a snake. "She could be brash and arrogant, and some people thought she was wild, but she would have yanked down the moon to light my way at night."

"You think she's watching over you?"

I used to imagine death swapped our roles. She was the invisible shadow to my flesh and blood. I'd whisper to her at night, pretending we were separated by a curtain of dark that would disappear and show her face as the sky exploded with sunlight.

"I used to imagine she couldn't move on from me, and not the other way around," I say. "But I bet she's off having her own adventure."

"No," Anne whispers, resting her head on my shoulder. "I think she's here. I think this is her adventure."

Footsteps shuffle a few feet away. That's when I notice him. Hair dark as night in this dim cave. Lips pinched to hold tight to his thoughts. I think about what will happen when he opens his mouth.

Does it really matter why someone murders someone else?

"I know what you're thinking," I say.

Elliot's eyebrows jump. He glances at Anne, who leaps to her feet. "I need to check on Charlie," she says, leaving me with Elliot and the words he said that night in the woods.

"I know what you're thinking," I repeat.

He steps closer. "I honestly hope not."

"You're thinking it doesn't matter why someone kills."

"No," he says, continuing toward me. "I'm thinking about the other night and how I want you to kiss me again."

I stand. Dust off my shorts to give my hands something to do. "Well, *I'm* thinking I'm just like your mother. And I'm thinking about how much you hate her."

"Stop that. I'm trying not to think about my mother right now." His eyes skim across my face. "Are you okay?"

"I killed my sister."

"I know," Elliot says. I don't remember the steps that brought him so close. Did I walk to him or did he come to me? "It was the murder out of love, just like the legend says. It was mercy."

"You said murder's unforgivable."

His fingers whisper against mine. "That's where I was wrong, Ruby. Nothing's unforgivable as long as there's someone there to forgive."

I feel his words the way I feel music, with every last bit of me.

"Is that what you want?" I ask. "To forgive me?"

"I've already done that." He steps closer. "I want you to be okay. I want you to realize you're not a monster."

Elliot quirks an eyebrow. I didn't even know he could do that, but it's so perfectly, smugly Elliot that I can't imagine his face in any other arrangement. "Kiss me, Ruby."

"If you want a kiss, then why don't you just—"

He crashes his lips to mine. My skin sings as his fingers cup my face, as his hand traces my spine. He walks me backward until my back hits stone. When we kiss like this, I think maybe it's possible to feel too much. To be too alive.

This is the year you live, Rubes.

Elliot stops to catch a runaway tear. "Ruby?"

"I can almost hear her laughing."

Maybe Anne's right and Sadie stuck around. Maybe she saw heaven and said, "Not so fast. My sister's not done learning and growing just yet, and I'd like to be there along the way."

Maybe her ghostly fingers put *Treasure Island* in Elliot's hand that day at the museum. "Here you go, Rubes," she'd have said. "You can't have me, but you can have all of this."

FORTY-FIVE

COOPER

My nightmares go like this: two shots, two bodies. White fog, red sand.

A boy. A boat. And a woman with wild hair.

Two go, one returns. She's crusted in salt and silent as death. It can't be real.

It can't be real because my memory is broken. Has been for half a year.

It can't be real because he was a man and that was a boy.

But it's only a nightmare. And it was only a deer.

I hitch the bag of treasure over my shoulders. Time to go back to what I know is true: the island that brought me here.

Time to bury a treasure.

I wander through town. Drink my fill of Wildewell. One

day I might forget all this, turn blank as the day Bishop found me. I hope not.

Diamonds of fabric soaring through the sky.

Flowers growing where cement has split.

The scent of baking bread. Taste of salt in the air.

I'm doing my best not to let it go.

Doris spots me on my way to the docks.

She's sitting on her front porch, wearing a dress that looks like a nightgown. It makes me want to wash my eyeballs.

"Want company?" she asks as I approach her house.

"Go back to bed, Doris. I'm doing a thing."

She gestures to the backpack. "You're burying a treasure on Gray Wolf Island."

I pretend it doesn't bother me. That Bishop told her about the backpack full of treasure. "Why are you even awake?"

It's so early in the morning it's practically night.

"Morning moves backward as we move forward, Coop." She cuts across the lawn to my side. "And besides, it's never too early for adventure."

"I might not come back."

She shakes her head. "You'll come back."

It's a half mile to the docks. Doris hums the whole way. It's not the kind of thing I want to hear before sunrise. Or ever.

"Check that out, Coop." She stops in front of a lobster boat.

I guess it's nice. Kind of old and worn, though. "Bishop's sailboat is better."

"Not the boat." She's staring at the lobstermen. She's really focused, too. Like she's counting them.

"You thinking about bumming a ride?"

Doris laughs. I have no idea why. "Sure, that's exactly what I was thinking."

Thirty minutes later, we're on the water. The air washes me with salt and mist. When the sun finally rises, it feels like the first I've ever seen.

The crew's a mix of sailors from northern Maine and Canada. They teach me how to watch for their buoys. How to thread bait needles with herring and pogies. The captain hauls a wire trap into the boat, and the men teach me how to sort through the catch.

It's all a little too much productivity for before noon.

"Won't be going with you," says the big one, Rich. He sold Bishop the first lobster I ever cooked. Right from the back of the boat. Jud Erlich was sure that was illegal, but Bishop ignored him. "That place gives me the willies."

I shrug. "It's really green."

"That's not so weird. But that damn hole is."

"Don't curse," I say.

The crew laughs. Doris grins.

Fifteen minutes later, the island pokes through the mist. Rich does the sign of the cross.

"Can't get any closer," the captain says. "It's bad luck for a ship to touch the island."

"There's a dock," I say.

"No, no. That's the same thing. The luck will just slither from the island, over the dock, and onto the boat. Can't have that." He peers over the edge of the boat. "How's your swimming?"

"I have absolutely no idea."

"Guess today's the day you learn." The captain checks the underside of a lobster. The egg-carrying female gets tossed overboard. "Go on, jump out. I'd like to get away from this place as quickly as possible, if you don't mind."

I know how to sail with a raw egg in a spoon. I don't know whether I'm about to sink or swim.

Clearly common sense wasn't a big part of my mysterious past.

"I think I'm going to drown."

The captain nods. "You'll get a sailor's farewell."

"Okay then." I beg a plastic bag off Rich. Secure Bishop's letter inside. It goes in the red backpack.

I stop in front of Doris. "You'll have to stay here."

"Alone with a boatful of rugged sailors? I will do my best to endure it."

"Yes, fine," the captain says. "We'll come back for you to-morrow. Now hurry off the boat before we're sunk by bad luck."

I drag Doris away from the men. We can't go too far with-out knocking into stacks of lobster traps. Makes me wish we'd gotten a lift from someone with a yacht.

"I might not come back," I say.

"You'll come back."

"Maybe. But if I don't, there's something you should know."

I tell her about the poem. About the book.

I tell her that when the time is right she should make sure the twin, the true believer, finds it.

And then I tell her goodbye.

Bishop said I'm going to be okay, so I heave the bag over my shoulders. And I jump overboard.

I learn two things when I hit the water: I can swim. And the Atlantic in fall is fecking frigid.

The waves lick my face. Make my eyes burn.

As I near the island, I let the ocean do the work. It catches me on a cresting wave. Carries me closer and closer to shore, like it knows I'm home.

FORTY-SIX

RUBY

HIDDEN STAYS HIDDEN
until the ray
that guides your gaze
does a secret betray.

Static sings against my body. I jolt awake.

Anne stands above me, water bottle poised over my head. She snaps it up, letting only a drop fall to my forehead. "Oh, good. I didn't want to waste this."

"What's going on?" The hair on my arms stands on end. Even the wispy pieces around my face strain for the ceiling.

"C'mon." She drags me to the center of the Star Stones, stopping beneath a skinny ray of moonlight. It's the first time I realize we slept from night through morning full into the next night. "I must have crossed this cave a hundred times while you all slept. Maybe a thousand—it did go on forever."

As my mind clears of sleep, a memory hits me like a stone. Falling rocks, red blood, white flowers. After a tragedy, waking is particularly cruel. "Not nearly long enough."

"Yes, well, while you were unconscious and not thinking about him, I haven't been able to do much of anything else." She blinks and blinks. Blinks again. "Anyway," she says with a teary laugh, "the point is, I stood right here, gathering up the sunshine, and I never noticed it at all."

I follow her gaze. Pale moonlight laps at the base of one of the Star Stones, highlighting a dulled engraving. The symbol is unmistakable. In this light, the slashed square practically glows.

I press my fingers to the grooved stone.

Almost everything is cold. Cold ground. Cold stone. Cold air wrapping itself around my body. But the symbol is warm.

" 'Hidden stays hidden until the ray that guides your gaze does a secret betray.' "

My heart's not quite sure what to do with this. It's still breaking apart for the boy buried beneath flowers. Does it stitch back up for Sadie and the promise I made?

I rub at the engraving. "I've only ever imagined this moment with the five of us."

"That was always a dream," Anne says. "But it was a very, very good one."

For two heartbeats, neither of us speaks. And then she says, "I'm glad we're discovering this together."

"Me too," I whisper.

She studies the ground, lips blooming into a small smile.

A tall shadow devours the moonlight. The silver symbol winks out with it.

We turn to find Charlie. His hair's a mass of tangles on the right side and a flattened lump on the left. "What's going on?"

"Move out of the moonlight, and we'll show you," Anne says.

He shakes his head. "He's only been gone a day and you're already thinking about the treasure. Like his death doesn't even matter."

"What a strange thought," Anne murmurs, "that anyone could ever forget a death like that."

She could be talking about his fall to the earth or the way his blood winged out from his back. Maybe the delicate stems pushing through stone, maybe the petals hugging his body. But I think she's talking about him saving Charlie's life. About him dying so I can keep a promise to my sister.

And with that last bit, I'm certain. We must find the treasure. "If we stop now, what will have been the point? He'll have died for nothing."

Charlie nods, steps to the side. Releases a long, low breath when the slashed square glows with life. "He's missing the best part."

"Elliot!" I yell, though I know Charlie is referring to a different boy.

The cave echoes the name, again and again as Charlie wrestles Elliot awake. The boys rejoin us beside the monolith, a bittersweet expression on Charlie's face and a spectacularly sour one on Elliot's. "I realize a 2012 study in *Neuropsychopharmacology* advised against sleeping too soon after a traumatic event because it could lead to more symptoms of PTSD, but this is ridiculous. It's still dark out."

"Light, dark. Either way, he's gone," I say, rising to meet him. I stare at the wolf inked on his skin. Howling mouth. Sharp teeth. Fur-covered ears pushed back on its head. It's real enough to jump off his body and to the ground. My fingers skim over the intricate artwork.

"Ruby," he groans. Rests his forehead on my shoulder. He snatches my hand from his side. My thumb traces his battered knuckles.

"We found it," I say. Elliot's head snaps up. "I think my secret unlocked our final clue."

I may be a liar, but I can spot the truth, and right now it's silver zinging off my tongue. In answer, the symbol inhales. It sucks down the night's light. Through the crack in the ceiling, the sky is velvety black.

Gorged on moonbeams and starlight, the mark glows with an unearthly light. My eyes water at it, so outrageously beautiful. Charlie looks away, and I wonder if we could be thinking the same thing. That it seems impossible we should experience anything so blatantly breathtaking after Gabe's death. That it should have exhaled night, covering the cave and the moon and the stars with gloom.

"Oh," Elliot says. He's kneeling beside the stone now, though I don't remember him moving from my side. His fingers rest in the grooves of the slashed square. His eyes are open, but his body is motionless. If it weren't for the rise and fall of his chest, I'd assume he was turned to stone.

"Why is he not moving?" Charlie's voice is frantic. "It's like the light is sucking out his soul."

"My great-grandmother says the Thornes are born with half their souls on Gray Wolf Island. Maybe he's trying to get his back."

❖

"He'll wake up." Charlie is squashed between me and Anne, our backs to cool stone. It's been over an hour since Elliot went still.

"Of course he will." Anne says it like she hopes her words will turn into truth. "Now would you quit repeating that?"

Charlie squints at the back of Elliot's head. "You think he'll wake up, Ruby?"

"Of course he will," I say, though I don't feel nearly as confident as I sound. Gabe's death stole almost all of my hope, and Elliot's catatonic state took the rest.

"The island's already swallowed Gabe." He rakes a hand through his sleep-rumpled hair. "And now it froze Elliot. He could be just as gone."

"I'm going to tell you something—and I'm talking to you, too, Ruby, because you're just as worried as Charlie but better at being silent." Anne kneels before us, and I can almost taste the insect repellent she recently reapplied. "Gabe never slept very long. No, that's a lie. He slept a long, long time—time stops and stretches during the night when everyone but you sleeps—but he didn't waste half the next day. He used to climb out of his tent while the sun was rising and keep me company until we had to wake the rest of you.

"The morning after he told us his secret, Gabe said the island wanted the truth. I told him that was unfair, considering the island hadn't given up the truth of the treasure for hundreds of years. Gabe got real serious—well, more serious than the serious he had been acting since he kissed Ruby—and he told me what the island had been whispering to him through the leaves and the grass and the dirt stirred up in the wind."

"It should have been whispering a warning about his death," Charlie says with a rasp to his voice. "If it cared so damn much about him."

"It did," I say, though I don't know why. It lobbed a rock at his head. But something about his death—the way the cave cried tears of light, the way flowers blanketed his broken, bloody body so it became beautiful once more—tells me this place mourns Gabe as much as we all do.

Charlie grunts. "What'd it whisper?"

"That the island devours the truth like . . ." Anne searches the ceiling for the right words. "Like the slashed square swallowed the light from the sky."

"But we already know that."

"Charles Kim, one day I'd like to get through a story without your interruptions," Anne huffs. "As I was saying, Gabe was certain there was more. After the island drank our secrets from our lips, we'd be worthy of one of its own."

"But Charlie—"

"Told me his a few days ago," Anne says.

"So Elliot was worthy," I say.

Anne nods. "And now he's learning the truth."

Charlie is out.

"I don't care what the island told Gabe, I'm not hunting for a treasure while my best friend is . . . *that*," he says, thrusting a hand in Elliot's direction.

He hasn't moved. I thought, for a little while there, I'd stay rooted to this spot, too. That I'd be forever staring at Elliot's fingers, at the way the light seems to curve around his hand. All that staring, and it still took me three hours to spot it.

Now it's all I can see.

"I'll find it alone." The words don't taste half as sweet as they did at the start of this quest.

I stand in front of the Star Stone. Head-on, it's nearly impossible to see that certain slant of light. I study the upper left corner of the square and . . . there. An odd beam breaks from the rest and bends outward. It's slight, so slight. But it's enough for my treasure-starved mind.

I hold my hand in front of the beam, watch it pale my skin. I take a step back. And back. And back until I hit the cave wall. I click off my headlamp. Shadow swallows this section of the cave.

If it weren't for the dark, I'd never notice the light. It's faint, barely brushing the wall, but it's there. I run my hands along the stone. Searching, searching, searching for something. Anything.

A button.

A lever.

A hidden door.

My fingers brush dirt, something slimy, and sharp stone. I'm sure I'm bleeding, but I'm not sure I care.

I follow a crack down the wall. It yawns wider as I reach the base, where I can faintly make out a small cranny. I flick on my headlamp. There's a whole lot of black. And a flash of red.

"I think I found it," I say, and the entire cave brightens.

Anne and Charlie race to my side. We slither on our stomachs until we're inches from the opening. "There could be spiders," Charlie says with a shudder.

"There could be snakes," Anne says, and Charlie groans.

"There could be treasure," I say, reaching a hand into the small space. My fingers brush dry earth, cool stone, and something else. Fabric. When my fingers have closed around a strap, I pause.

"I've got your daydreams in my grasp," I say softly to my sister. And I know that whisper is traveling out of this cave, across the island, and all the way to the cemetery, where Sadie will hear it and celebrate with enough glee to shake the entire town of Wildewell.

I pull out the treasure.

FORTY-SEVEN

COOPER

I'M FILLED WITH A BIZARRE BUZZING. IT MAKES MY SKIN ITCH and mind twitch.

There's something I'm supposed to remember. I don't know what.

Tell the truth, the grass whispers. I crush it beneath my shoes.

The closer I get to the cave, the more my body tingles. It's the worst in my brain. Static that's trying to say something.

What am I supposed to remember?

The wind tosses dirt into my eyes. *The truth,* it hisses. *Tell the truth.*

Dirt clouds follow me across the valley. To the waterfall. To the cave.

Then I'm there. Standing in the center of the underground Star Stones.

I wait for the moon to show up. Just like Bishop's letter instructs. Except his letter makes it sound exciting.

It's not.

The island hounds me the whole time about the truth. I toss out a few.

"I am Cooper Rollins!"

"I'm a treasure hunter!"

"I really have to pee!"

None stick, and the longer the air whispers about the truth, the more my head swims. By the time moonlight hits the symbol Bishop chiseled into one of the Star Stones, I can barely feel my limbs.

And I'm still forgetting something.

I shrug it off. Follow the light to a crevice in the cave wall. Either it's really well hidden or my brain's as sluggish as it feels.

Red backpack. Dark hole.

A push. A kick.

For all the hours of planning it took to get here, burying the treasure is pretty anticlimactic. I bet it'd be a million times better with Bishop by my side. Now it just reminds me he's gone.

I shake my head. There's something specific I'm supposed to remember.

My beginning on Gray Wolf Island.

The search for my lost identity.

A deer on the beach.

Lies, whispers the darkness. *Tell the truth.*

"He killed Toby," I say. "On the beach."

But that's not all. I can taste the hint of memory on my tongue.

I flop onto my back. I'm loose legs and liquid arms. Brain sloshing all over in my skull. Rinsing away fiction and replacing it with fact. I shout the truth to the ceiling.

"I didn't wake up on Gray Wolf Island."

"I had a home all along."

The island roars. Every piece of dirt and every other hidden thing this far in the earth rumbles with its cry. *Tell the truth!*

"My dad tried to kill me," I whisper. "He killed my brother and I was next."

FORTY-EIGHT

RUBY

Only the worthy
can see the clue
to the greater treasure:
to know what is true.

We sit in a circle, knees pressed tight to one another's. Anne's bounce up and down, faster and faster.

"All of the magic of Gray Wolf Island might be stuffed inside that bag," she says. "But we'll never know unless you unzip it."

She's talking about the backpack lying inches from my fingers. Its underbelly is coated in a layer of dirt, but the rest is shockingly red. It seems to me the treasure must have been buried recently, but Anne's convinced the island protected it for us.

Charlie shakes his head. "Honestly, the island took Gabe and it did something to Elliot. I don't give a shit about the treasure."

"Don't curse," a voice croaks.

There's no beam of light. No illuminated square. No magic at all.

There's only Elliot.

I drink him in, noting every strange and wonderful piece. "You're better," I whisper.

Charlie is less contained. He springs from the ground. Crushes Elliot in a hug punctuated by slaps on the back. "I thought you'd be stuck like that forever."

Elliot sinks to the ground. I'd like to run at him. Wrap my arms around his waist so I can know for sure. That he's alive. That he's flesh and bone. That he's going to be all right.

Instead I say, "Are you okay?"

He scrubs a hand over his face. "Not really. But I think I will be."

"Dude, you wouldn't move. You didn't even blink—it was actually really creepy." Charlie's voice is teasing, but there's an undertone of worry to his words. "What happened?"

"I—" Elliot exhales, the kind of breath that's more about holding something back than letting something go. "I know the truth, and I'm going to tell everyone everything. Set things straight. But not right now."

Anne nods. "Two things in this world my great-grandmother says you can't rush: bowel movements and grief."

Charlie laughs.

Elliot narrows his eyes. "What makes you think I'm grieving?"

"Oh, Elliot," Anne says. "It's written all over you."

She's right, though I think it's more than that. It's like he's added a whole world of troubles on top of it. Like he's been through the kind of event that knifes your life in two. Before and after.

He clears his throat. "You found the treasure."

"We think. We got as far as wondering, then you came to." I tug the bag onto my lap. My fingers play with the zipper. I look from Charlie to Anne to Elliot, and I feel such immeasurable love for my twin, who knew that the end of this quest would be a terrible place to reach without friends.

I open the pack.

The light from my headlamp bounces around in there, reflecting off silver and gold, winking around in a pile of jewels.

Nobody speaks. I inspect an ancient figurine while Anne presses a gemstone between her fingers and Charlie weighs gold coins in his palm.

"There's one more thing," Elliot says.

"Always one more thing with this damn island."

"Don't curse, Charlie." Elliot swallows. There's something like guilt in his eyes when he turns to me. "You made a promise to your sister, and I know how important that is to you. We'll keep the treasure, Rubes, if that's what you really want."

"We *have* the treasure."

"Wait. I have to get this out." Elliot's fingers clench the fabric of the bag. "We can keep everything in here, but I'm hoping we don't have to. We're meant to leave this behind."

"It was never about keeping the treasure," I say. "We'll hide the book. We'll let someone else find it."

"Then all of this was pointless," Charlie says. "Gabe died for nothing."

Anne stares at the leather band around his wrist. "That first night, around the fire, I said you could beat fate. Do you remember?"

"Of course I remember. I fell a little bit in love with you then."

"Because it's what you wanted to hear. That you weren't going to die. But I was wrong about destiny," she says. "You glimpsed his death for a decade, Charlie. Gabe was always going to die here."

I lean my head on Charlie's shoulder. Take his hand in mine. "Even without the treasure, this wasn't nothing. Not to me."

"No." Elliot's eyes are on the slashed square etched into the Star Stone, but his mind is somewhere else. "No, it wasn't all pointless."

He rummages through the treasure like he's searching for something specific. He plucks out an object and, without showing the rest of us, stuffs it in his pocket. He dives in for more.

"This reminds me of you." Elliot tosses Charlie a small Buddha statue. It's blindingly gold. The kind of gold that comes from daily polishing, not aging in a hidden cave.

"Sure, give the Asian kid the Buddha," Charlie says, snatching it from the air. "You know I'm Catholic, right?"

"I'll take it back, then."

"No." Charlie squints at the statue's face. "His smile kind of looks like mine."

Elliot laughs. "You don't say."

He reaches back in the bag, rustles its contents all around. It sounds like a hundred glass marbles rolling over one another. Elliot unfurls his fist, revealing a small cameo. He holds it out for Anne. "It's three-layered agate," he says, and none of us ask how he knows this. "One stone, but the horse figure is carved in the white middle layer. You can see the light brown layer below. And here, see? Its mane and tail are carved from the upper layer."

"I used to have a horse." Anne's finger runs the length of the cameo.

Elliot nods. "Riding it made you happy."

"It did," Anne says. "But my aunt thought all the time I spent with Violet was making me weird. I tried telling her I'd be weird without Violet, but nobody trusts the weird girl. So she sold him."

"Violet was a boy?"

"Yes, Charlie. I didn't know to look underneath when I was little."

Charlie shakes his head, but he does it with a smile. "Looks like you're up, Ruby." He peeks in the bag as Elliot rummages around. "How's a guy with a bag full of treasure say, 'I want to keep making out with you'?"

"I'm going to throw you down the pit," Elliot says.

Charlie laughs and laughs until Elliot pulls a grape-sized diamond from the bag. "Dude, that says, 'I want to keep making out with you for the rest of my life.'"

"Charlie," Elliot says between clenched teeth. "Mind shutting up?"

Anne purses her lips. "Charles Kim, you make one more joke and I'll drag you across the cave. Then neither of us will hear what he says."

Charlie mimes locking his lips.

"Can you maybe pretend you didn't hear any of that?"

Elliot's ears are red. Cheeks, too. "I'm not proposing, so you know."

"I'm crushed."

He drops the diamond in my hand. "It reminds me of you is all."

"Sparkly?"

Elliot laughs. "Um, no. Kind of think that was Sadie, right?"

"Right. I'm more of a ruby."

Charlie leans into Anne. "I was thinking I'd have to make a ruby joke if one of them didn't."

"So much for zipping his lips." Elliot clears his throat. "It's like this: You have these carbon atoms and they're put under extremely high temperatures and all this pressure. And because of that they form bonds. And you don't care about the details, but the end product is this really hard material. I'm not saying you're sparkly, Ruby. I'm saying you were under some pretty serious pressure when your sister died, and it made you tougher than nails."

I close my fist around the gift, so tight the point bites my palm. "One day," I say, kneeling in front of him, "I'd like to see myself the way you do." And then I kiss him.

"So cute."

"They're adorable."

"I'm being serious, Charlie."

"Know what I'm serious about? Getting off this island."

I pull away from Elliot. Stare at the crack in the ceiling. In the midnight cave with only a sliver of moon, it's as if time has tossed us a million extra minutes. As if it's waiting for us to feel safe before speeding back up again. But Charlie is right. Morning is close, and we need a plan.

"Tomorrow morning," I say, "we follow the tunnel back to the musical cave. Those rocks were stacked. I bet we can climb to the cliff above."

"You do remember the cave-in, right?"

"No, Elliot. I must have slept through it." I sigh. "Look, right now it's our only way out. But if the entrance into the cavern is blocked or the exit to the cliff has crumbled, then we'll try another path."

Charlie nods. "And then we leave Gray Wolf Island."

FORTY-NINE

RUBY

THE GOING IS EASIER THAN THE COMING.

I guess that's life. Took sixteen hours of labor to bring Sadie into this world, kicking and screaming and red in the face, and six minutes to take her out, pale and broken but full of peace.

"It seems unfair we made it out so easily." Charlie's voice is low and wet.

We stare at the rumbling ocean. It hurtles into the cave below, and even from here—standing on the shoulders of the musical cave—I can hear its song. The melody is what comforted me as we climbed damp, stair-shaped rocks up the face of the island. It comforts me again as tears drip down my cheeks and I think of the boy we're leaving behind.

We'll tell them where to find him. Across the island and

into the caves and beneath a flowery grave. We'll tell them he died saving Charlie's life. Some might believe us. His mom will. But Wildewell likes to make up its own legends. Someday down the line, they might tell stories of pirates' treasure and the boy who made the island cry. Some will say they knew from the start he was wicked. And some will say that with a birth like his, he couldn't be anything but divine.

Anne slips her hand into Charlie's and says, "Bishop Rollins once said nobody could bake the way Gabe baked and be human. My great-grandma always believed he was something . . . other. Maybe part of the island. Maybe part angel."

Charlie raises an eyebrow. "That's ridiculous."

"I don't know," she says. "Is it?"

The western coast is a line of cliffs and jumbled rocks. We follow it for as long as we can before Elliot leads us inland. Past the waterfall, through a forest thick with birch. The woods deepen, then thin, and then we're there: staggering, stumbling, running through the underbrush and over warm sand, shedding our shoes and splashing knee-deep in the cool ocean.

"It's like waking up from a dream," Anne says. "Those first moments when you're not sure if you've slipped into real life or out of it."

"Nightmare." In the setting sun, Charlie's face is ferociously orange. "It's a nightmare when your friend dies."

He tears off his shirt, plunges under the waves. Anne jumps on his back and won't let him go. Won't let him feel the guilt and the pain. She clucks her tongue and Charlie's lips twist into a mournful version of his Cheshire cat smile before he dives into the next wave.

"Will he be okay?" I ask.

Elliot nods.

"Will you be okay?"

"Half of me thinks I'll never be okay. The other half thinks I'm already there."

Anne sits piggyback as Charlie wades to shore. They're a huffing, soaking tangle of limbs.

Elliot and I let the water lap at our shins, let the sand suck our feet under. I can hear Charlie and Anne making camp. Charlie wanted to leave tonight, but sailing with him or Anne at the helm is scary enough during the day. So we'll eat a meal that makes us miss Gabe and sleep under the stars, then return home.

But without treasure. We stuffed that back into the crevice. Gabe's rescuers won't find it. It's not for them. It's for the explorer who discovers *Treasure Island*. For a true believer.

"What treasure did you take?" I ask.

Elliot fumbles in his pocket. Pulls out a small sailboat. "I stole this."

"Are we calling it stealing now? That sounds so . . . illegal."

"Jud Erlich would say it *is* illegal."

I grin. "Isn't the idea of a treasure hunt sort of finders keepers?"

"Yes. But this isn't part of the treasure. This I stole." Elliot drops the boat in my hand. It doesn't look special at all—more like a child's toy. The kind you can get for ten tickets at the arcade.

"You knew about them—the Buddha, the necklace, *this*," I say, handing him the boat. "How could you know what the treasure was?"

"I spent a summer working for Bishop Rollins." He says the words like he's taking them out for a test drive.

"I remember."

For a moment he's frozen. "Right. That happened. And I—" Elliot takes a breath so deep I half expect to go light-headed from too little air. And then he says, "I'm the one who hid the treasure."

My mouth springs open, but I've lost my words.

"There was a horrible thing, and my mom tried to make me forget it. But she somehow wiped an entire summer from my mind."

I don't doubt that. Sometimes the mind would rather forget the truth, even if that means remembering fiction.

"I didn't know the map was mine. I didn't know . . . a lot. Then the island gave me a story twisted around the truth." He runs a hand through his hair. "But all these new memories are still muddied up in my head."

"One day, maybe you'll tell me about it."

"You might not believe me."

I rest my head on his shoulder. "You can't imagine the impossible things I'm willing to believe. Like right now, I believe there's more to us than on the island."

He's looking at me like he's discovered a treasure, like I was buried for years before he dug me up. "Was that ever even a question?"

And then he dips down and kisses me so deeply it sinks the sun into the ocean and draws the moon up into the sky.

I sit on a boulder under the full moon, knees tucked close to my chest. It's the middle of the night and the boys are asleep. Anne says she's reading a book, but she's really watching me. I catch her sometimes out of the corner of my eye. She smiles like she knows what I'm thinking, and maybe she does.

I'm thinking I love them all, these people who barged into my life and turned it upside down. It feels like there should be something supernatural about it. But there's no magic in love, just a gradual giving of yourself and trusting that whoever holds a piece will transform it into something magical.

"You were right," I say. "You were right all along."

The wind whispers and it's Sadie's voice, looking for a different kind of truth. So I stare at the sky and I tell her all of it. Her laugh ruffles my hair, and I say, "You would have loved it, Sadie. You would have loved every last bit of it."

When I'm done telling my story, the breeze kisses my cheeks and it says, "This is the year you live, Rubes."

The voice is so bright, so full of love and joy and peace. I hold it in my heart, in the space I've always left for Sadie.

I hold on.

And on.

When the wind dies down, I rise from the boulder and I tell the greatest truth of them all. *Everything is going to be okay.*

ACKNOWLEDGMENTS

I HAVE KNOWN SUCH KINDNESS WHILE WRITING THIS BOOK.
Simple letters and words are woefully inadequate (and a backpack of gold and gems unfortunately hard to come by), but I
will do my best.

My agent, Sarah LaPolla, is a treasure herself. Thank you
for having confidence in my writing from the beginning and
encouraging me through it all. I'd be a mess of nerves and
hopelessly lost without you.

I count myself among the very luckiest to have Karen
Greenberg on my team. A thousand thank-yous for your brilliant feedback and unfailing support. You are the editor I
dreamed of when I dreamed, all those years ago, of publishing
a novel.

I'm so fortunate to have an amazing team at Knopf, who
pushed me to make this book better and smarter and more
grammatically correct. Thank you, Jenny Brown, Artie Ben-
nett, Alison Kolani, Melanie Nolan, Janet Renard, and Dawn
Ryan. And much gratitude to Ken Crossland and Ray Shappell
for designing a book that looks beautiful both inside and out,
and to Mike Hall for his gorgeous map. Special thanks go to

Julia Gray at the Abbe Museum for her thoughtful read and for help making my fictional people and made-up history authentic to reality.

This book wouldn't exist were it not for the talented writers who read it when it was still a messy infant of a story yet loved it all the same. Riley Edgewood, Rebekah Faubion, Lola Sharp, and Katy Upperman—thank you for your excitement and especially your advice. You gave me confidence when it was seriously lacking, and for that I am truly grateful.

Liz Parker has been on this journey with me, right from the beginning. Thank you, dear friend, for urging me to write this book, for your faith in my ability to finish it, for all the times you read this story and all the genius ideas you shared. It seems only fitting that, as I wrote about life-changing friendship, we were forming our own.

For the words of encouragement, fellowship, and keen insight, thank you to Lindsay Currie, Kelly Jensen, Shannon Grogan, and Alice Fanchiang. To Nova Ren Suma, who, with unfathomable kindness, has taken me under her wing, thank you for being so very generous in every aspect of your life. I respect you all more than you probably know.

I owe my sanity to my fellow debut authors, and the Class of 2K17 in particular. It is a privilege sharing this milestone with you.

Once, when I wasn't much older than Ruby and the gang, I traveled around an island with a group of girls who became forever friends. Thank you, each of you, for showing me why friendship is a lot like magic and for inspiring the strong bonds in this story. And much gratitude to the friends I made later who have proven that we can weather anything if we have the right people by our side.

My family has been my first and most loyal supporters. To my grandfather, who can tell a tale like no other, thank you for fostering a love of storytelling in me.

I am forever grateful to my mother and father for reading to me at bedtime—even if that bedtime came outrageously early. Thank you for never doubting my dreams and for believing, with the utmost certainty, that I would one day realize them.

To my sister, Jill, who was there the day, so long ago, when I started my very first book and has been here every book since: sufficient gratitude seems like an impossibility. Thank you for the pep talks, the brainstorming sessions, and, most of all, your constant enthusiasm for my stories.

And, finally, thank you to Matt, who always believed. Who captained our lives when I couldn't. And with whom I feel the opposite of invisible.